Richard Barnes studied Medicine at Cambridge and University College Hospital and pursued a career in teaching and research at Cambridge for many years. He is passionate about theatre, education, and equality of opportunity. He now writes murder mysteries which draw on his experience in both university and secondary education. He is married with four grown up children who are out there, saving the world.

This book is written for my many students, and for my family, whose very best qualities are exemplified in the behaviour of the good guys in my stories.

Richard Barnes

THE SCALES OF JUSTICE

AUSTIN MACAULEY PUBLISHERS™
LONDON * CAMBRIDGE * NEW YORK * SHARJAH

Copyright © Richard Barnes 2023

The right of Richard Barnes to be identified as author of this work has been asserted by the author in accordance with sections 77 and 78 of the Copyright, Designs and Patents Act 1988.

All rights reserved. No part of this publication may be reproduced, stored in a retrieval system, or transmitted in any form or by any means, electronic, mechanical, photocopying, recording, or otherwise, without the prior permission of the publishers.

Any person who commits any unauthorised act in relation to this publication may be liable to criminal prosecution and civil claims for damages.

This is a work of fiction. Names, characters, businesses, places, events, locales, and incidents are either the products of the author's imagination or used in a fictitious manner. Any resemblance to actual persons, living or dead, or actual events is purely coincidental.

A CIP catalogue record for this title is available from the British Library.

ISBN 9781398485808 (Paperback)
ISBN 9781398485815 (Hardback)
ISBN 9781398485839 (ePub e-book)
ISBN 9781398485822 (Audiobook)

www.austinmacauley.com

First Published 2023
Austin Macauley Publishers Ltd®
1 Canada Square
Canary Wharf
London
E14 5AA

I am grateful to the medical members of my family for validating the medical passages in this book, and to them, and the non-medical members of the family, who patiently read the drafts and spotted the howlers.

Table of Contents

Prologue	11
Chapter 1	12
Chapter 2	15
Chapter 3	18
Chapter 4	22
Chapter 5	26
Chapter 6	32
Chapter 7	34
Chapter 8	40
Chapter 9	43
Chapter 10	46
Chapter 11	52
Chapter 12	58
Chapter 13	64
Chapter 14	69
Chapter 15	72
Chapter 16	76
Chapter 17	81
Chapter 18	96
Chapter 19	104

Chapter 20	114
Chapter 21	123
Chapter 22	137
Chapter 23	152
Chapter 24	158
Chapter 25	164
Chapter 26	172
Chapter 27	176
Chapter 28	184
Chapter 29	195
Chapter 30	203
Epilogue	213

Prologue

Tom Pike sat by his sister's bed in the acute care ward. She was drowsy and still being intensively monitored but the ward sister had told him that she was on the mend. They were still giving the N-acetylcysteine, although the protocol suggested that this was coming to an end. The urea and electrolytes, and blood pressure, were now approaching normal. Liver function tests were also normal. It had been a tough 24 hours, but it looked as if Rowan would pull through without significant renal or liver damage. And then they would have to try to find out why she had taken the overdose. The regular beep of the heart monitor matched the perfectly normal ECG trace running across the screen of the bedside monitor.

The lighting in the room was subdued and Tom was tired and sleepy.

Rowan opened her eyes, Tom squeezed her hand and leaned over the bed and kissed her on the cheek.

"You need a shave," said Rowan.

Tom teared up. He 'sort of' knew she would be alright.

He got his iPhone out and took a quick picture of Rowan smiling, to send to Mum and Dad.

Chapter 1

The problem had begun just 72 hours earlier when Meera, one of Rowan's medical student friends at St Joseph's, had gone to wish her luck for the viva the next day, and had found her, very drowsy, lying, semi clothed, on her bed with several empty paracetamol packets beside her. Meera had rushed to the porter's lodge and the head porter, Donna Golding, had immediately called the ambulance. The Senior Tutor had been informed and had then informed all the relevant authorities and made a very difficult telephone call to Rowan's parents. Tom was a fifth-year medical student at another Cambridge College and his parents had immediately called him. He had gone up to Addenbrooke's and watched helplessly while the extent of the poisoning was assessed, and the appropriate medical protocols were put in place. It seemed that the paracetamol overdose had been caught in time. The administration of N-acetylcysteine to mitigate against toxic damage to the liver had begun immediately because it appeared that Rowan had taken a lot of tablets, and there was no knowing for sure that it was less than eight hours since she ingested them.

There was no rational explanation for this overdose. All the way through school, Rowan, tall, blonde, curly haired and deep blue eyed, with a trace of emerald and gold speckled through the iris, was popular, eminently stable, and obvious head girl material. She duly became head girl. You name the sport, Rowan played it. She was a member of the theatre club, mainly working on the technical side, although she could turn her hand to acting if the occasion demanded. She had set her sights on medicine very early in her secondary school career. It had not been a damascene conversion, more a gradual realisation that she liked science, she liked people and people liked her, and confided in her.

Mrs Patti Pike, Rowan's, and Tom's, Mother, was a ward sister at the local maternity hospital. She was vivacious, hardworking, and dedicated. She had the same curly blonde hair as Rowan, and a few more freckles. Their dad, Matthew, was a consultant in Accident and Emergency Medicine. When these facts are observed it seems, perhaps, inevitable that Rowan and her older brother should have gone into medicine, but it was more the caring nature of both, and their desire to make a difference, rather than any direct impact of family upbringing, that sent the two children on the path to medicine.

They had chosen Cambridge because they wanted a science degree before embarking on the more human side of medicine. Although they were mature for their age, they both thought that they wanted more time to develop their own personalities, more time to grow and be ready for the obvious cut and thrust of patient contact.

They had chosen to apply to different colleges simply because Tom liked the idea of 'en suite' and good kitchens and plumbing, and Rowan, a much more romantic character, liked the ambience of old buildings and the patina, the mellowing of the surfaces of stone, and wood, and metal, that comes with centuries of learning. Rowan always teased Tom, when they were both in residence, that she also had the plumbing. St Joe's had renovated almost all the accommodation, while he had to come and borrow the patina of learning from *her* college.

They had both excelled academically. Rowan had taken three 'A' levels and one AS. She knew that several of the students at St Joe's had more 'A' levels than she but, as her teachers had advised her when she was thinking of applying, 'you need to have a life as well.' There is a well-known saying that the proof of the pudding is in the eating, and Rowan's scholarships and college prizes in her first two years, had certainly demonstrated that she had made the right choice. At the time of the overdose, Rowan did not know, but she subsequently went on to be granted a Clarke Scholarship, for clinical study, by her college, for the first class she received in her third year, and a university prize, the 'Glover's Prize,' for the best dissertation in a Part-2 biological subject.

Whatever way it was looked at, and whoever was looking at it, the idea that Rowan would have taken an overdose did not compute. But it was a fact that she had been admitted with a massive quantity of paracetamol in her stomach, and a high blood level.

Tom, sitting by the bedside, was at a loss to understand why Rowan would have taken an overdose. Surely it could not have been related to her studies. She was in the third year of medicine and had managed to get two firsts so far in her exams. She was taking a third-year course in physiology, with a project looking at the factors relating to foetal lung development in the uterus, and she had seemed to be enjoying it. She had completed all but one of her final exams, including all the written papers, and this suicide attempt had come on the day before her final examination, which was an oral exam, based on her write-up of her project. The main purpose of that exam was to check that the student had done the work described, and the oral was not considered onerous. Certainly, it was not something that was likely to precipitate an exam crisis.

Tom and Rowan were reasonably close, but not living in each other's pockets. Each of them had developed their own separate set of friends, and mainly socialised within their own colleges and year groups. Rowan's tutor, and her set of friends, had no idea that Rowan was, in any way, distressed.

To sum it up, this attempt at suicide came right out of the blue in a young woman who had, throughout her childhood and adolescence, never shown any signs of depression or any other form of mental illness. It also came in the middle of the summer after all the stress of study had ended and she should have been looking forward to rowing in the May Bumps, she was Ladies' Captain of Boats, and going to a May Ball. The situation was inexplicable by normal criteria. It remained so for many months to come.

Tom knew only too well that a liver transplant, or for that matter, the medical treatment of liver failure in paracetamol overdose, did not necessarily have the best of outcomes. Ten-year survivals were modest, and beyond ten years, there was a shortened life expectancy. The liver transplant also involved regular treatment with immuno-suppressive drugs, which also created potential medical hazards for the recipient. Tom was so grateful that this all seemed to have been avoided.

Chapter 2

It was a good few days before Rowan was released from hospital, and that was only after a lot of consultation with a psychiatrist, who remained completely puzzled as to why the event had happened. In the end, he discharged her with no real advice about future treatment. There seemed nothing to work on in terms of psychology and Rowan went back to college, just in time for the May Bumps and the May Ball. The high level of fitness she had built up in advance of the event stood her in good stead, but she was not ready for the intensity of the May Races, and so her friend Paige, who had subbed in for her during the period of hospitalisation, retained her place in the Ladies' First Boat. They did well, but they missed the power of Rowan in the three position and just missed out on the fourth bump that would have won them their oars. Rowan promised the other girls, many of whom were in their second year, that she would return and row for the college next year.

"And we'll get that darn oar!" She said.

The speed with which the old Rowan reappeared in every detail lent further incredulity to what had happened in that first week of June.

Rowan's boyfriend, Vincent, took her to the May Ball. They had a great time, but both knew that this was a farewell date. They liked each other; they had shared a lot of good memories, but Vincent was off to Imperial to do a PhD in engineering, and Rowan still had three more years as a student before she would even begin on the pathway to a Hospital Consultant's Post.

Rowan wore a black ballgown that was beautifully cut, and a fluffy feather stole, to keep her shoulders warm when the early hours came. It moulted, not badly, but enough that when the two of them went back to Rowan's room for a coffee before the survivors' photograph was taken early morning, Vincent's dinner jacket looked as if it had been in a snowstorm. Almost a whole roll of Sellotape later the plain black colour was restored, and Rowan substituted a white pashmina shawl for the feather construction. There were still a couple of weeks to go before the General Admission ceremony and Rowan and Vincent, with several other friends, enjoyed every minute. For some, this would be their last few weeks in Cambridge but for the medical students, and for those going on to post graduate study, it merely marked a turning point, away from the more didactic undergraduate learning and towards either vocational training or original thinking.

Rowan's tutor had applied, on her behalf, for the award of the honours degree to be based on the course work project write-up that she had submitted, and the four papers that she had taken. The examiners have discretion to award a classed degree based on the examination papers and course work completed, if it constitutes a substantial part of the examination requirement, and they counted missing the viva, especially as they had supervisors' reports and the write-up of the project to look at, as falling within their terms of discretion. They felt entirely justified in awarding her a first-class degree, and much to Rowan's surprise and delight, they gave her the Glover Prize for the best project.

So, Rowan sat there, with a first-class degree and her career in medicine still intact.

Rowan was able to enjoy the General Admission degree ceremony with her peers at the end of June. The college served the graduands with an excellent graduation dinner and Rowan took full advantage of the excellent food, and the wine; grateful that the prompt treatment of the overdose had left her able to enjoy them both.

The terms associated with the degree ceremony reflect the history of Cambridge Degrees. The gathering to confer degrees is called a Congregation, reflecting the religious background of the education process at Cambridge. It is one of those slightly arcane things about Cambridge that the normal method of receiving a degree is for students to be presented at a Congregation, to the vice-chancellor, or the vice-chancellor's deputy, in person, by a don known as the Praelector. There is much muttering of Latin mumbo-jumbo, much lifting of Doctors' Bonnets or mortar boards, and forming of processions in and out of the Senate House. Rowan, like everyone else, knelt before the vice-chancellor and had 'wisdom' transferred by his clasping of her hands and muttering the Latin mantra.

Afterwards Rowan, her family, and three of her close friends, retreated to Midsummer House, a Michelin Starred restaurant on Midsummer Common, for what was probably the most expensive, but also one of the most delicious, meals that any of them had enjoyed. Rowan was unable to resist a small glass of an excellent Burgundy with her meal.

Over dinner in the glass roofed dining area, with white starched tablecloths and beautiful place settings, the main topic of conversation was about the future. Rowan and her three friends had, for the moment, had enough of abstract scientific learning, and were chomping at the bit to begin the clinical phase of their training. The four girls were going to share a house together, up at the far end of Mill Road and relatively close, by bicycle, to the Medical School.

The 'elephant in the room' was still Rowan's suicide attempt, but nobody spoke about it and everyone was looking at a Rowan who seemed no different from the one that they had known for almost three years now. Everyone was confident that what had happened was a one-off event and extremely unlikely to be repeated.

Chapter 3

The clinical students return to Cambridge almost a full month before the undergraduate teaching term begins; thus, it was, at the beginning of September, that Rowan, Madeleine, Paige, and Meera all turned up at the Mill Road house with their luggage, including their new Littman stethoscopes, and an inordinate degree of enthusiasm. The day was spent deciding who would have which room and making sure that everything needed for living was in place. The great thing about Mill Road is that it has a huge variety of food shops, from oriental to middle eastern to vegan and vegetarian. All four women enjoyed cooking and so, nobody in this household was going to starve. They had chosen the house because it had four bedrooms of a decent size, a living room, and a separate large kitchen dining room with a huge table, ideal for entertaining. It also had two bathrooms, with showers and a bathtub. Tom had told Rowan that a bath was a great way to relax and unwind after a whole day on your feet in the operating theatre. He had forgotten to add that he usually did it with a glass of whiskey and a good book, topping up the tub with extra warm water as the bath cooled down, and sometimes, topping up the glass of whiskey as well.

It was the fourth week of September, and the undergraduates would soon be coming back. A few of them had already returned, such as Suzannah, the student union president, to prepare things for the incoming students, or to take pre-term specialist courses in technical methodology for their third-year research projects. The Senior Tutor, Adrian Armstrong, who was also the pre-clinical Director of Studies for the medics in the college, was sitting in his study going through the morning emails. It was fascinating how things had changed during his fifteen-year tenure of this post. When he started, his PA had been a secretary, the morning ritual consisted of his secretary opening all the correspondence and sorting it into the wastepaper basket, the we-can-deal-with-this-later folder, or the urgent and needing attention now. The two of them had then sat there with Adrian dictating to the secretary, who had excellent shorthand, and signing any letters from the day before that needed signing. There had been social contact; there was an understanding. As time went on, the secretary had developed the ability to come with drafts for the more routine matters, and through shared experience, had come to be a sounding board for more delicate decision making.

The situation now was entirely different. He now had Ellie as a PA, who dealt directly with the more routine matters which Adrian hardly ever saw. The difficult matters came straight to Adrian's computer and were dealt with by Adrian himself, often without any input from Ellie. The idea that something would not be dealt with immediately was almost an anathema. The one thing the PA did do was to sit in her office all day and be accessible to students calling about any matter that the students considered urgent. Requests for face-to-face meetings with the Senior Tutor were managed, alongside the diary, by Ellie. She would leave a note on the desk for him to pick up when he returned to his office from his laboratory.

This morning, there were two matters which demanded immediate attention. One was a request from the president of the student union to see him urgently to discuss a slightly delicate matter, she had refused to say what that was. The other, which, strangely, proved to be related, was a request from the Cambridge Constabulary to see Adrian with a request for his assistance. All the other matters by email were quickly dealt with, either by deletion or by a rapid one, or two, line response. Meeting announcements were referred to Ellie, and the diary began to fill up. Adrian was the secretary of the Senior Tutors' Committee and a member of the University Council. Both these roles meant attendance at committee after committee; the laboratory was a welcome respite.

With her usual remarkable efficiency, Ellie had suggested appointment times which suited Adrian very well; they would even allow him time to nip up to the parlour for a cup of coffee with the Bursar, after Adrian's morning visit to the laboratory to check up on his research group.

Adrian's laboratory was on the top floor of a building built in the early nineteen hundreds, and there was no internal lift. It meant five flights of stairs before he could open the door to the lab and check on everyone. The department's chemical and general stores were on the ground floor. There was an external goods lift which could carry equipment and materials to the upper floors, but it was not a passenger lift. It was also slow and relatively inaccessible at the end of a long corridor, so Adrian and his research group got a lot of exercise. Indeed, they became so fit that they decided to form a running club and call it the Prairie Scooters, with a logo of a road runner, in dark blue on a gaudy yellow background. They regularly entered local 10k events and even half marathons. A few of the people who came through the lab over the years did go on to run marathons, but that was on an individual basis and not as members of the Prairie Scooters team.

All was well in the lab. Adrian sat for a while with the PhD students, discussing the next steps in their projects and talking over the results with them. Rowan had been part of the team during her third year, and one of the PhD students had picked up the project where Rowan had left it. It was an outstanding student project, hence the award of the Glover Prize, and the post-graduate student was taking it further, adding to the data to create enough power in the analysis to give the result statistical significance. It was very close to being publishable, and from it, Rowan would get at least one publication in a major scientific journal, as one of the principal authors. Jake, the student, was in regular touch by email with Rowan, about the project and its write-up.

This was the first time since Rowan's suicide attempt that Jake, who had been working away at Cornell for the past six months, had been able to talk to Adrian about what had happened. Both Adrian and Jake agreed that the incident seemed completely out of character. Both agreed that the write-up by Rowan had been spectacularly strong and needed only more data points before submission. It was simply the constraint of time, not quite enough data points, that had meant it could not be published as it stood. All Jake was doing was simply to repeat some of Rowan's experiments to provide those data points. The abstract, the introduction, the methods, the results, the discussion, the conclusion, not a single word needed changing. Adrian went over to his computer in the laboratory office and dashed off an email to Rowan to explain the situation and congratulate her, yet again, on an amazing piece of work. He then, confident that all was going well in the lab, returned to St Joe's for a morning cup of coffee, before the first of his meetings, with Suzanne, the president of the college student union.

Coffee with Mark, the Bursar, was a regular thing. Mark usually sat there with the newspaper open at the puzzle page doing the Killer Sudoku, although he only ever did the harder ones. The Bursar of a college is essentially the Finance and Resources Director. The Senior Tutor is the Education and Welfare Director. Adrian and Mark often sat together and discussed college business informally over coffee when they were not discussing more important matters, such as football. Although not directly responsible for welfare and education, Mark was an outstanding Bursar but, also, a very wise educationalist, and his opinions often challenged, and to an extent, guided Adrian in the forming of action plans. Over coffee this morning, Adrian speculated on the reason for Suzanne's visit later.

"You know, Mark," said Adrian, "I think this is going to be about one of two things. It will either be about the macho culture in the bar at the beginning of freshers' week, or it will be about the recreational drug issue. There have been a lot of funny tobacco smells around in recent years."

"I think you're right," said Mark. "My guess is it will be both and that both will be linked. Subtle coercion of naïve young freshers by the old hands. Isn't that why you banned anyone, apart from freshers, from going to the bar on the first three nights of term?"

"That's right. Got a lot of stick from the student press for it but it was the right thing to do. So was limiting alcohol on the first night there. You remember the students asked me to do that because not everyone has a drinking culture and many freshers had little previous experience of alcohol. That stringer at St Alfred's, what was his name, Hugo Gill, he told the *Daily Herald* reporters about it, and they came to see me. He told them I was a teetotal spoilsport who had banned alcohol from the bar on the first night. I will never forget the guy's face when I sat him down, asked him if he wanted a sherry, and poured one for myself. I think he said something like 'I've been had, haven't' I?'" The story got killed.

"But it needs more than that to protect the more naïve youngsters. We just need to work at changing the culture so that macho male and predatory behaviour is unacceptable. We need a culture of reporting and then we need to act on the reports. I can see a lot of permanent banning from the bar and a slight massive dip in my popularity in the opinion polls."

And Adrian laughed.

They finished their coffees and went their separate ways.

Chapter 4

When he got back to his office, Suzanne was waiting for him, and he called her in.

"How are you, Suzie?" He asked.

"Fine thanks. How are you?" Suzanne said.

They got the pleasantries over and then got to the business. Over the previous two terms during which Suzie had been president, the college officers and the student union had built a very strong working relationship, each grateful to the other for support and cooperation.

This conversation was indeed about drink and drugs, basically marijuana, and inappropriate behaviour in the college bar. Suzie wanted Adrian's assurance that the same arrangements as last year would apply this year when the freshers came up in a week or so, and that she and the Junior Common Room committee could report on bad behaviour, confident that it would be dealt with. She also wanted permission to continue the system of fines, and requiring people to clean up their own mess, if they got drunk and vomited, or otherwise messed up the bar.

This was a no-brainer for Adrian. If he could get the students to police themselves, they were always far stricter than he was, and he only had to step in when things were a bit more serious.

Adrian reassured Suzie that nothing would be changed about the successful arrangements from last year, and that if there were a need, he would put notices on the tables in hall warning about good behaviour. He also reassured her that there would be zero tolerance of sexual harassment.

Suzie departed, content that the college was doing the right thing.

The next visitor was an Inspector Jacobs of the drug squad. His request was a little unusual; he wanted to use a room in college overlooking the bus terminus to conduct surveillance on the activities there. The police were quite sure that there was a great deal of drug dealing going on in the public lavatory attached to the bus station, and they needed somewhere where they could not be seen, to monitor the activity for a week or so. The question was whether the college would allow them to use the room on the corner of one of the college's residential blocks overlooking the scene. Jacobs was adamant that it was not university students they were concerned with but a group of local drug-dealers resident in the town.

This was, as it turned out, not a difficult question to answer. It happened that the ideal room was a fellow's study belonging to one of the fellows who was currently on a year's sabbatical in New Zealand. Adrian would contact him by email to get his agreement to use the room and would then let Inspector Jacobs know as soon as an answer came back. If that did not work, there was an overspill computer room on the floor above, which could be temporarily closed, and used for the surveillance. It was now Tuesday afternoon. The inspector would prefer to set up the surveillance from Thursday, if possible, that would cover the heavy dealing activity, associated with recreational nights out, over the weekend. Adrian agreed to that and was gratified to find that the email he had bashed out to Mellor, the fellow on leave in New Zealand, while he was still talking to Inspector Jacobs, had already been responded to positively. He told the inspector and suggested that, when he left the office, the inspector should go to the porters' lodge and get the porter to give him a key and take him over to see the room.

Adrian, who had an immense appetite for caffeine, offered the inspector a cup of coffee; the inspector accepted and the pair of them sat talking for a while. The inspector talked about the hidden level of recreational drug usage in universities in general and Cambridge, in particular. The use of recreational drugs was mainly confined to marijuana, a bit of ecstasy, and a few other trendy recreational drugs. Alcohol was still the drug most used by students.

"The problem for Cambridge," said Inspector Jacobs, "is that the fast train to King's Cross is only a forty-five-minute journey; it goes very frequently, King's Cross is a huge drug dealing centre. My worry is that the dealers can bring strong stuff up here and prey upon inexperienced users. That can lead to bad accidents. In general, the students tend to be victims rather than the cause of the problem. But university towns attract people playing on the generosity and naivety of the young, so we do have a problem in this city."

Adrian thought about this. As secretary of the Senior Tutors' Committee, he had a role to play in bringing issues to the notice of the other Senior Tutors and their colleges. Realising just how ignorant he was himself about the drug scene in the city, he decided to ask the inspector if he would like to come and address the next meeting of the Senior Tutors' Committee. The inspector thought it would be an excellent idea.

Adrian ended this meeting realising the level of ignorance that he himself possessed about the drug scene among the modern youngsters. Having grown up in the late sixties, he could smell funny tobacco a mile off. As a student in London, he had joined a volunteer group of students taking soup and bread to the rough sleepers of north central London. The group met in Camden Town and made huge urns of soup from produce donated by local businesses. Unsold bread from half a dozen bakers was chopped into chunks. The soup and the bread were loaded into an ancient and battered, and smelly, Volkswagen camper van, and the half dozen student volunteers disappeared to do 'The Soup Run.' First stop was the queue of job seekers lying on the pavement in carboard boxes and sleeping bags outside the Marchmont Street job exchange, waiting for the possibility of casual labour in the morning. Second stop was outside the grating venting the kitchen of the Strand Palace Hotel. It was warm there, warmed by the heat of the kitchen inside. The third, and final stop, was under the arches outside Waterloo Station. That third venue was always the most populated and the most depressing. Many there were very young, desperate escapees from abusive or simply dysfunctional families, just waiting to be picked up and pimped, or turned to drugs, or both, by predators. The police regularly came along and checked for under-age runaways, but it was a soul-destroying task. Adrian had got to know a few of the junkies and when they were brought into casualty, with their infections and pneumonias and other complications of the junkie lifestyle, as a medical student on casualty, he would often be able to talk to them and get much more information than a stranger would have done. This drug scene bore no relationship to the university student drug scene, and Adrian recognised his complete ignorance in that respect.

The university and colleges had drugs policies which complied strictly with the law while, at the same time, trying to offer welfare support to students struggling with either alcohol or drugs. Dealing and supplying was a criminal offence and students caught dealing or supplying would be reported to the police. Possession of illegal substances would also be liable to reporting, but possession of legal quantities of drugs, while they might not be criminal offences, might lead to college sanctions and disciplinary procedures, or to a review in which the student would be offered help to deal with their issues. Like all other Senior Tutors, Adrian hoped that he would not be called upon to implement the sanctions in the drug policy. So far, he had been lucky.

Rowan, meanwhile, was enjoying her introductory course. It was a mixture of theoretical and practical advice on how to examine a patient, take a history, take blood, and importantly, how to behave professionally. Life-like plastic arms saved pain and frustration for both student and potential patient. The big advantage of living in Mill Road was that a short cycle ride got you to the hospital, a short cycle ride got you back to college, and a slightly longer, but still manageable, cycle ride got you to the river and the boat house or the playing fields. Rowan and the other three housemates settled into a routine where one person cooked for all four of them, on a rota basis. They had to sign themselves in or out by lunchtime on the day before, and they could invite guests and sign them in, also before lunchtime on the day before. The girls ran a weekly contribution system and were charged extra for each guest. The meal allowance was £1.50 per head and guests were charged at £2.00. For the first two weeks, all four girls had been in the house all the time, but for the second two weeks, they all four went out on placements. Rowan and Paige were at Hinchingbrooke, a hospital in Huntingdon very close to Cambridge. It was convenient because Paige had a car, and on days when Paige could not give Rowan a lift, there was a guided bus from the station, very near to the Mill Road house that the girls were sharing, all the way to the hospital. The same bus could, if necessary, take them back from Hinchingbrooke all the way to Addenbrooke's, useful if they had to attend an evening lecture or seminar. Meera and Madeleine were at Stevenage, the big Lister Hospital there. Student overnight accommodation was arranged there, so, unless there was an urgent reason for returning midweek, the two girls left early on Monday morning and returned, not too late, on Friday afternoon. The house felt a bit empty, and Rowan and Paige, always very sociable, tended to arrange compensatory dinner guests in the week, and a dinner party, with any of Meera's and Madeleine's particular friends, for one of the weekend evenings.

Chapter 5

On the last Monday in September, Nigel Crofton-Jones rang his girlfriend, Angela Huddlestone, when he got back from Cambridge late that afternoon:

"Hi, Angie. You free for dinner tomorrow night. Thought we could go to that nice Greek restaurant off Gower Street down in Soho?"

"Hi, Nige, I would love it, and guess what, my flat mates are all away, so we can go back to my place afterwards. Have you been up to Cambridge for the usual? My stocks are running low," said Angela.

"I can help you there," said Nigel. "I still have plenty here, but I have brought back something else a bit exciting to hand over to you for safekeeping; could make a shed load of money out of it."

The two of them, even though nobody had managed to pin it on them, during their three years in Cambridge, had been part of a syndicate that made a business out of supplementing their student grants by dealing in recreational drugs. Everyone suspected they were doing it, but apart from their customers, who had a vested interest in keeping quiet, nobody knew for certain that Angela and Nigel, and some of their friends, were dealing.

They had both come up to Cambridge with a history of having used drugs recreationally in the sixth form at school. Angela had been at a sixth form in a Hertfordshire suburb of London and had first smoked pot at the age of 16, when her then boyfriend took her to a rave at a disused airfield about 20 miles away. Angela and her parents were often in conflict, right from the time she started to get piercings and tattoos, in year 10 at school. It was difficult for them to completely understand her. She was academically very able, and they rather let that distract them from any behavioural issues. When they went to parents' evenings, and they did go to parents' evenings, they almost felt they needed to take a passport along to check they were talking about the same child. Angela was, apparently, a perfect student in school. Her parents knew her as a complete disaster at home.

In the sixth form, Angela had become less of a perfect student, she tended to rely entirely on her wits and to be very lax about homework and class assignments, but she was so much cleverer than her contemporaries that the school, just like the parents, began to turn a blind eye. There was one episode when she turned up at school apparently drunk, but they just sent her home and told her not to do it again. She wasn't drunk, she was stoned, but the school did not realise. The school might have recognised that Angela was beginning to keep company with some of the more disruptive elements, the students who had poor disciplinary and attendance records, but it was a very large comprehensive, and there were a lot of disruptive pupils; so Angela just became part of the backdrop.

Nigel had been a boarder at a minor public school up near Leeds. His mother and father had divorced shortly after Nigel was born, and his mother had emigrated to Australia with a doctor she had met during the pregnancy. Hugh Crofton-Jones had come home unexpectedly from work one day to find his one-year-old child playing in his play pen while Mrs Crofton-Jones was romping away in the matrimonial bed with the local doctor. Nigel's mother's affair with the doctor had led to the divorce but a deal was struck whereby, in return for not having to pay her any alimony, Hugh Crofton-Jones allowed his wife to sue for divorce. The doctor was then able to disappear to the Antipodes with his new wife, and practise medicine in Melbourne without a stain on his character.

Nigel's father was a very senior civil servant; Nigel was an only child, and neither Hugh Crofton-Jones nor his second, and trophy, wife wished to have their lives disrupted by the need to look after a child. A nanny was employed for the first few years and as soon as they could, when Nigel turned seven, they sent him off to prep school as a boarder. He took the common entrance at 13 and from 14, he was at this ancient, and a little second rate, establishment on the edge of the Yorkshire moors. To be fair to the school, they did their best for him academically. The small class sizes, and the persevering watchfulness of the staff, meant that Nigel overachieved in his 'A' levels and managed to get into Cambridge, but not without a scare.

During Nigel's time in year 12, it became clear to the headmaster that someone was supplying cannabis and other recreational drugs to the boys and girls in the sixth form. A search of all the studies found cannabis in the four-bed study that Nigel shared with three other lads. The head could not prove which of the four the drugs belonged to. He called them in and interviewed them separately and concluded that it was Jonas Clarke, one of the less academically able and slightly more disruptive boys, who was the ringleader. Jonas took one for the team and was relocated in a school about thirty miles away. The remaining three had the sense to cool it for a bit, but they did get back into it after about a term. They decided that smoking cannabis was a dead giveaway so they switched to supplying other recreational drugs, like ecstasy, as well as the cannabis, and they insisted that cannabis could only be taken orally. The home economics teacher was gratified that the entire student body became very interested in making cakes. The school tuck shop ran out of Betty Crocker's Brownie mix almost every month.

Angela finished her latest project a little early on the Tuesday afternoon. Her company was working on an advertising campaign for a well-known brand of chocolate and trying to widen its appeal to include younger and more trendy consumers. As one of the other members of the team had said, "Not just Radio 4 listeners." Angela had been proofreading the final drafts of the newspaper campaign. It had not been particularly demanding, and she had finished it quicker than she and the rest of the team had anticipated. She passed the printed copy and the electronic files on to the person who was going to be working on the layout, and then left the office and went home.

She had a little time before she was expecting Nigel to call to collect her, so she rolled herself a spliff with some Golden Virginia tobacco and a little of the marijuana from her stash in the coffee tin on the windowsill. She ran herself a bath, put some bath salts into the water and lay in the tub smoking her spliff, relaxing, just chilling out. A few puffs were enough, so she carefully extinguished what was left and put it in a tiny tin that had once contained drawing pins. She shaved her legs and under her arms. She washed her hair, then she lay there soaking until the water got quite cool and she got out, dried herself and got dressed ready for the evening. Angela tended to dress a little theatrically still. She had to tone it down a bit for the office, for example, some of the facial ironmongery, as her father used to call it, was removed for work, but when she went out in the evening the jewellery came back, and you might have described the rest of her clothing as having been designed by a charity shop, for British Home Stores. She was an avid charity shop customer. She really did not like wasting money on clothes when there were bargains to be had. She was attractive enough, and still young enough, to get away with it. She could look good in a sack.

Nigel arrived on time, dressed still in his work suit. In describing Nigel's dress sense to someone else, Angela once described it as utterly non-existent. As a student, he had been just scruffy; lazy about shaving, lazy about bathing, except with Angela, and lazy about washing his clothes. Angela thought he had probably worn the same set of jeans every day, until they crawled into the rubbish bin by themselves, and the same 'Radiohead' t-shirt, the same underpants, and the same socks. She knew that was not quite true, about the socks and underpants anyway, but that was a marginal adjustment to her thoughts about him. When he graduated and moved to London to the law firm, his father had taken him out and bought him work clothes, and as far as Angela knew, the work clothes, suits, shirts, ties, and shoes, were all the clothing he possessed, apart from those bloody Radiohead t-shirts, he must have got a job lot, and a couple of pairs of jeans. Even Angela, with her aversion to wasting money on haute couture, had a couple of decent outfits that could take her to a posh cocktail or dinner party.

But Nigel was Nigel, and she did not know why, she loved him, and she believed that he loved her. So off they went together to dinner, but not before he had left his briefcase in her flat. They were off to dine with a mutual friend from university, Henry Castleton, and Henry's new girlfriend.

Angela and Nigel walked from Judd Street down to Russell Square and then over to Tottenham Court Road and the restaurant. Henry, and his new girlfriend Judith, were waiting for them. Angela and Nigel had their usual starter of hummus, then Angela had the stuffed vine leaves and Nigel had lamb skepasti. Judith ate very little, she simply picked at a few of the dishes that comprised Henry's selection of meze. She also had a small piece of Henry's chicken skepasti.

This was the first time Angela and Nigel had met Judith; so, there were a lot of introductions, and asking about each other. Judith was a fellow pupil at the same law firm as Henry. She had done her undergraduate degree at University College, and lived in Hampstead, near to the Heath. She was good company, and the four chatted happily for a couple of hours. Nigel and Angela rarely bothered with dessert but on this occasion, they shared some baklava. The other two also shared a portion of that very sweet honey laced pudding. They had two carafes of the house red, which the waiter said was Limniona from Thessaly, and they each had a coffee to finish their meals. It was delicious. Nigel paid the bill, and they all left shortly after 9:30 pm. Henry and Judith headed off towards the bus stops on Tottenham Court Road, to get a bus towards Hampstead. Nigel and Angela said goodbye to them and headed on towards Judd Street.

"We can go back to my place for a change," said Angela. "The others are away in Tenerife."

"Great," said Nigel. "It so happens that my dad is staying at the flat tonight, so I was thinking we might have had to get a hotel room."

"I've missed you," said Angela.

"I've missed you too," said Nigel.

They practically ran back to Angela's flat. They acted out one of those scenes you see on films where they are practically falling over trying to get their clothes off, when, if they took a little more time about it, they would be quicker, and safer, stripping methodically; they flopped into Angela's queen size bed, and made love.

Angela dug out her spliff and re-lit it, and Nigel rolled himself one, using her tobacco and what was left of her marijuana.

While they smoked, they talked.

"I've got you some more marijuana," said Nigel. He went over to his briefcase, took out the weed and put it in Angela's coffee tin.

"Not much this time, Angie," he said. "But it will keep you going until I can get back up to Cambridge again and meet our old friend from the Market Square."

"Thanks," said Angela. "What were you doing in Cambridge yesterday? You said you had something for me to store; I presume that is so that your dad doesn't find it. And you said it might make big money."

Nigel walked over to his briefcase, took out several small, sealed, packets of white powder and put them on the bedside table.

"Do you know what these are?" He asked.

"I'm guessing they are either cocaine or heroin," said Angela.

"They are about the purest heroin that anyone has seen for years. Each one of these little packets will make up into at least fifty individual packets. That would give us fifteen hundred doses. At ten quid a shot that gives us about fifteen thousand pounds. And there is loads more where that came from."

"My god," said Angela. "Who did you get it from?"

"Needle," said Nigel.

"You know, Nige," said Angela, "marijuana and recreational drugs are one thing; you might even get away with a reprimand if the Law Society found out, but heroin means you will get banned from practising law completely, and your dad will not be able to save you. I really am unhappy about doing this. This is moving in with the big boys and we are just a couple of kids. Have you told

Henry about this? I'll store this stuff for now." And Angela started to put the drugs under the pillow on her bed.

Henry had been a friend of Nigel from before Cambridge. They had been at the same boarding school up in Yorkshire, and during the lower sixth year, it was they who had shared, with two other boys, that four-bed study where the drugs were found. After Jonas had got himself expelled, there were just the three of them, Nigel, Henry, and Charles Ma, sharing that set. In the upper sixth year, they all had individual studies but the three remained firm friends.

"I rang Henry," said Nigel. "He was quite excited about the idea."

"I'm really not happy," said Angela, "I'll store the packets for you this time, but please don't bring any more of them round here, and please move these on as soon as you can. I expect Henry will know how to do that. He was always the brains of this outfit in terms of handling the drugs. As I said, marijuana and ecstasy, fine, but I do not want anything to do with heroin or cocaine or any other class A drugs."

Nigel rather glossed over that and started to turn over to kiss Angela again.

"OK," he said.

"Promise?"

"Promise!"

And they started to make love again.

Eventually, they fell asleep with Angela wrapped in Nigel's arms.

They woke about 6 am and made love again. By this time, the packets of drugs had been scattered all over the room by their somewhat energetic love making.

They then got up and had breakfast. It was just toast and marmalade, orange juice, and coffee, but at least it was sourdough toast. They did not have time to put the drugs away, and as the others were away, Angela did not bother to tidy them up, she just left them scattered on the floor.

The pair of them got dressed for work. The charity shop clothes went back in the closet, and the smart office wear came out. Nigel had only the suit he had arrived in, but he shaved, using Angela's razor, and so was half presentable when he left with her to head out for a day's work.

Chapter 6

Once Angela had turned off towards the advertising agency, Nigel continued towards his law firm. Angela and Nigel had agreed to meet up for dinner on the Saturday evening at the Pizza Express near the British Museum. Nigel paused briefly in Russell Square and sat down on a bench. He got out his burner phone and dialled the first of the two numbers on it. It was Henry's burner number. Henry answered immediately.

"Give us a sec. I just need to go out of the office for a moment."

Nigel waited for Henry to speak again.

"OK, I hope this is urgent, we mustn't overdo using this number," said Henry.

"You think I don't know that?" Nigel said. "Of course, it's urgent. I just wanted to tell you that I picked up the stuff in Cambridge on Monday and Angela is minding it for us, but she has said she will not be doing it again. She doesn't mind the goods we handled in Cambridge, she didn't know about the other stuff, but she does mind, very much, the class A stuff, and she will not do it again. I don't think we need to worry about her telling anyone, but I sort of feel we ought to let her bow out gracefully now. I think I need to move on anyway. There's this new girl, Samantha, I met when I was delivering some papers to Carter and Pritchard's, and I must admit I am getting a bit tired of Angela and her working-class chic. I'll find a way to move on. When I gave the stuff to her yesterday, I managed to get a video of her putting the white powder away under her pillow and telling me that this was the last time she was going to store heroin or cocaine for me, I'll let her know about that. I've got a bit where she just says, 'I'll store this stuff for now.' I can edit it so that it is a separate sentence and then she is absolutely compromised. No need to tell the boss, I don't think we need to anyway. I'll cut out the bit where she mentioned you and me by name."

Henry listened, acknowledged what Nigel had said, and rang off.

Then, Henry called a number on his burner phone:

"Boss, Henry here. We have a problem. Angela is backing off from being part of the team. Nigel has some video of giving her some H to look after, but he seems to have managed to record a conversation in which Angela implicates both

Nigel and me in drug dealing at Cambridge. It would not be much of a step for the narcotics squad to work from that to where we are now. I am not comfortable. Nigel says he can delete that bit and just leave the bit that compromises Angela, but it worries me. It would probably be alright if Nigel were not going to dump her, but he is going to chuck her in the next couple of days. I think she is crazy about him, and I can honestly see her landing us all in it. Got any ideas?"

The scrambled voice at the other end replied, "Leave it to me. I'll sort it. Just keep your head down and get ready to put the screws on Nigel if you must. We need to tie up a couple of loose ends here. Angela wasn't, and Nigel still isn't, as committed as the rest of us to making a load of money out of dealing. I'll sort it."

Henry rang off and went back to his office; the other participant in the conversation made a telephone call to a person in Scotland.

Angela came home that evening at about 6:30 pm. The agency had kept everyone on, a little after the normal end of the working day, to get this chocolate advert into shape for sending off to the newspapers and magazines in time for the weekend supplements. The advertising space had been booked, but the detail still needed thrashing out.

She let herself in, as usual, and made herself a cup of coffee, which she left on the table while she went into the bedroom to change into something a bit more casual than the power dressing suit she wore to the office. She flopped down in her chair, reached for the remote and turned on the news channel. She decided that she would clear up the room, including the packets of powder, after she had drunk her coffee. That was the last decision she ever made.

Chapter 7

Back in Cambridge, it was the fifth week of the introductory course and the week on which all the freshers had arrived. The first week of Full Term.

Adrian was fully occupied with overseeing the settling in of the freshers and the return of the other years. The college was buzzing with life. Adrian was sitting in his room in college, having a brief respite from the hectic schedule, when Ellie buzzed through to him.

"I have an Inspector Gregory from the Metropolitan Police on the line for you," she said.

Adrian took the call.

"Adrian Armstrong here, what can I do for you, Inspector?"

Adrian listened in shocked silence as Jerry Gregory told him that one of his recent graduates, Angela Huddlestone, had been found dead in her flat in Judd Street, sometime the day before.

Detective Inspector Jerry Gregory had been called to the flat in Judd Street early on Sunday morning, and he and another detective, Sergeant George Trinder, given the inevitable nickname of 'Tommy,' had begun the collection of evidence. When they arrived, Nigel Crofton-Jones, the boyfriend who had made the 999 call, was still there with the body. They introduced themselves and asked him what had happened. The first thing he said was:

"I found these packets of white powder on the floor and put them on the table for you. I checked that Angela had no pulse and was dead, but otherwise I have just been sitting in this chair waiting."

Jerry and 'Tommy' were furious but kept their feelings under wraps. The little bugger had interfered with the crime scene. It might not matter, but it might be very important.

There was a used syringe and needle and a tourniquet. The body was sitting in a chair next to a small table. The body was relatively flaccid, and the detective surmised that death had occurred at least two or three days earlier. Looking at the bare arms of the girl, she was not a regular intravenous drug user, there was only one puncture mark over the antecubital fossa, and it had bled a little, making it obvious to see. Exact time of death would need a pathologist's report. They could see no signs of a struggle and no signs of injury, no bruising or cuts and scrapes. The syringe, the needle, the tourniquet, and the packets of drug were all collected in evidence bags and taken away for analysis. There was also a coffee cup on the small table next to the chair in which Angela was sitting. That too was put in the evidence bags for analysis. Jerry and Tommy looked at each other. This did not look like a typical overdose at all; nor did it look like a suicide; there was no note and no evidence of a reason for suicide, and the flat was tidy and clean. And who makes themselves a cup of coffee before committing suicide? They found some cannabis hidden in a small coffee tin on the windowsill next to the bed, no more than one might have expected someone to have for personal use.

The detectives began to make enquiries. The obvious first person to speak to was Angela's boyfriend, Nigel. He was here and must be a prime suspect.

Nigel Crofton-Jones had studied English with Angela at Cambridge, but not at St Joseph's. He had changed Tripos in his second year to law, but, through theatre and previous association, he remained her boyfriend. He and she had been members of the theatre set. The pair of them had obtained jobs, she at a major advertising agency in the city, and he at a law firm, and they had moved together to London. Angela had moved into the flat near King's Cross with two other girls, but the two girls had been on holiday for the past week and were only due back the following weekend. It seemed that they had gone to Tenerife. Nigel was living in his daddy's flat in Mayfair; Nigel's father was a very senior civil servant.

Nigel was still at the flat with the detectives. He had waited with the body until they arrived.

"Sit down please, sir," said Jerry.

The questioning was obvious and direct. It began with gathering some background.

"How long had you known Angela?"

"Since our first term at Cambridge. I met her at the freshers' fair, we were both looking at taking part in the theatre. That was just over three years ago."

"When did you last see her alive?"

"Last Tuesday. We went out for dinner at this Greek restaurant in Soho. Afterwards we came back here. We usually go to my place, but because the other girls were away, we came here for a change. I stayed the night, so, strictly, that would have been Wednesday morning when I left, and she was very much alive then."

"Do you know where Angela's two flat mates went?" Jerry asked.

"I think it was Tenerife that she said they had gone to. They are not due back until next weekend."

"How close were you?"

"Very close. We would probably have got engaged soon."

"Did either or both of you use drugs regularly?"

"Angela used some things, but only recreationally. Only a bit of marijuana, now and again. I think she had used cocaine a couple of times."

"When did she start using drugs?"

"She told me it was at school, in the sixth form. Someone gave her a spliff at a rave, and she quite liked it."

"Did you ever use drugs or obtain drugs for anyone else?"

"No, never," lied Nigel.

"Those packets of white powder in Angela's room, the ones you picked up and put on the table."

Tommy practically spat out the words.

"Do you know what they might be and how she got hold of them?"

"No idea, Inspector. I assume they are some sort of drug, and I could speculate, but I have never seen Angela with anything other than the odd bit of marijuana."

At this point, Nigel was beginning to sweat.

"Would you mind if we take your fingerprints, sir? We need to go over the room to check if there are any fingerprints here that should not be here. Since you said that you came here last Tuesday and stayed overnight, we need to eliminate your prints."

"OK," said Nigel. "I am really happy to cooperate. I really want to know what happened. I can't believe Angela would have taken an overdose."

"Nor do we, sir," said Jerry.

And he noticed that Nigel had a sharp intake of breath, almost as if he had been hit in the stomach. The guy was hiding something.

"Are you sure you have never seen packets of white powder like this before?" Jerry repeated.

"Only on telly, Inspector," said Nigel.

"Do you know if Angela had any other friends who might have called on her here at the flat?" Tommy asked.

Nigel gave them quite a long list of Angela's friends, mostly from her time at university, both college and theatre related, who were now living in London. Jerry and Tommy groaned; this was going to be a lot of interviewing.

"We shall need a complete list of your movements since last week, sir. I am sorry to have to ask, but I am sure you do understand that we need to eliminate you from our enquiries. If you could write it out and email it to me, here is my card."

And Jerry handed Nigel his card.

"If possible, we would like the names and contact details of anyone who can corroborate what you tell us. Just routine, sir," said Jerry.

"Please let us have a number where we can contact you and please stay local. We need your address too in case we need to call you as a witness at the inquest. We will almost certainly need to talk to you again. Meanwhile, I would be grateful if you would keep any details of what you have seen here to yourself, and if you would not talk about the case to anyone else, especially not the press. Now, if you don't mind, sir, I think the crime scene people want to get on with their work and it would probably be best if you were to leave. One of my officers will give you a lift home."

Nigel acknowledged the request and picked up his coat, put it on, ready to depart.

Jerry Gregory went outside quickly and spoke to one of the constables.

"Chris, take the guy home and go in and sit with him. Ask him if he minds your having a look round, and if he says he does, then just sit there until we get there. I am going to get a warrant to search his place in case any more of these little white packets are around."

Detective Constable Chris Howes came back into the flat and collected Nigel to give him a lift back to his apartment.

As soon as Nigel had gone, the two detectives looked at each other and raised their eyebrows.

"Not a very trustworthy character," said Jerry. "I bet we find his fingerprints all over the white packets. I bet they were there in the first place. Not just because he kindly picked them up for us. What a smart little bugger he is."

"My guess," said Tommy, "is that the boyfriend supplied drugs to Angela, and something went wrong. But I don't see her as a regular user. Marijuana, bit of ecstasy, yes, but heroin? No. I don't see that. I don't believe that he never touched the drugs either, but I suppose he had to tell us that, because he wants to be a lawyer."

"Well, we need to interview all those friends and see what they know about the lifestyle of these two. We'll need to be gentle because my guess is that they will all be a bit cagey in case anything they say might damage their high-flying careers, especially the lawyers he mentioned. I think we need to be in touch with the two flat mates sharpish. The caretaker will probably have their names and some contact details. Better get Jenny Patel on that one; she is very good at breaking bad news. We need to talk to them, but we can probably do it over the phone to begin with. No point in dragging them back from Tenerife or wherever it was he said they had gone."

Jerry turned to one of the constables working the room.

"See what contact details you can get Jeff and pass them on to Sergeant Joseph. Did you find a mobile phone yet?"

"Yes, Guv. We have it. It's an iPhone, so unless we have the pin number we are going to struggle."

"Try the boyfriend," said Jerry. "He may know her password and pin numbers. People often share their password with their partner."

"I have a bit of a hunch here, Tommy," said Jerry. "I wonder if this is a big mistake and the overdose happened because the heroin was much stronger than expected. Can we get the lab to check the purity of the white powder, and can they also check that it is the same in the packets as the syringe? It just doesn't feel right, does it? I want a full toxicology report on her blood."

Tommy agreed with Jerry:

"That Nigel really did seem a bit smooth but also, he got very nervous with a couple of the questions. Let's get the search warrant just in case he is uncooperative. Oh, and make sure they bring her laptop, and ask the boyfriend if he knows the laptop pin number and password. It will save the guys a lot of hassle."

As they left the building, some reporters accosted them.

"We understand there has been an unexplained death in the flats here, sir," said the taller of the two. "Would you be able to give us any further information?"

"No comment at the moment," said Jerry. "We will issue a press release in due course."

The two reporters resorted to their usual secondary line of investigation and began talking to neighbours and bystanders.

Tommy commented to Jerry:

"Going to be all over the papers tomorrow morning and on the websites this evening. Better get the press office to sort out a statement to keep things under control."

Chapter 8

At about the time that Adrian received his telephone call from Inspector Gregory, Rowan received a text message from Amanda Sayers, one of the girls who had shared a staircase with Rowan and Angela last year. Amanda had gone to Oxford to study for the BCL. The text contained some shocking news. Angela Huddlestone had been found dead in her flat near King's Cross. It appeared that she had been dead for a few days and had only been discovered on the Sunday morning, yesterday, because her boyfriend Nigel had been expecting her to join him for dinner on the Saturday evening, and Nigel had become concerned when she had not turned up. She had also failed to answer any of his phone calls. The police were treating the death as suspicious. It was in the morning editions of the papers in London. Amanda had gone up to London to visit a friend and had seen the report in the early editions of the *Evening Standard*. It was from that and the press releases on the local news stations, that Amanda had obtained the information she had relayed to the girls in Mill Road.

Inevitably, there were several telephone calls from friends who had known both Rowan and Angela, and the conversations were not always kind. They all knew that Angela had been one of the girls who regularly smoked marijuana and dabbled in other recreational drugs. Jane, one of Rowan's other friends, said that she thought Angela's boyfriend, Nigel, had often obtained very strong stuff from London, for Angela and some of the others. There was a sort of bet going on that this had been an overdose. Over lunch in the medical school common room, Meera, Rowan, Madeleine, and Paige discussed all this. Meera commented that she had often smelt, very strongly, the aroma of marijuana on the landing outside Rowan's college room, especially in that final year.

"I don't know how you put up with it?" Meera said.

"It was tough sometimes," said Rowan. "I often went to the library to work, because of the smell, and I never did drugs, as you know. But I felt I couldn't report them because two of them on the landing were lawyers and would have lost their careers if they had been done for drugs, and Angela was a 'thespie' and had that awful boyfriend Nigel, and I sort of thought they were both a bit alternative. It was Amanda, one of the two lawyers, who emailed me this morning. I assume the three of them had been keeping in touch with each other."

"Bet this is drug related," said Madeleine. There was a lot of nodding of heads.

It was now almost three months since Rowan's suicide attempt, not long as time goes, but long enough that she was beginning to be able to remember some of the events leading up to it. Until this moment everything after the final exam paper on the day before the overdose had been a complete blank but now, she was beginning to remember the morning of the event. What she did recall was that she had woken early and gone for a run as part of her fitness programme for the rowing. She remembered enjoying breakfast and she remembered going to the library to read over her project in preparation for the viva the next day. Then, the blankness descended again, and she was unable to recall anything further about that day. The next thing she could remember was waking up in hospital with Tom squeezing her hand and giving her a kiss. She smiled to herself when she remembered what she had said to him, but he did need a shave!

At St Joseph's, Adrian Armstrong, having received the news that Angela Huddlestone had been found dead in her flat, and that the death was unexpected, thought back to her time as a St Joe's student. She had been a very good student actor, and he had watched her a couple of times at the ADC, the Cambridge University Student Theatre. She had made a quite outstanding Blanche DuBois in Streetcar, and a very impressive Yerma in the Lorca play of that name. It did not seem possible that such a talent could have been snuffed out, and only a few months after leaving St Joseph's.

Adrian tried to remember if there had been any disciplinary or other incidents, and the only thing he could recall was that some of the other students had suggested that there was a boyfriend, from another college, who seemed to be spending a lot of nights in St Joe's. The boyfriend was not well liked by the other students on Angela's staircase. He was a little noisy and he tended to get drunk, or maybe stoned. There had been a couple of complaints that he might have been smoking marijuana in Angela's room, but that had never been proved. Adrian did recall that he had spoken to Angela about this, and she had promised him that it may have been a one-off event and she would make sure that her boyfriend never did it again, although she never admitted explicitly that he had been a marijuana user.

Adrian had rung the Senior Tutor at the boyfriend's college and had been told that Nigel Crofton-Jones was the son of one of the most senior civil servants in the UK, and Nigel did have a bit of an attitude, but he was not totally out of order. The other Senior Tutor promised to have a word.

Now, he came to think about it, Adrian recalled that he had seen this Nigel character in a couple of roles at the ADC. He was not in Angela's league, but he was a competent enough performer.

Adrian did the usual thing. He contacted the Master and the Tutorial Office and the University Press Office. Everyone was advised not to talk to the press but to refer any telephone calls to the Master. A brief note was prepared for distribution to all the staff, including the fellows, giving them the bare facts of what had happened, expressing sympathy to relatives and friends, and advising them to pass any enquiries to the Master's PA.

Adrian recalled that Rowan had been on Angela's staircase in her final year, so he sent her an email suggesting that she contact him when she had a moment. Given the recent events in which Rowan had been involved, Adrian wanted to make sure that she was not too upset by this fresh tragedy.

Rowan was sitting in the canteen having her lunch with the other girls when the email came through. She decided to wait until she got home that evening before talking to Adrian, but she sent him a very brief text saying that he should not worry, she was fine, and she had already heard the news about Angela.

Supper that evening was Meera's speciality, coq-au-vin. With some nice French bread, from the bakery in Mill Road, to mop up the gravy, and a good green salad to clean the palate afterwards, in true French style, the four girls enjoyed their evening. Rowan almost forgot to call Adrian, but she managed to get through to him at 7 pm, just before he went over to hall for dinner. It was mainly a case of reassuring him that she was still alright, and then talking about the papers that they were writing, together with the PhD student. Adrian told Rowan, again, that he really would like her to try to find some time to come into the lab and do some more science, and he pressed her to consider doing her SSC (Student Selected Component) with him. Rowan felt flattered but probably more importantly, excited at the idea of more science. She agreed to talk to him about a proposal for the first SSC, due over Christmas and early in the New Year. She then went back and enjoyed a glass of Beaujolais with a little camembert that one of the other girls had brought back with her from a visit to her parents.

Chapter 9

Back in London, Jerry, and Tommy, had been reviewing their notes for that day. Constable Howes had taken Nigel back to Nigel's father's flat and had been refused permission to search the premises. Crofton-Jones Senior, alerted by his son, had been waiting at the flat having rushed up from the family home in Kent, and had been less than pleasant in his manner towards the constable. Despite their best efforts to obtain a warrant in time, the two detectives knew that there was a likelihood that any evidence, if there were any, would have been got rid of by the time the search took place. There was no clear evidence that Nigel was in possession of drugs, or had supplied drugs to Angela, and so there was no realistic chance of getting a search warrant. Crofton-Jones Senior basically told the police to get lost.

As soon as the police had left him at his father's flat, Nigel was on the burner phone to Henry.

"Angie's dead," said Nigel.

"How do you know?" Henry said. He was clearly shocked by the news.

"I found her dead in her flat on Sunday morning. I was supposed to go out with her on Saturday and she didn't turn up. I was going to tell her this weekend that we were finished, but someone finished her off first. I went round to the flat on Sunday morning to check on her and found her dead from what looked like an overdose. But we both know she didn't use the stuff. Did you tell anyone I was breaking up with her? Did you tell the boss about our conversation?"

"Of course not," lied Henry. "This must just be random bad luck. Was it a robbery or something?"

"I don't think so, there was nothing missing, and it wasn't a junkie because they left all the drugs there. I had to pick them up and put them on the table, because my fingerprints were all over them. I left her iPhone, but whoever killed her had taken her other phone, so we are safe there. I gave them the pin to her iPhone but there aren't any incriminating calls on it. I also gave them her computer password, but that doesn't have stuff on it either."

"What do the police think?" Henry asked.

"They're suspicious. They don't think it was an overdose, and nor do I. If I didn't know what a bloody chicken you are, I would suspect you, and are you sure you didn't tell the boss I was busting up with her? After what happened in Cambridge, I am not sure it was not organised by the boss."

"I think you're being paranoid. What did they ask you?"

Nigel told him.

"Did you give them my name?" Henry asked.

"No, I bloody well did not," said Nigel. "But I bet they will go and ask people in Cambridge and that someone is bound to tell them who you are, and how you spent lots of time with Angie and me, so I suppose you had better have your alibi ready."

"I was in Paris from the following Thursday after we went out to dinner, and I am still there. I don't come back until next Wednesday. They cannot interview me until then anyway, and I reckon by then they will have seen most of the other contacts. When do they think she died?"

"Well, I think they believe it was sometime on Wednesday or Thursday, so you'd better be ready for that. You were still here on Wednesday night and Thursday morning, I presume?"

"I was. I expect they will check up on me. Fortunately, I took Judith out to dinner on the Wednesday evening and the Eurostar went quite early on the Thursday, so I think that'll stop them hounding me."

The names on the list given them by Nigel Crofton-Jones were supplemented by an additional list that Jerry had obtained from Adrian Armstrong on the Monday morning, after the news of the death had broken. Jerry had asked about Angela as a student and Adrian had confirmed that he had had to have a disciplinary talk with her about her boyfriend and 'funny tobacco,' although the use of marijuana had never been proved for either of them. Adrian had also confirmed which students had been on Angela's staircase in the final year, and that she had been almost totally wrapped up in theatre, and Nigel, the student at St Alfred's. Adrian mentioned that he had had some suspicion about Crofton-Jones and the supply of marijuana to other students in the university. He had talked to the Senior Tutor at St Alfred's about the matter. There was also another friend of Nigel's, a Henry something, who spent a lot of time in St Joe's. That gave Jerry and Tommy a few more names for the interview list.

On Tuesday morning, Jerry and Tommy sent members of the team off to conduct most of the interviews with the recent contacts in London. That included the people that Angela worked with and some new social contacts that she had made through work and in the building where she lived. They decided that they themselves would interview the Cambridge contacts.

Chapter 10

The conversation with Freya Phillips took place in Regent's Park during Freya's lunch break. It seemed like a convenient place to meet someone studying at the Royal College of Music. The detectives and Freya sat wrapped up warmly in gentle autumn sunshine on a bench overlooking the Japanese Garden just inside the inner circle. The only information that Freya conveyed was that Nigel and Angela had been good friends. She did inform the detectives that there had, in her opinion, been some cannabis usage, and sometimes there could be a bit of a fug on the landing, but she said that the use appeared either to have gone down, or to have become more discrete, after Robert, one of the other people on the staircase, had complained to the Senior Tutor. She was asked about Angela's friends, and she told the detectives that they were mostly theatrical people, especially in the third year. When asked whether there was anyone other than Nigel who seemed to be a particular friend, Freya did say that there was another actor who spent a great deal of time in Angela's room, whether Angela and Nigel were there or not. She could not remember his name, but he was tall, with light brown hair, and Freya thought he might be from St Alfred's, the same as Nigel. Certainly, he was always wearing a St Alfred's scarf, with its horribly clashing orange, pink and yellow stripes. Freya had seen Nigel and Angela once since they had all decamped to London. It was in early September, and they had met, with Robert and Robert's friend Stefan, at the Pizza Express near the British Museum. Robert and Stefan had come up from Oxford for the visit. It had been pleasant enough, but nobody had made immediate plans to meet up again, although Freya had seen Robert and Stefan since then. Robert and Stefan had friends in the University Chaplaincy student house near Gordon Square and Freya had been there for one of the communal meals.

"Not much useful information from that," said Tommy afterwards. "Might be good to find out who that other chap was who spent time in that room. Otherwise, it just confirms Crofton-Jones's story, and despite his denial, I reckon it puts him as an occasional marijuana user."

******

The following day, Tommy and Jerry went to speak to the next obvious person on the list. Robert Parker had lived, in the last year, on the same staircase as Angela, Freya, Amanda, and Rowan. Robert was currently in Oxford studying for the BCL with a view to taking a pupillage the following year and becoming a barrister. Amanda was also in Oxford on the same course as Robert, so they arranged to meet her too.

The two policemen went together to Oxford by train. Jerry always found going on any GWR train a romantic event. As a child, he had a wooden jigsaw puzzle, an antique almost, since, these days, and even when Jerry was growing up, most jigsaw puzzles were made of cardboard. The puzzle was called 'Ancient and Modern' and pictured two locomotives in GWR livery running alongside each other, one a 'sit-up-and-beg' model that Stevenson would almost certainly have recognised, and the other a streamlined steam locomotive that, in terms of design shape, would probably sit comfortably alongside one of today's high-speed diesels. If any child in the Gregory household was ill, they would sit up in bed with a large red oxo tin, suitably stuffed with sweets, a tray in which to assemble the jigsaw puzzle, and the magic jigsaw puzzle itself. It occurred to Jerry that, if you had not been ill when you first opened the puzzle, its exposure to bug after bug over the years would make sure that you were ill by the time you finished licking your fingers from the sweets and put the last piece of the puzzle into place.

Oxford Railway Station, rather like the one at Cambridge, is nothing to write home about, but they were not there on an architectural survey trip. They hopped on a bus from the station to the centre of Oxford and then walked to the college where Robert had arranged to meet them. As they approached, a slim, well-dressed, young man who was talking animatedly to a slightly chunkier individual, walked away from them and went into the middle common room, the place with papers and a coffee machine where graduate students can pass the time together.

Robert Parker was a slightly fidgety, slightly fussy, slightly chunky, sort of person. He seemed quite uncomfortable with the two policemen, but both thought that it was a general discomfort in new social situations, rather than having anything to hide. Robert had a strong, deep, voice, and both Jerry and Tommy thought they could see him making impressive opening statements, and concluding remarks, in a court of law.

The two detectives introduced themselves as always, professional and to the point.

They found what Robert had to say interesting. He explained that he had chosen the room at the top of the Cumberland Building because he knew that Rowan and Freya were there, were studious and yet sociable and popular, and he himself wanted a degree of privacy in his life. Amanda, another lawyer, was also there, and he and Amanda often used to work together over legal cases and their interpretation. The top of Cumberland provided just that degree of privacy he needed. He told the two detectives that he had complained to the Senior Tutor about Angela, although it was not really Angela, it was more the boyfriend, Nigel, and his seemingly endless stream of rather smelly visitors, especially one lad from St Alfred's. Robert explained that he was particularly upset about the smell of marijuana, because he needed to be squeaky clean for a career in law, and he was worried that he might be unfairly convicted of complicity in the drug use. He had consulted Amanda before making the complaint, and she had agreed to back him up. He was a bit surprised because Nigel was also studying law and he needed to remain absolutely without any criminal convictions or cautions. He said that sometimes, in the daytime, the smell of marijuana had become so strong that he, Robert, was almost under the influence himself.

The complaint to the Senior Tutor seemed to have dealt with that problem, but after the exams started, and in the couple of weeks leading up to Rowan's overdose, it seemed to have intensified. It was only Robert and Rowan who would have noticed that because Freya had finished her exams early and had gone home to practise for her RAM audition. Freya lived in North Hampstead and was from a somewhat musical family.

"I sometimes wondered whether it was her wish to be a musician, or her predestination," said Robert.

"What about Rowan Pike?" Tommy asked.

"One of my favourite people," said Robert. "She always found the time to listen to me when I had problems, and she always made time for me when I needed to try out a speech or a line of argument. It wasn't just listening passively either. Rowan has a very sharp mind, and she would often pick holes in my arguments and help me to improve them. I would love to hire her as a speech writer if I ever went into politics, which I may yet do."

"We understand that she took an overdose at the end of last academic year?" Jerry said.

"It seems impossible now," said Robert. "And it seemed impossible then, but she was found having taken a massive overdose of paracetamol, and I understand it was touch and go at one point whether she might need to have a liver transplant. Thank God for Addenbrooke's and how amazing a hospital it is. But she is doing well now. She recovered in time to join us for graduation, and she has been in touch with me since she started back at clinical school. I am going up there the weekend after next, with Stefan, to stay over with some friends, meet the four girls, and go to a formal hall dinner in college."

Then Robert took his courage in both hands, he had still not come out to his family, and he said, "I swear, if I were not gay, I would be chasing after Rowan. As it is, I simply adore her, and I just wish I had been there to stop her taking those tablets. She was the one who helped me come out to myself. She was the one who helped both Stefan and me to accept ourselves. I come from a very religious family, my father is a vicar, and I still have not been totally honest with him or my mother, but I think they are slowly realising who I am and what I stand for. They are good people, and it will come right. I think I will ask Rowan to come with me when I tell them."

It was a brave thing for Robert to say to complete strangers, but it was the right thing to do, and Robert felt very good about himself afterwards. The two policemen liked this young man and hoped for a good career for him. They were grateful for what he had said so far but they wanted one thing more.

"Do you know the name of the character from St Alfred's that you did not really like?" Jerry asked.

"You mean apart from the Nigel bloke?" Robert said. "Yes. It was Henry. Henry Castleton. He was another lawyer in my year. Very smart in a clever sort of way. Not just clever, sort of clever-clever. A bit too fly, for my liking. I think he got firsts in the first two years but a 2.1 in his final year. He was a regular opponent in debate at the union. I think his father is a high court judge in the north somewhere. Anyway, he's got a pupillage lined up down here in London in one of the Magic Circle chambers. Good luck to him. I think he will come unstuck unless he improves his work ethic!"

"Another tricky interview to organise," thought Tommy.

"All these 'posh school' boys with powerful dads," said Jerry, quietly to Tommy.

"Robert. Thank you very much for talking to us. Here is my card. The same number gets Tommy here, so, if anything else occurs to you, call at any time. If we are not there, it will go through to an answerphone and our answerphones are monitored frequently. Good luck with your BCL and I look forward to bringing a case before you in the high court one day. Now, we'll let you get back to your, no doubt more interesting, conversation with Stefan. Thanks for your time."

Amanda Sayers was waiting for them in her college room. They called at the Porter's Lodge and were directed to the correct staircase by a burly ex-soldier who was now the head porter of the college.

Amanda was quiet, rather plain, and very clever. She wore very thick horn-rimmed glasses which indicated a remarkable degree of short sightedness. She had protruding front teeth, with a gap between the upper incisors, and had clearly not had any orthodontic correction. She had little to add to what Robert had told them except that she did say that she found it very frustrating sometimes to have to go to the floor below to use the bathroom, because Nigel and his friend Henry would sometimes spend a very long time in there.

"And if it wasn't one of those two, it would be Angela and Nigel, having a long bath together," said Amanda.

"Did you complain?" Tommy asked.

"I did, but they called me a useless frustrated old bag and took no notice at all. In fact, they were rude to me most of the time. I just ignored them and used the loo and shower downstairs. It didn't bother me because Freya, Rowan and Robert were always very friendly, and over the years, I have developed a combination of a thick skin, and an utter contempt for those that think it clever to be rude to people they think might be vulnerable. I intend to go into human rights law to support people who are less tough than me and need the law to help them sort out bullies. I suppose the only thing that did hurt me was that we had all been quite friendly before that third year. I wondered if Nigel had been the thing that changed our relationships."

Jerry and Tommy walked from Amanda's college back to the station, enjoying the ancient town on the way.

The two of them came away from the interview almost in awe of this remarkable young woman. They talked a little more about human rights, discrimination, and prejudice, and found themselves discussing it further on the train back to London. Both made a note to watch out for Amanda Sayers, a potential QC of the future.

That evening, Jerry sat talking to his wife Marianne in their terraced house in Finsbury Park. It was an area described by estate agents as up and coming.

Jerry and Marianne were only too glad that when they had managed to buy the property it had not yet started on its up-and-coming journey. Marianne was French and taught French at a local school. They had two children, James, and Audrey, who were bilingual and smart with it. James was basically a scientist and Audrey loved literature and theatre. Both Audrey and James had their sights set on top universities and, in the meantime, they went locally to school and enjoyed the benefits of being young in London.

"I'm off to Cambridge tomorrow," said Jerry. "Need a bit more background on that girl who died of an overdose last week."

"Ça va bien," said Marianne. "If you don't mind, I will not be going with you."

Jerry laughed. They both knew that business trips were business trips.

"We will have to take James up there to have a look sometime soon," said Jerry. "He needs to think about applying next October. I suppose we ought to take him to see Oxford too. But I think he is set on Cambridge. I think he will also want to see several other places. London is easy, we're here. But he might want to look at Manchester and I think he talked about Durham as well."

"Plenty of time," said Marianne. "Might as well take Audrey too. She is only a year behind him, and we can have a rare family outing."

"OK," said Jerry.

"When are you going to give up smoking?" Marianne asked.

"When you stop bringing me those French cigarettes back from your day trips to Paris to see your mother," said Jerry.

Chapter 11

Jerry and Tommy caught the fast train from King's Cross direct to Cambridge. They got the number 1 bus to the city centre and got off outside the Grand Arcade. They walked to St Joseph's.

Their first interview was with Adrian. It was Adrian's second appointment that morning with the police.

Inspector Jacobs of the local police had called on Adrian first thing to thank him for the college's cooperation with the surveillance, and to report that they had managed to gain a huge amount of intelligence on the local dealers. They had recorded several days of CCTV footage and caught several drug deals online. Inspector Jacobs said that there were likely to be a lot of arrests soon, and at least for a short while, the supply of drugs would be hit quite hard. The dealers were all local people and nothing directly to do with the university but, disappointingly, a few students had been buying, although, as far as the inspector could tell, there were no takers from St Joe's.

They had drunk another cup of coffee together and parted having done quite a lot of good for town and gown relations.

Jerry and Tommy came in and introduced themselves. They thanked Adrian for agreeing to meet them.

"No problem, gentlemen," said Adrian. "I was sad to hear about Angela Huddlestone. She was a slightly troubled soul, but intelligent, and a rather brilliant actress."

"From talking to some of her friends and associates, we get the impression that she may have been dabbling a little in drugs, just recreational as far as we can tell. Can you tell us any more about that?" Tommy asked.

"Indeed. I had occasion to call her in and ask her to sort out that boyfriend of hers, Nigel Crofton-Jones. He was practically living here. We don't really allow that, although it is a bit difficult to police now that we have fewer bedmakers making up the rooms and the rooms are not serviced every day. I had received a minor complaint from Madge Cooper, the housekeeper, that Angela's room was getting a bit smelly. I think she also thought they might be growing cannabis there, but it turned out to be coriander and basil. Apparently, they made a lot of middle eastern and Italian meals. Probably, just pasta with tinned tomatoes if I know the culinary skills of the thespian brigade. Anyway, shortly after the housekeeper complained, one of the students, Robert Parker, also complained but his complaint was about passive smoking of cannabis. He complained that there was so much cannabis smoke around sometimes during the day that he was almost getting high himself. He also complained that a lot of people were coming up to Angela's room during the day, and only spending a few minutes there before moving on. There was one lad, also from St Alfred's, who spent a lot of time there in Angela's room even when Angela and Nigel were out.

I called Angela in and gave her a very strict telling off and warned her that I was not prepared to turn any sort of blind eye to this. If she or Nigel were dealing in cannabis, or any other drugs for that matter, I would be notifying the police. I referred her to the college policy on drugs and addiction and gave her a copy of it to read. She assured me that it was only occasional use by herself and that no dealing was going on. I had no direct evidence, but I asked the porters and the bedmakers to keep an eye open, and I think Angela knew it. I don't know what happened after that but the complaints from Robert ceased and everything seemed to settle down. I did, however, notice that Angela was absent from college more than she was present, and Nigel hardly ever came here again. I did contact his Senior Tutor to offer a friendly warning, but she was already aware that Nigel might be using marijuana and just promised to warn him that it could prevent his having a career in Law. It might be OK for an English student to have a police caution, but it would not be helpful to a potential lawyer."

The rest of the information from Adrian corroborated things that other interviewees had told the detectives. Adrian did not know the name of the young man from St Alfred's who had been such a regular visitor, but he suggested that when they interviewed the Senior Tutor of St Alfred's; they might have more luck in finding out who he was and how to get in touch with him.

Adrian's appetite for coffee extended to offering the two policemen a cup of real coffee at Savino's, the best coffee shop in Cambridge. It was on the way to St Alfred's, so the three of them walked over and ordered coffees and a couple of the delicious homemade amoretti biscuits each. Adrian liked to go out to Savino's for coffee, it made him feel almost human and not just an academic hack.

The two policemen went off to St Alfred's and Adrian went back to St Joe's.

****

Marjorie Grey, the Senior Tutor at St Alfred's, welcomed the two detectives into her study. There were the usual introductions, and the detectives were offered yet another cup of coffee. Tommy, a little older than Jerry, immediately asked if there was a loo nearby that he might use but said yes to the cup of coffee. While he was out of the room, Marjorie asked Jerry whether he had been to Cambridge very much in the past.

"You know, I think this is my first visit. But I hope it will not be the last," said Jerry.

Marjorie asked him to explain.

"I have two bright teenagers," said Jerry. "I expect you hear this all the time, so I won't bore you with it. One wants to do Physics and the other wants to do English, although I rather think she wants to come here because of the ADC. She is heavily into theatre at school and with local drama groups, and she's funny. I think that, among other things, she has 'Footlights' in her sights."

"That's good to hear," said Marjorie. "And you are right. I hear all the time from people with very bright children, especially former fellow students who have not contacted me for sixteen or seventeen years, depending on exactly how old their ewe lamb is!"

"Well. I leave my children to it," said Jerry. "My wife is French and teaches in the local comp, I never went to university, so I leave it to the school to advise them. They'll do what they need to do, and I just hope they find a course and a career they enjoy. I started life as a railway man, and I joined the Met when my mum and dad moved to London. Hendon was my tertiary education!"

At that point, Tommy returned.

"Sorry," he said. "Got lost when I dived into that old building with the spiral staircase inside. Apparently, I shouldn't have gone that far."

"How can I help, Inspector?" Marjorie asked.

"You probably know that we are investigating a suspicious death in London of a former St Joseph's student. Her body was found by a former student of yours, Nigel Crofton-Jones. We wondered if you could give us any information about Crofton-Jones and one of his associates, whose name has also come up in our enquiries, a Henry Castleton, we think his name is?"

The look of pained resignation in Marjorie's eyes probably said it all.

"You know, Inspector," said Marjorie, "in every year there are some students you hate to see leave and there are others you cannot wait to see them go. I regret to say that you have mentioned two in the 'thank goodness we don't have to put up with them anymore' category. I am sure Nigel was into the drug scene, but we could never prove it; it was all really hearsay and happenstance. I had complaints that he was sometimes either drunk or stoned in supervisions, and he was always a bit disruptive and trouble making around college. I am convinced that he was responsible for smashing the glass doors to the bar on one occasion but the CCTV camera covering the door had chewing gum stuck on its lens just before the incident. I called him in and threatened to get a DNA analysis and asked him for a sample, but his father, one of the Whitehall Mandarins, phoned me and was aggressive beyond belief.

I really believed that Henry Castleton was the other involved, but his father is a high court judge up in Leeds, so it wasn't worth pursuing. I think Castleton might also have been on the margins of the drug scene, but again, we never had any proof. I remember them all sitting on the grass by the duck pond after their exams finished, eating brownies, and drinking champagne. My bet was that those brownies contain cannabis. The pair of them were law students so what they were doing was doubly stupid.

I must say I feel a little guilty in hindsight. I tried to crack down but could not find any physical evidence; in the end, it seemed to be just a few students that were involved. The girl who died in London used to come here and join them, so I kept a watching brief and was glad when they left.

If they were using cannabis, I don't think they were distributing the drug to others, just using it, and our policy on drugs is basically to admonish and advise, unless it is clearly breaking the law. If I had thought they were distributing, I should have informed the police immediately. As you can tell, I tried the admonishment and got a bloody nose from powerful parents. Advice was, in the end, a big waste of my breath."

There was not much more to be gleaned from this conversation. The two detectives asked for contact details for Castleton and, since withholding that information would have impeded the investigation of a crime, the information was given. It was just an address, an email address, and a mobile telephone number.

The officers finished their coffees, thanked Marjorie Grey for her help, and went out to the street. Jerry lit up a cigarette. It was his first of the day. He was trying very hard to cut down, with a view to giving up, as Marianne was constantly nagging him, and he knew she was right.

"I'm hungry," said Tommy. "You would be too, if you didn't smoke those blooming things."

After two more quick puffs, Jerry put the cigarette out in one of those black litter bins, with the sand tray for cigarette butts on top.

"OK. Chicken and chips or noodles?" Jerry said. There were several big franchises along Regent Street where they were now walking.

They settled for the chicken and chips.

After lunch, they caught the bus out to Addenbrooke's Hospital where the clinical school was situated. They had arranged to meet Rowan there at about 2:30 pm and she was sitting in the common room waiting for them when they arrived.

Jerry looked at her. She looked the epitome of health. Tall, graceful, full of life, and with a dazzling smile. It was difficult to believe that she had so nearly died only a few months ago.

"Rowan Pike?" Tommy asked.

"Inspector Gregory?" Rowan asked.

"Not actually Rowan, I'm Sergeant George Trinder, but everyone calls me Tommy. My colleague here is Inspector Jerry Gregory."

Introductions over, they settled down to talk about Angela, Nigel, and that chap Henry, that seemed to be cropping up in all the interviews conducted so far. They didn't really learn anything new about these people from Rowan, but there was a moment, when they asked her if she could recall any occasions when the cannabis smell on the landing had been particularly strong, when they noticed a flicker of what looked almost like pain cross her features. Rowan had another of those flashback type moments and was walking back to her room after seeing Angela on the Rec; she could remember as far as entering the staircase, but then things blanked over once more.

There was something very disturbing about these memories and she could not pin down quite what it was, but, somehow, she knew that she was working her way to understanding what had happened that day of the overdose, and she decided that letting it come back slowly, rather than trying to force things, would be a good idea. It hurt her too much to try and dig deeper now.

Rowan talked a little about Freya, Amanda, and Robert; it was clear to the detectives that she liked these three people, and that she was, at best, neutral towards Angela.

"I was grateful to Robert for making the complaint about Angela and Nigel," said Rowan. "I find the smell of marijuana nauseating, and I really didn't want to be inhaling it. It caused a bit of friction when he put the complaint in, but Robert did the right thing there."

Rowan did not know anything about Henry, only that she had seen him around in college rather a lot, especially towards the end of the Easter term, the exam term, of their final year.

Jerry and Tommy thanked Rowan for her time, received a beaming smile as their reward, and went back out to get the bus and train back to London.

Chapter 12

Sitting in the train on the way back to London, Jerry got a text message. It said simply:

"Lab and Path reports in. Very Interesting. Get your little backside over here as soon as you can."

It was from their chief inspector. It was intriguing.

The train pulled into King's Cross and Tommy and Jerry rushed for the taxi rank. It was about 4:30 pm, so the traffic was not bad, so by 5 pm they were sitting round a conference table with DI Lusinga and the rest of the team.

"The first thing you need to know is that the pathologist puts time of death as sometime on the Thursday, about 48–72 hours before the body was found. We checked with her advertising firm where she was working, and she did work a full day on the Wednesday but did not come in on the Thursday. That sort of fits; and it puts Nigel Crofton-Jones out of the picture for the moment, although we need to look at CCTV and get a slightly different slant on any alibis he comes up with. The second thing you need to know is that the heroin, yes, it was heroin, in the packets is about the purest that the lab has seen in twenty years. The third thing is that the heroin in the syringe is not the same batch as the heroin in the packets. The chromatography shows traces of different substances in the syringe sample. Finally, there were very high levels of flunitrazepam, Rohypnol to you, in Angela's system. Traces of Rohypnol were also found in the coffee cup."

There were sharp intakes of breath all round. Tommy and Jerry were clearly right to have been suspicious. *This was murder. It looked very much as if someone had given a high dose of Rohypnol to Angela, and while she was unconscious, had overdosed her with heroin. How did the Rohypnol get into the coffee cup? Who put it there?*

It was now a murder enquiry, but there was still no idea of why this girl had been killed. There was no obvious motive and no obvious suspect, apart from Nigel. The team would now need to examine the CCTV in the entrance hall to the building for the relevant periods. The caretaker would be worth another chat too.

The very pure heroin pointed towards a motive associated with drug dealing, but that was not much help. Clearly, they now had to carefully scrutinise Nigel's alibis for the Wednesday and Thursday and have a much more in-depth conversation with him. He would probably want his lawyer to be present. They decided to contact Nigel immediately and let him know about the findings of the pathologist. At the same time, they would ask him to come in and talk to them, and advise him that he could, if he so wished, bring a legal representative with him.

It had been a long day. They went off home. Tommy called in at a branch of Harry Ramsden's on his way and bought himself and his wife cod and chips. Jerry telephoned Marianne and arranged to pick up a couple of pizzas for the family on his way home.

****

Over this next week, the second four-week block of the introductory course for the clinical medics began. The four girls who had been out at district general hospitals for the past two weeks were all back together at Addenbrooke's for two weeks. They would be back out at their District General Hospitals for the second two weeks of this block. They were now considered almost safe to go on the wards and into the outpatient's departments and GP surgeries, depending on where they were being sent on their clinical rotations. This meant that the amount of clinical contact time was increasing, and they were putting into practice some of the things they had already been taught.

During this second four weeks of the course, much of Rowan's spare time would be spent planning her laboratory involvement for her first Student Selected Component, the part of the course where the students could choose how they spent their time, either on the wards or in the laboratory. She was going to do a lot of bench work, chemically analysing the hormone content of various foetal rat blood samples, and then measuring the biochemical activity of certain enzymes in their lungs. It would be quite intensive, but these were assays that she had done before during her project work last year, and so the preparation was about deciding which samples deserved the intense attention that the project entailed.

The girls in Cambridge, and Adrian, knew nothing about the Rohypnol and the fact that this enquiry was now definitely being treated as murder, not just as suspicious circumstances. While the detectives in London continued their investigation, life in Cambridge went on very much as normal for the time of year. Adrian and the college were busy with the new batch of undergraduate and postgraduate freshers.

All the students who were coming back to Cambridge for fourth year undergraduate courses or graduate study were now back, so the girls arranged a dinner party for the coming weekend, to welcome back some of their friends.

And that is how, on Saturday of that week, eight St Joseph's students sat down together for an evening meal, at the house in Mill Road.

The inevitable topic of conversation was the dreadful news about Angela. She had not been a particular friend of any of those present, although Dorcas, who had read English with Angela, had known her rather better than the other seven. Ashok had taken Angela to a May Ball at the end of the first year; he had been quite besotted with her for a while, but that had come to nothing because, by then, she was really quite heavily involved with Nigel.

"I hear the police came to see you this week, Rowan," said Ruaridh. "What was that about?"

"I think they were trying to get some background on Angela because they went to see the Senior Tutor as well, and then they came to see me and asked me about Angela. They wanted to know about drugs, and I told them about Nigel, and about Robert's complaint about him and Angela smoking cannabis."

"I never liked Nigel," said Ashok. "And it wasn't just because he was going out with Angela. There was something a bit too smooth about him and I swear he was always nipping down to London to get drugs. To be frank, once she started going out seriously with Nigel, Angela became a bit skanky herself. I know you shouldn't speak ill of the dead, but she was quite lively and fun and natural in the first year, and then she became different. I thought some of the vivacity went out of her and she was moodier and a bit aloof. She also stopped hanging around with the rest of us in the JCR bar and spent all her time at the theatre. I know the bar at the ADC is pretty good, price wise and ambience, but it was as if her first year friends didn't matter anymore. I admit I felt a bit hurt at first, because we had been on the same staircase together in the first year and shared lots of cups of coffee and late-night discussions, and then, suddenly, it was as if she didn't want to know me. From what the others on her staircase told me, they hardly saw her in that second year. She was either in a play, or getting ready to be in a play, or in bed with that Nigel bloke. I think she did go to the odd lecture, and she must have got her essay portfolio done, or she would have been chucked out at the end of the year."

"Did anyone in college get to know her that year?" asked Dorcas.

There was a consensus that Angela had completely abandoned her St Joe's affiliation, gone 'thespie,' and devoted the rest of her time to Nigel, in that second year.

"Rowan," said Jim, "how come you and she ended up on the same staircase? Did you get to know her at all?"

Rowan started to talk, and for a moment, as she talked, she had a further short flashback to the day of the overdose. She remembered meeting Angela on the Rec, the large open space with the tennis courts, volleyball courts and croquet lawn, when she came out of the library, but no sooner had that recollection come to her, than the windows of memory closed again, and she came back into the present.

"I don't know why she chose that room. It was right at the top in the attic, it had a nice attic window that looked out onto the Rec, we had a decent gyp room on the landing, and there was a bathroom with a bath. I guess a lot of women prefer a bath to a shower, and I remember Angela spending hours in there soaking, often with that bloody Nigel. She didn't have any friends on the staircase. I think the rest of us, me, Robert, Amanda, and Freya, were all rather hard working and busy with other things, so we didn't make all that much effort to break the ice with her. We were friendly enough when it came to casual meetings, but she didn't really give anything back in conversation. I was busy with the lab, rowing, and these three idiots I now live with; Amanda had her law, and that boyfriend who visited her from time to time; Robert had his mooting and his Union Society; Freya had her music; do you remember the Mendelssohn at the end of the Lent Term?"

Everyone did. Freya was a music student, a former finalist in Young Musician of the Year, and had been a leading light in the University Music Scene. When she left St Joe's, she had gone to the Royal Academy of Music for postgraduate study.

"You know," said Rowan. "The four of us were not loners in the traditional sense, but I think we all chose that particular attic landing in the Cumberland Building because we wanted quiet and some privacy. I know it was not the most modern part of the college in terms of facilities, but it was adequate, and we all wanted a bit of peace and quiet, for our own different reasons. None of us minded

Freya playing her violin, it was a pleasure to relax to at times, and she never played in her room outside sensible hours. All her piano playing was on the Bosendorfer Grand in the music practice room. I sometimes used to go down there and listen. Robert had a very good friend called Stefan with whom he spent a lot of time. I think they were in love, but Robert was a bit shy about it. He comes from a very religious family I think, and he still has not come out to them. I really liked Robert. We sat and talked until quite late on more than one occasion. I think he felt, because I was a medical student, that he could talk to me and know I would be supportive. He was right, of course. For such a powerful intellect and such a powerful orator, he was a surprisingly shy person behind the public façade. I sort of hope that life leaves him alone a bit, to be himself. I remember him taking the health secretary to bits in that debate at the Union in his first term as president. Mind you, by the time the health secretary had finished, it was a miracle that any of us medics still had a career to look forward to."

"What about Angie?" Dorcas asked.

Having been with Angela in supervisions during the first two years, Dorcas was more familiar with Angela, and used her nickname in talking about her.

Rowan went on:

"Well, I guess, it was a place where she and Nigel could just do their own thing. They had a lot of visitors, and it was almost as if Nigel lived there. I was not around much during the day but the bedders told me that there was almost a procession of people coming up to see Angela and Nigel. I think there was some cannabis smoking going on there. I could sometimes…"

Rowan broke off talking and clutched her head for a second.

"Sorry. I just had a brief sort of stabbing pain in my head for a moment," said Rowan. Then she went on:

"I think after he had a discussion with Amanda one day. Robert reported it to the Senior Tutor, but nothing happened. I think the Senior Tutor spoke to Angela and then nothing happened, except that the marijuana smells became less frequent, and Nigel and Angela moved camp to Nigel's place in St Alfred's for a while. They came back though because our food at St Joe's is better."

The consensus was that nobody had any thought about why Angela might have died unexpectedly, nothing from the time at St Joe's anyway.

So it was, a week after the death in London had been discovered, the people from St Joe's most closely associated with Rowan, laid the matter to rest in their minds and moved on to the excitement of graduate study. Dorcas was working on a thesis about the role of music in nineteenth and twentieth century novels by female authors. Ashok was studying some aspect of graph theory which left the rest of them far behind. Someone once described undertaking research in mathematics as being equivalent to building a four-storey house from the top down, in the middle of a housing estate. You are somewhere up in the sky, standing on one leg on a scaffolding pole, trying to locate the right foundations from all those possible down there, and trying to choose the correct building materials to connect you back to those foundations, all the while drinking a cup of tea which you are holding in one hand. Ashok had not yet mastered the cup of tea! Sarah and Julie were two of the other medics on the course with the four girls. Sarah and Julie were 'an item.' Everyone liked the pair and liked them as a pair.

Thus, despite the sad news at the beginning of the week, they all left the dinner table on that Saturday looking forward excitedly to three more years of close friendship, three more years of shared experiences, and three more years of study. It is not always understood by everyone that simply studying and learning and acquiring new knowledge is something that creates the biggest turn on for a lot of people. The privilege of finding something out is, to many, the greatest privilege of living.

Chapter 13

The telephone call from Sergeant Trinder to Nigel Crofton-Jones had clearly shocked Nigel to the core. Sergeant Trinder could hear the panic and shock in Nigel's voice when he was given the news that Angela's death was now a murder enquiry, and Nigel was invited to the Islington Police Station for further questioning on the Saturday morning.

"You will remember to bring the notes of your movements over the whole of the week before her body was discovered, please, sir?" Sergeant Trinder said.

"Yes, Sergeant," stammered Crofton-Jones.

"Please feel free to bring a legal adviser with you, sir," said Sergeant Trinder.

The interview with Nigel was conducted in the presence of a very eminent lawyer who had, no doubt, been contacted by Nigel's father. It did not make a great deal of difference. They hardly expected Nigel to turn round and say that he and Angela had been dabbling in serious drugs, even if they had. The most useful thing was the list of movements, which they could check, and the fact that Nigel was now very uncomfortable, and anxious for his own safety.

"Of course, you are not obliged to say anything, sir, but for your own safety, if you did know anything about those packets of very pure heroin that we found in Angela's flat, I think it would be advisable to talk to us. We believe that whoever supplied those packets was probably responsible for Angela's death, and we would not put it past them to want to tie up any loose ends. I do hope, sir, that you are not a loose end," said DI Gregory.

Nigel looked at his lawyer. There was a slight shake of the lawyer's head.

"I have nothing to say," said Nigel.

When Nigel left the premises, the detectives passed on the list of movements to one of the team for checking. While they were there, Tommy and Jerry asked the team reviewing the CCTV about progress. The CCTV at the flats did not make a continuous recording; it was a motion activated camera system that recorded everyone entering or leaving. The block of flats had about a hundred occupants. The team had seen Angela and Nigel leaving together on the Wednesday morning, as Nigel had previously told them, and Angela returned alone that evening, presumably after her day's work. There were several other entrances and exits over the evening of the Wednesday and well into the night, but the caretaker, who was helping the squad, identified all but four of them as residents or well-known regular visitors. There were just four people whom the caretaker could not identify, and all four of them had kept their faces hidden from the camera, either by accident or design. One was wearing a raincoat with a hood, which he kept up. He came in around 6 pm and left again at about 7:30 pm. The others came in at 8 pm, 1 am and 2 am respectively. Again, the CCTV had not shown up their faces as they came in. The one who came in at 8 pm left around midnight. On this occasion, his face was visible, and they were able to get a screenshot to use for identification purposes. The two other visitors had not left until the following morning, and on this occasion, their faces were visible. The caretaker did not know them, but as they each left hand in hand or arm in arm with a resident, the police were not inclined to enquire too closely about what they had been up to. They did, of course, confirm later with the residents, that the two gentlemen had remained in the flats with their hostesses all night.

That left two possible suspects, the one in the raincoat with the hood, who had been there early evening, and the one who had come in at 8 pm and left at around midnight. The police put a copy of the still photograph of the 8 pm visitor on the inner door of the block of flats, and then they knocked on each of the flat doors, showed the picture, and asked if anyone knew him. They had a positive response from a couple living on the third floor of the block. It was their son and he had come home for an evening meal that evening.

That now left just one possibility, the tallish guy in a dark raincoat with a hood. They had no idea who he was, but he was the only unaccounted for person entering and leaving the block of flats that night, during the time when the murder must have taken place.

"Great," said Jerry. "A man in a raincoat with a hood. Ought to be easy to find under the circumstance. Pissing with rain all day that day, 12 million people in and around London. I think I'll buy a lottery ticket on the way home, better odds of winning the jackpot!"

****

There was now just one more London-based person of particular interest to the police that they had not yet interviewed, and that was Henry Castleton. Castleton was difficult to pin down. He had been out of the country temporarily, visiting a friend in Paris, according to his colleagues at the chambers where he had his pupillage. He did, however, return on the Thursday of that week, and in accordance with the message that the detectives had left for him, he telephoned to make an appointment to see them. So, it was that, on the following Monday morning, Henry Castleton turned up at Islington Police Station with his lawyer in tow.

There are some people you take an instant liking to and there are others to whom you take an instant, and usually lasting, dislike. For Jerry and Tommy, Henry Castleton fell into the latter category. He was tall, blond, and clean shaven with a roman nose, deep blue eyes, and a cleft chin. He exuded overconfidence.

He answered questions readily enough about his relationship with Nigel and Angela, but the detectives always felt that he was holding things back. He refused to comment at all about the suggestion that he himself had taken drugs of any sort, including marijuana. He pointed out that there had been no disciplinary record against him at Cambridge and he claimed to have been squeaky clean. When challenged with the comment that several people had implicated him in smoking marijuana with Nigel and Angela, he simply laughed, and suggested that this was just a device to divert attention from their own misdemeanours.

Henry indulged them for about twenty minutes, perhaps slightly more, and then tried to terminate the interview by saying:

"Well look, Inspector, I am so sorry to hear about Angela's death; she was quite a sweet girl, a little overly theatrical but very pleasant. In fact, I have hardly seen her since graduation. We all had a little drink together at The Eagle just after our degree ceremonies and then we went our separate ways. I've met Nigel and Angela a couple of times for a drink and a snack after work, but we haven't seen much of each other at all since Cambridge. So, I really cannot help you, and, if you don't mind, I have a lunch engagement, so if there's nothing else."

"Just a couple of more things, sir," said Tommy.

"When did you go over to Paris and precisely when did you return?"

Henry thought for a moment.

"I caught the 7:55 from St Pancras last Thursday week. Got me in at just after 11:15 and I was having a light lunch with my friend in a nice little bistro on the banks of the Seine, round about one o'clock. I came back on the 19:13 train from Gare du Nord on Wednesday this week. Sorry, I didn't contact you immediately, but I was rather busy catching up and did not get your telephone message until late on Friday."

"Thank you, sir. So, you were in the country on the Tuesday and Wednesday before the body was found?"

"Yes."

"Well, I'm afraid, we are going to need to know your movements on those two days, right up until you caught the Eurostar. Just so that we can eliminate you from our enquiries, of course."

"Right you are. I'll have a hard think, a lot of my days are routine, and I don't think there was anything special last week, apart from the trip to Paris, so I need to look through my diary. Can I get back to you?"

"Of course, sir. We would appreciate it if you could do so quickly, and if you can list anyone who can corroborate each part of your statement, that would be helpful."

"Am I under suspicion then?" Henry asked.

"At the moment, sir, we are not ruling anyone or anything out. This is a murder enquiry, and we need to follow up every possible lead."

Henry blanched.

"A murder?" He asked. "I thought it was an overdose."

"No, sir. People do not take Rohypnol and then give themselves an overdose. And Angela's fingerprints were not on the syringe or needle or tourniquet."

Henry looked shocked. Whether it was because he had, until then, no idea that Angela had been murdered, or because he had no idea that the police had realised that this was a murder, was impossible to say.

"Well, Inspector," said Henry, "I will get on with producing my itinerary for those two days for you, and if you don't mind, I really would like to keep my lunch appointment."

"Well, that's all for now, sir, thank you. But we would prefer that you did not leave the country and remained available in case we have any other questions for you. Thank you for your help."

And Henry, and his lawyer, left the police station and took a taxi back to the chambers.

As soon as he had gone, the two policemen looked at each other. "What a slimy git," said Tommy. "I don't rule him out," said Jerry. "I think we need a very careful scrutiny of his itinerary and I think we should get the Eurostar CCTV images for the 7:55, a week ago yesterday. We need to be careful about this, but the CCTV guys may be able to ID Henry in some other relevant footage from around the flat area. We can't use that as identification evidence, but it might give us a steer as to how hard to push our enquiries about Henry."

Chapter 14

Both Tommy and Jerry looked forward to the weekend. They had instructed their team to look at the CCTV footage around the area of the flat, especially in Judd Street and along the Marylebone Road, to see if they could locate footage of the person who had entered and left the flats without being identified in any way. Some members of the team were very good at spotting mannerisms, gait, body shape, and similar identifying features, which might be picked up on one of the other cameras. But for the time being, Jerry and Tommy would be off duty over the weekend unless something happened requiring their urgent attention. They had also asked the team to investigate the two Eurostar journeys, any CCTV footage on the train, and put in a request to Interpol to check the arrival and departure from Paris, Gare du Nord. A 07:55 departure on the Thursday did mean that Henry was still in the UK at the probable time of Angela's murder.

Over the weekend, the police enquiry about Angela's murder ground relentlessly on.

When Inspector Gregory and Sergeant Trinder returned to Islington Station on the Monday morning, they learnt that Nigel's itinerary for the days surrounding Angela's death checked out in every detail. There was just one curious element, which Nigel had not mentioned to them before. He had gone up to Cambridge on the Monday of the week Angela was murdered, ostensibly for a meeting at a legal office near the station. The two detectives were puzzled by his failure to mention this in his original conversation with them, but he had a perfectly plausible explanation, that he had simply forgotten to mention it because it was work related, and he thought it was well before Angela's death. For the moment, they accepted that at face value.

Eurostar footage confirmed Henry's departures and arrivals and his Tuesday and Wednesday itinerary checked out. It seemed that he, and his new girlfriend Judith, had gone out to dinner on the Tuesday evening. He had not mentioned the restaurant and the detectives made a note to ask him about that. It occurred to them that Nigel had also gone out to dinner on the Tuesday evening with Angela. They couldn't have met up, could they? They needed to ask Henry where he had taken Judith for dinner that evening. On the Wednesday, Henry had a full diary of appointments during the day and had gone to the theatre with Judith to see Les Misérables, and Judith was able to confirm that. She also confirmed that Henry had taken her home by taxi to Hampstead and she had got home around midnight. Turning their attention back to the Tuesday evening, the detectives discovered that both Angela and Nigel, and Henry and his dinner partner, Judith, had gone to the same Greek restaurant in Soho.

"I bet they shared a bloody Cyprus Mezze," said Tommy. "They are clearly hiding something. That extra pure H is involved, I am sure. And one or the other of these two is distributing, if not dealing."

The two young men were brought in for questioning again. This time, the questions were more focussed and more insistent. The kid gloves had come off, but both young men brought with them extremely competent lawyers and refused to answer any questions that might have incriminated them. They continued to deny all knowledge of drugs and drug dealing. They expressed absolute horror at the thought that Angela might have been dealing in heroin sales.

When asked why they had not mentioned meeting together at the Soho restaurant, Henry simply pointed out that he had not been asked for that degree of detail about his movements on the Monday and Tuesday. Nigel had simply told the detectives that he and Angela had gone out to dinner at the Soho Greek restaurant, and neither detective had asked if anyone else was present. It had not occurred to Nigel to cite the presence of Henry and Judith as corroboration of the alibi. As Nigel's lawyer said to Jerry, "My client has been fully cooperative. He told you originally where he and Miss Huddleston ate on the Tuesday evening, and as soon as you asked, he volunteered the information that Mr Castleton and his friend Judith were also dining with them at the restaurant. I am sure you are not suggesting in any way that my client was trying to conceal information from the police."

Jerry ignored it.

Henry's lawyer made similar comments.

Jerry ignored that too.

"Did anyone else go with you to Cambridge on the Monday?" Jerry asked Nigel.

"No," said Nigel. "I was alone. I was taking some confidential documents to another law firm with whom we are working on a case at the Crown Court."

"Did you meet anyone else in Cambridge?" Jerry asked.

"No, Inspector," said Nigel. "I went straight from the station to the solicitor's office; I gave you the address in my itinerary. Then, I caught the bus back to the Drummer Street bus station and walked from there to the railway station. I thought I needed some exercise."

"You are sure you did not collect any drugs, marijuana or anything, while you were there?"

"No. I have told you before, I have never used nor purchased marijuana nor any other drugs."

Jerry thought to himself, *We don't believe you, sunshine. I need to check with the drug squad in Cambridge. I just wonder if you kept your supplier when you moved to London. It's a long shot but you never know.*

The rest of the interview with both the young men was not helpful. There was nothing that they could pin down, nor could they describe the answers they were given as obstructive. Asking about suppliers would certainly be ruled unacceptable by the lawyers who were present, given that both Nigel and Henry were looking to have careers in law, and had flatly denied ever having used any illegal drugs, recreational or otherwise.

When Jerry and Tommy sat down to think about it, they had definite links between Angela and drug usage, but they had only circumstantial evidence that either of the two young men had even used cannabis, nothing that could be used to caution them, certainly nothing to charge them with.

"I want to know where that pure stuff came from," said Jerry. "I reckon if we know that, it might throw this case wide open. I wish we could get one of those two boys to talk to us."

Chapter 15

Back at St Joseph's College the Cumberland building was being upgraded, a staircase at a time. It was one of the last parts of the college to come in for the renovation treatment. The staircase that Rowan had been on was receiving the treatment this term. The rooms that had been occupied by Rowan, Robert, Freya, Amanda, and Angela were unoccupied this year, and the 'in-house' team of carpenters, electricians and plumbers were busily working on the upgrade. It involved stripping away the plaster and reducing the building, floor by floor, to a bare shell. Wiring, plumbing, fitted wardrobes, these were just a few of the things that were happening. Insulation and sound proofing were being improved, and best of all for the students, individual bathroom pods were being put into the ancient rooms, so the communal washing facilities were being removed. The space next to the gyp room, the room in which the cleaners kept their housekeeping materials, was being converted into a half decent kitchen area.

It was the dismantling of the communal bathroom area that led to Andrew, the head of maintenance, standing in front of the Senior Tutor holding some rather antique looking apparatus. It was a chemical balance.

The other items were things you could buy in a kitchen shop or steal from a chemical laboratory.

Adrian took one look and thought to himself:

If ever, there was a system for dishing out drugs, this was it.

He had no idea what the funnel and rubber tubing might have been for. He assumed the pestle and mortar were for grinding up tablets, or, perhaps, dried plants into powder.

"Where did you find these?" He asked.

"Behind the panel behind the lavatory in the bathroom. Someone had fitted the panel with hinges and a tiny pair of turn latches. In front of it, they had put a false wall panel which hid it completely from view but slid aside for easy access."

Adrian was thinking to himself how he was going to deal with this.

"Thanks, Andrew," he said. "I'll take it from here."

It was almost certain that whoever this balance belonged to was no longer a member of the college if they ever had been. It may well have been Nigel Crofton-Jones or his friend Henry Castleton, or it may have been neither. Adrian thought about it and decided just to put all the stuff away on a low shelf in the bookcase for now and forget about it. He couldn't see any reason to do otherwise. It was not as if anyone was going to claim it.

****

Jerry contacted Inspector Jacobs of the Cambridge drug squad and told him about the murder investigation. He mentioned that he was almost certain that the girl who had been murdered, and two of the possible suspects, had all dealt in marijuana, if not something more serious, when they were in Cambridge, and he wondered if Jacobs knew where the main suppliers were.

Jacobs told him about the two main student suppliers of marijuana; someone who hung around the fountain in the middle of the Market Square; and the one-legged baggage minder in Christ's Passage. He pointed out that there were other drug dealers in Cambridge, but as far as marijuana went, these were the two they knew best. The other dealers were into class A drugs as well as the recreational ones.

"We've just done a seven-day surveillance on Christ's Pieces near the bus station lavatories," said Josh Jacobs. "St Joe's was very helpful: let us have a corner room overlooking the area. We set up CCTV. We are still going through it. Lots of hits so far. I think we are going to be able to clean the place up quite a lot."

Jerry's ears pricked up.

"Any chance you were recording on Monday the week before the girl was found?" Jerry asked.

"Yes," said Josh Jacobs. "We were on it from Thursday to Thursday over the weekend and including that Monday."

"Could I send one of our guys up to look at the Monday footage?" Jerry asked.

"Well sure. What are you looking for?"

"We want to check whether one of our suspects did any drug dealing while he was in Cambridge and we know, because he told us, that he was at the bus station at some point in the late morning or early afternoon."

"Well," said Josh. "I could send you a digital copy of the tapes, but you wouldn't know who the dealers are, and we do. I will send you a digital copy and you can have a look. If you see your suspect, then you can tell us the time, and we can check whether he met up with a dealer. How does that sound."

"That sounds great," said Jerry. "Let's do it."

"One other thing," said Jerry, "we are very interested in the origin of some ultrapure heroin we found in the murdered girl's flat. You haven't come across any packets of ultrapure H in your area, have you?"

"We haven't logged any," said Jerry, "but we have heard rumours here that there is some ultrapure stuff around and some of our snitches have said that all the heroin users have been warned to be careful. There is a chance it could be coming down to London from here, although usually our stuff comes here from London or from..." and he mentioned a midlands town.

They exchanged details for the encrypted exchange of the information, and Jerry rushed out to talk to Tommy.

It took about half an hour for the encrypted tape to arrive, and Jerry and Tommy went straight to it. They viewed it slowly and carefully from about 11 am.

When the tape got to about 11:45, Jerry suddenly said, "Bloody Hell, it's Nigel."

They watched as Nigel walked from the direction of Emmanuel Street where he had presumably just got off the bus, towards the public lavatories on the edge of Christ's Pieces. He seemed to stop for a minute or two and talk to a big issue seller, and buy a copy of Big Issue, and then he talked to someone else, who had also bought a copy of Big Issue. Both the Big Issue purchasers disappeared off camera, for about thirty minutes, and then Nigel reappeared from the direction of the town, and the other Big Issue purchaser reappeared from the Christs Pieces side. Nigel handed his copy of the Big Issue to the other guy and the other guy gave Nigel a tray of large disposable coffee cups. They went on their respective ways, Nigel headed towards Parker Street, presumably walking towards the Station.

The two detectives noted the precise times of all the meetings between Nigel, the Big Issue seller, and the other Big Issue purchaser with whom Nigel exchanged the magazine and the coffee cups. They sent the information to Josh Jacobs.

It took about fifteen minutes before Josh called them.

"Big Issue seller squeaky clean. Really nice guy, down on his luck, well known to us, but not in a criminal context, and never any trouble. Other Big Issue buyer, we reckon, he is one of the biggest heroin and cocaine dealers in the Town. Your boy contacted him, did business with him. We reckon the money was in the magazine, the drugs were in the coffee cups. It is one of the two ways in which that dealer regularly does business. He tends to deal in quite large amounts, and he usually supplies other slightly smaller dealers, bit further down the food chain, but not simple punters. The coffee cup method is for modest deals, for big deals, he uses a briefcase swap."

Jerry thanked Josh and thought to himself that Nigel Crofton-Jones was going to have a lot of explaining to do tomorrow.

Chapter 16

That Monday was one of the days when Rowan had to catch the guided bus. Paige, Rowan's regular lift to Hinchingbrooke, had an appointment to talk to the people with whom she was planning to do her SSC. Paige was particularly interested in paediatrics and was hoping to do an audit, a sort of meta-analysis, on the outcome of three different treatment-regimes for croup, an upper respiratory tract infection, usually caused by the parainfluenza virus, which causes airways obstruction and a strange sort of barking cough in a particular age group of young children, 6 months to 3 years being the peak occurrence. It was not going to be the most exciting project, since it would be mostly ploughing through records and journals, but it was important as it would guide the future choices of treatment for the clinicians. Paige also knew that the team she was working with would include her in any ward rounds and case conferences, so there would be clinical exposure as well as the paperwork. Rowan had offered to help Paige with some of the literature search. Rowan was not a workaholic, far from it, but she had boundless energy and drive and an almost insatiable appetite for learning. One SSC project was never going to be enough for her, and much as she liked lab work, it was on the wards and with patients that her real passion was developing. She hoped to get herself included in some of the ward rounds with Paige and the paediatric team.

Rowan sat there on the bus as it made its way out past the new Cambridge North Station, the Science Park, several villages along the way to St Ives, the slightly quaint old town on the river, and then to Oliver Cromwell's hometown, Huntingdon, and Hinchingbrooke Hospital. Rowan was now completely recovered from the trauma of the summer although she still could not remember anything after the meeting with Angela on the Rec that morning. It was very frustrating. Something was telling her that there was more to come, that she would, given time, remember more, but she was still quite disturbed that she could not remember why she had decided to take a huge overdose. Even now, it did not make sense. She was on a medical ward today. Most of the patients were quite elderly and the commonest theme was cardiovascular disease. Like Paige, Rowan was thinking about paediatrics as a career. She liked the cleanness of many paediatric diagnoses and treatments. Sometimes, a syndrome involved multiple organ systems but often a single system was failing, and if you could sort that out, you were looking at lots of QALYS, the quality adjusted life years, that were so beloved of NICE, the National Institute for Clinical Excellence. Well, that is the jargon. What it means is that if you sort the kid out, they are likely to have a long and fruitful life. She wasn't naïve about it. Not every child was going to pull through, but there was often a very good chance, and you were likely to win more than you lost. She was looking forward to working with Paige, undoubtedly her closest female friend, over the six or seven weeks they could devote to their SSCs.

The day went by with plenty of clinical contact and lots of chance to hone her history taking skills and her skills at physical examination. She had a way of making friends quickly with the patients, those sparkly eyes and that happy smile helped no end.

On the way home, the bus stopped at the railway station and Rowan popped into the supermarket there for a few ingredients. It was her turn to cook this evening, fresh pasta, onions, basil, garlic and tomatoes, and some parmesan, and a bit of lettuce and other green salad items. Simple arrabbiata pasta, using the chillies at home, and a salad to accompany. Not a long walk home to Mill Road from there, and she picked up some olives, gherkins and some ciabatta bread and a bottle of Chianti on the way down Mill Road.

****

Nigel, meanwhile, had no idea what was going to hit him tomorrow when the detectives summoned him again before them. He went out that Monday evening, with his new girlfriend, Samantha, to the same Greek restaurant where he had taken Angela, on their last date before her murder. Nigel did not see the man in the dark grey raincoat, with a hood, following them to the restaurant from Sam's office, where Nigel had picked Sam up after work. Samantha knew nothing about Angela, and Nigel's association with her, and Samantha was not involved in drugs. She was just a trainee, at a rival legal firm, that Nigel had met during their work. After the meal, Nigel offered to see Samantha home to her flat in Kentish Town. They walked to the Northern Line at King's Cross Station and went to the platform for the Kentish Town branch. It was about 9:30 pm when they caught the underground. Fifteen minutes later, they were walking along a quiet road towards Sam's flat. Nigel felt someone, a man in a dark grey raincoat with a hood, hit him hard in the chest a couple of times. The man stepped back and disappeared into the darkness.

Nigel suddenly found it hard to breathe; he suddenly found it hard to walk; he suddenly found it hard to think, and then he died.

Samantha was in a state of shock. The man in the raincoat returned out of the shadows and spoke to her.

"Get away!" He said, in a strong accent that she could not quite place.

"Stand back!" That accent again, what was it?

Samantha did as she was told and stepped back. The man moved over to Nigel's dead body and went through his pockets. He was wearing soft leather gloves. He removed something small from one of the pockets. It looked like a small mobile phone. He took out Nigel's iPhone and put that and the other small object in his pocket, stood up and looked hard at Samantha.

"Sorry to frighten you," he said.

He turned on his heel and walked away.

Detective Inspector Gregory and Detective Sergeant Trinder got the news shortly before ten thirty. Samantha had dialled 999 immediately but was, of course, too late. She had gone with the ambulance to the accident and emergency department at the Whittington Hospital, but Nigel had been declared dead on arrival. Samantha was able to give Nigel's name to the police and they had rung in the news of the crime to the central Met switch board. The duty officer at Islington recognised the name immediately and contacted Jerry at home. Jerry had just gone to bed, but he got up, got dressed and went, as quickly as he could to the Whittington. He asked the duty officer to notify Tommy as well and Tommy, who lived a bit nearer than Jerry, got to the Whittington before Jerry.

Not surprisingly, Samantha was sitting there in a state of shock. The poor girl had gone out for an evening date with someone she had only recently met and the next thing she knew, he had been murdered in front of her. She could tell them little about the attacker, except that he was quite tall, taller than Nigel, and was dressed in a dark grey raincoat with a hood. She said he was clean shaven and had dark coloured eyes.. She thought he might be Asian but she could not be sure. She said he had a strong accent which she could not quite place; it was almost Scottish, but not quite. It was clearly articulated but some of the words did not sound quite right.

Samantha said she had thought he had simply punched Nigel in the chest two or three times and then disappeared into the dark. It was not until Nigel collapsed that either she or Nigel realised what had just occurred. Samantha had not seen a knife at all, although she caught a glimpse of what might have been a blade, a flash of light reflected, as the man moved quickly away. He had not run away, just walked off quickly and calmly, and waited in the shadows while Nigel died. He had then come back and taken something from Nigel's pocket; she thought it might be a phone. It was when he came back that Samantha had been able to make out a bit more of him. This time when he left, he went in the direction of the main road. There had been nobody else around, not even a dog walker, or someone else coming off the tube and on their way home. In fact, Samantha had not seen anyone else at all until the ambulance and police arrived, about fifteen minutes after the attack. She thought the whole episode from the knife attack to the man leaving had taken no more than seven minutes. As soon as the man had turned to walk away, she had dialled 999.

The two policemen questioned her hard about the accent. All she could say was that she thought it was someone speaking with a Scottish accent, but someone who had probably started with a strong ethnic accent of their own. She was very sorry that she could not pin it down better for them.

"Could he have been Asian?" Inspector Gregory asked.

"I suppose so," said Samantha, "But it was difficult to be absolutely clear about that in the dark. I did get that impression."

Samantha answered a few more questions about her relationship with Nigel. She did not know Angela; she did not know that Nigel knew Angela. She had to be reminded that Angela was the girl who had been found dead in her flat less than two weeks ago. Samantha had never taken drugs in her life; she did not smoke, and she drank alcohol only with meals, and then only occasionally. She was shocked to be told that the police thought this attack might be drugs related.

Jerry Gregory called the station and asked for a liaison officer to be sent to the hospital immediately. He was rather pleased when Sergeant Patel was sent as the liaison officer.

"Jenny, this is a really sad situation," said Jerry. "This poor girl went out on a first date with some bloke she knew from work, and he ends up being murdered in front of her. She seems to be coping remarkably well right now, but I think the whole thing is going to hit her quite hard very soon, and I am so glad that they sent you to help her deal with it. You're my go to talent for this sort of thing."

Jenny smiled. "Thanks, Guv," said Jenny. "I don't find it easy, but I do tend to feel very sorry for folks and I try, I try hard, to help them cope. I think it will just be a case of being there for this young lady, making her a cup of tea and feeding her some sugar when the shock starts to set in. How long do you want me to stay with her?"

"See how she goes tomorrow and call in in the morning, and we can assess it from there. Between you, me, and the gatepost, this murder is a bit of a bummer. We had just got some evidence linking Crofton-Jones to drug dealing, and we would have had him in for questioning in the morning, and it might just have cracked open the Angela Huddlestone murder case. Now, we are way back; a line of inquiry has been cut off, and I don't see this murder, or the other one, getting solved unless we get something from an informer. But that is my problem, not yours. You go and take care of that poor girl over there."

Sergeant Jenny Patel went over and introduced herself to Samantha. She sat beside her on one of the benches in the casualty department. After a couple of minutes, Jenny went to the vending machine and came back with a couple of cups of hot chocolate. It took about 5 minutes, but Samantha suddenly started to cry, and Jenny put an arm round her shoulders and comforted her. The process of dealing with the trauma of the evening had begun. DI Gregory knew that Samantha could not be in better hands.

About five minutes later, a squad car arrived at the door of A and E and Sergeant Patel picked up Samantha's bag and raincoat, put them over her arm, and with an arm around Samantha's shoulders, escorted her to the police car. It took them back to Samantha's flat in Kentish Town.

It has sometimes been said that when one door closes, another one opens; at this moment on a dark autumn night in North London, Jerry couldn't see it.

Just after 10 pm, a man in a light grey raincoat, with a dark grey lining and a hood, caught the number 134 bus from Kentish Town to Euston Road. When he got there, he walked at a measured pace across to Euston Station. He took out a burner phone that he had purchased earlier that day. He rang a number and left a message. It said, simply, "One loose end fewer, I have the phone with the video." By midnight, the man with the raincoat was in his seat on the Caledonian sleeper heading north.

Chapter 17

In the morning, Jerry and Tommy both looked shattered. Neither had managed much sleep after the visit to the hospital, and the realisation that their most promising line of enquiry had just been shut off.

"I wonder why he didn't kill the girl too," said Jerry.

"Some sort of warped sense of morality," suggested Tommy. "Anyway, that was a break for us."

They talked about what to do next, and both considered that their most promising approach would be to push harder with Henry Castleton. If he was involved with Nigel in drug dealing, and Nigel had now been murdered, it might just frighten Henry enough to get him to tell the detectives more about the people with whom he and Nigel had become embroiled. The second line of enquiry would involve visiting Cambridge and trying to get a better idea of the drug scene there, especially the link between the professional dealers and the occasional rogue student dealer.

Jerry contacted Sergeant Patel.

"How is Samantha doing?" He asked.

"Thanks for asking, Guv," said Jenny. "It hit her again this morning when she got up. I am glad I was here. She is OK now, but her parents are going to come and collect her and take her home for a few days. I can't imagine what a shock it must have been. First date with a bloke and he gets murdered in front of your eyes."

"Did she remember anything else?" Tommy asked.

"No. She is beating herself up a bit about not being able to pin down the accent. She is definite it had a touch of Scottish in it."

"Right," said Jerry. "There aren't that many trains in and out of Scotland after 10 o'clock on a Monday. Let's see if anything shows up on the CCTV at Euston or King's Cross. I'm not hopeful, it's a bit of a shot in the dark, but we might get lucky."

He also made a note to access Nigel's phone records for the past year; under the Regulation of Investigatory Powers Act he could do that automatically. He also needed access to Nigel's computers, at home and at work. That was not quite so straightforward, he would need a warrant for that, but it should be forthcoming.

It still was not clear what the motive was for the murder of Nigel or Angela. It surely had to be more than that they were both involved in distributing drugs. There had to be something they knew, or were doing, that mattered enough to some relatively big fish for the big fish to have arranged a very subtle murder of the girl, and then a thoroughly professional hit on the bloke. What did they know, or what had they done, that had got them killed?

DI Gregory and Sergeant Trinder sent a police car to collect Henry from his office. They told him about Nigel's murder. He was visibly shocked, and he started to look a little frightened, but he did not crack, and he still maintained that he knew nothing about drugs and had never taken any drugs himself. They told him about the CCTV footage of Nigel and a well-known drug dealer in Cambridge, and all he said was, "Damn, fool. I had no idea he was mixed up in drugs."

Henry was very scared, he also blamed himself for the deaths of both Nigel and Angela, but he hid his anxiety well, and the detectives were completely unable to shift him from his story. In the end, they had no choice but to put one Henry Castleton on the back burner and try to crack this case another way. They arranged to go, later that day, to Cambridge to meet Josh Jacobs and see what help they could get about the student drug scene. Jerry also telephoned the Senior Tutor of St Alfred's and arranged to meet her later that day, and he called Adrian Armstrong at St Joseph's and gave him the news of the murder. Tommy was going to call in at St Joseph's on his way back to London.

They were quite used to the short trip to Cambridge by now, only this time they went first, not to Colleges Ancient and Modern, but to Parkside Police Station. It is only a brisk twenty to thirty-minute walk from the railway station, so the pair of them walked it. One route would have taken them along Hill's Road, but they chose the walk along Mill Road and were absolutely amazed to bump into Rowan, who was having a day off, because the consultant supposed to be teaching them had too long a surgical list, involving a major organ transplant, a liver transplant. Rowan thought that a bit ironical, she might, so easily, herself have been a recipient.

"Hello, Inspector," said Rowan. "And Sergeant Trinder. What brings you both here?"

"I'm afraid it's work. We are off to Parkside Police Station," said Jerry. Then he realised that neither Rowan nor any of the other St Joseph's girls would know about Nigel's murder.

"I am afraid I have some very bad news for you Rowan," said Jerry. "Can we go and sit down somewhere and talk?"

"We could go to Savino's," said Rowan. "It's not far from the Police Station."

"OK," said Jerry. "Tommy and I are buying. Last time your Senior Tutor bought us a drink."

There was little conversation on the walk to Savino's. Jerry and Tommy were rather lost in thought, and Rowan sensed their mood.

There was a table just inside the window and Rowan and Jerry sat down while Tommy went to the counter to order.

As they sat there, one of the owners, Tony, came over and started to make a big fuss of Rowan. It was obvious to Jerry that Rowan was a regular and well-liked customer. It was made even more obvious when Tony refused to take any money for the coffee, and added three slices of carrot cake. "Because we have missed you, Rowan!"

Jerry kept his counsel until the coffees and cake had been suitably distributed and then he began to talk.

"I am really sorry Rowan. I don't suppose you will have seen the papers yet but there has been another murder of someone you know. Maybe not as close to you as Angela but still very connected. Last night Nigel Crofton-Jones was stabbed to death by an unknown man while he was walking his girlfriend home. He died in front of her."

Rowan went very pale. She sat very still for a minute and then she said.

"That is so hard to believe. First Angela and then Nigel." Rowan paused, thought a second or two more and said:

"You did say he was walking his girlfriend home?"

"Yes," said Jerry. "I did say that."

"What a bastard," said Rowan, much to Jerry's surprise. Then she added, "We haven't even had Angela's funeral yet."

There was a long silence then Rowan asked,

"Do you have any idea who did it? Was it drug related?"

"No idea at this time," said Jerry. "But we do think it was drug related. We have some leads, and we are here following one of them up. I know you knew them both but at the moment we are pretty confident that you and your friends are not in danger, so we don't want you to worry, but we will let you know if anything changes."

Rowan went very quiet. There is not a lot you can say under these circumstances.

More out of politeness to Tony and his staff than for any other reason all three silently ate their cakes and finished their coffees.

They got up from the table and went back out to the street. The timing was perfect. Jerry and Tommy, both spotted him at the same time. The man who had bought the other copy of the Big Issue was just coming out of a coffee bar a little further along the road.

It was so tempting to try to accidentally bump into him and knock the coffee cup out of his hand, but it obviously did not make sense. Unless the owners or managers of the other coffee bar were directly involved in the drug dealing racket, the cup in the dealer's hands currently held coffee. Inspector Jacobs would know whether the café was involved. Jerry and Tommy did not; and there was no sense in tipping off the dealer. They needed more information first and that is what they were now going to get.

They said goodbye to each other, Jerry and Tommy just checking with Rowan that she was OK, then Jerry and Tommy went off to keep their appointment with Josh Jacobs. Rowan headed in the opposite direction, down into the town to go to the market for vegetables, and some personal items from the large chemist's shop on the way there.

****

As the two London detectives entered the Parkside Police Station, they noted a very scruffy looking man, who looked to be in about his late twenties, arguing and generally making a nuisance of himself with a young policeman and the duty sergeant on the desk. The language would have made a sailor blush. The f word and the c word were being mouthed off at a rate of knots. The man had a long straggly beard and dirty tangled shoulder length hair; the detectives could smell his body odour from the minute they walked in through the door. It was that sickly-sweet smell which is a combination of bacterially degraded sweat, stale alcohol, and acetone.

They were ushered through into an interview suite where Inspector Josh Jacobs was waiting for them.

"Hi, guys," said Josh, "I'm Josh Jacobs. Great to meet you in person. I gather you had a very unfortunate set back to your enquiry. Some hitman took out your potential star witness?"

"Hi, Josh. I'm Jerry Gregory and this is Tommy Trinder. Thanks for making the time to see us. Yes, one of our main suspects was murdered yesterday evening around 10. I reckon that murder will not be solvable in isolation. It was a very professional job by a hitman, who came out of nowhere and vanished equally quickly. We have the team looking at CCTV and retracing the victim's steps from 5 pm on that evening, but we are not optimistic that anything useful will turn up. So far, the only thing we have is that the victim and his date were followed out of the station at Kentish Town by a tall man in a dark grey raincoat with a hood. Not even a glimpse of his face. He knew where the cameras are and made sure he never got seen on them. Before that, the London scene was much too crowded for us to pick up anything in the way of people following the couple, either to the restaurant, or from the restaurant back to the tube station. Amazing how many tall men in raincoats there are, and surprising how many of the raincoats have a hood. Must be climate change or fashion or something?"

"That is such a bummer," said Josh. "So, how do you think I can help?"

"Well, as I said on the phone, the other major clue we have is this ultra-pure heroin that we found several packets of in the first victim, the girl, Angela's flat. We sent a team round to look at the flat Nigel Crofton-Jones was living in. The father was a bit sticky at first, but he eventually allowed us in, so we did not have to get a warrant. This time, we would have done. I guess daddy thought that nothing we might find could harm his son anymore. Makes me wonder if he knew his son was involved in drugs. But that's a bit irrelevant. Fact is we found some very strong marijuana in a tin in the boy's bedroom, and we found one packet of white powder that looked like the packets we had found in Angela's flat. The packet had slipped down the back of a chest of drawers in the bedroom. We are looking at it for fingerprints and checking if it is the same batch as the stuff we found before. We don't think it is, because it was wrapped differently, but it is probably heroin.

We think that magic white powder is the key to solving these murders. We think it is going to tell us how Angela and Nigel were linked to the drug scene, and more importantly, which drug scene they were linked to. Once we get that, we can begin to speculate why they were killed. Where the hell is this stuff coming from? Did Nigel collect it from your dealer on that Monday when he came up here?"

"Right," said Josh, "I'm going to introduce you to someone now, and the meeting you are going to have is not going to happen, it never happened. OK?"

"OK," said Jerry and Tommy almost simultaneously.

"We are going to the custody suite," said Jerry.

The three detectives walked along the corridor towards the custody suite. There were CCTV cameras everywhere, under the code of practice these were 'for the welfare of prisoners.'

A second door at the far end of the corridor led out to the main suite of offices. Josh unlocked the door and took Jerry and Tommy through. They doubled back along a corridor parallel to the custody suite corridor, and about a quarter of the way along, they stopped, and Josh unlocked another door into one of the cells in the custody suite. Lying stretched out on the bed in the cell was the young man they had seen when they first entered the building.

The young man sat up and moved over to the table and sat on one of the chairs. This cell had a table with four chairs, not at all a normal arrangement.

"This is, well, let's call him Arthur," said Josh. "Arthur is on an undercover assignment to infiltrate the drug scene here in Cambridge. He's been at it for about three years now. I think he may be able to help you. You will notice that this cell does not have CCTV and the furniture is not quite what you would expect!"

"Hello, guys," said Arthur, in a totally RP accent. "It will be quite nice not to have to be in character for a few moments. How can I help you?"

Jerry, Josh, and Tommy all sat down at the table.

"Where to begin," said Jerry. "Has Josh explained to you about the two murders we are investigating and the possible link to the drug scene?"

"Yes, he has," said Arthur. "I guess the first thing you want to know is if I have any information about the strong H that is on the scene?"

"Please," said Tommy.

"Well. It appeared around here about four weeks ago, and that dealer you saw on the CCTV, selling some to your victim, has been distributing it ever since. He has cut some of it now to make a bigger profit. I don't think anyone realised quite how pure it was until a couple of the addicts had a near miss and one OD. So, I am confident that your packets came from Sammy Needle, that's the dealer, and it is his real name. Where he got the stuff from is not quite so clear, but most of his stuff comes down from up north somewhere. He doesn't have a lot to do with the London drug scene. Needle was born in Yorkshire and he started in the drugs business up there, so he maintained his contacts when he came down south. I don't know what you make of that, Inspector, but that's all I can tell you about the origin. You might need to chase it up north, but for what it's worth, my guess is that your link stops here in Cambridge, or it might be in London."

"Thanks," said Jerry. "Now, I have a couple of photographs here and I want to know if you recognise any of these three, and whether you can tell us anything about them, and the drug scene here in Cambridge."

Jerry took photographs of Angela, Nigel, and Henry out of his pocket and put them on the table in front of him.

"I know all three of them," said Arthur. "Two of them I met through a combination of theatre and drugs, the other one was a friend of theirs. They were into marijuana and the two blokes usually bought more than they could use themselves. I am fairly confident that they were dealing, on a small scale anyway."

Arthur was too valuable an asset to have his cover blown by testifying to this in a court of law, but the information was very useful for the pair from London.

"How did you get to meet these three?" Tommy asked.

"Well, believe it or not, I am a graduate of this esteemed university, and I was very into theatre so, after my police training, I came back to Cambridge to 'do a PhD' and I re-joined the theatre scene. That is how I met the two actors. The girl was very good, by the way. The boy, Nigel, was an average performer. That one there, he is called Henry, was a surly and quite nasty piece of work. He also tried to be an actor, but he was a bit of an embarrassment as a thespian, so he was a bit of a backroom boy, scenery building and the like. I suppose he was quite good on lighting and sound as well, but odious in the extreme. The other two struck me as just foolish and a bit shallow. I would imagine they just got into recreational drugs at school and carried it on at university. I think Henry was the main dealer among that lot."

It was a lot to take in. The link to hard drugs was established through the meeting between Nigel and the dealer, Sammy Needle, and finding the packet of heroin in Nigel's flat. The use of marijuana and dealing in it at university was there. Henry was skating on thin ice, but there was no way they could tackle him yet. They only had Arthur as a witness, and they had no physical evidence to back it up. They were quite sure that they would not get a warrant to search Henry's accommodation just on suspicion. Where next?

"Are there any other student dealers that we ought to be aware of?" Jerry asked.

"There are a couple that you might like to know about," said Arthur. "There is a guy called Michael O'Grady at St Arthur's and girl called Justine Farrell at St Helen's. They are not in the theatre scene as such but one of them, Farrell, writes for the student newspaper and does the theatrical reviews. The other, I don't know much about; except he spends a lot of time in the union."

They took a note of the names, thanked Josh and Arthur, and left quietly by the back way. As they went down the parallel corridor, they could hear a commotion in the custody area; Arthur was back in character playing the role which, for him, was probably a matter of life or death.

Looking at all the evidence, Tommy and Jerry were now even more convinced that the key to the two murders was in the background of the Cambridge drug dealing scene. The only one of the trio of Angela, Henry and Nigel that they had left to work on, was Henry. They decided to go with the evidence they had so far and talk to their chief to see whether he thought it was enough to be able to get a warrant to search Henry's flat in the Barbican.

****

While the two detectives were interviewing Henry and visiting Cambridge, the crime scene boys at the Kentish Town murder scene had found absolutely nothing they could use. There appeared to be nothing missing from Nigel Crofton-Jones's pockets other than his phone. They had his wallet and other bits and pieces, like a pen, keys, and a handkerchief. Nothing appeared to be missing from his wallet. They were a bit intrigued as to what might have been taken by the murderer as well as the iPhone. It had to be a second mobile, possibly a pay-as-you-go used for internal communications within the drug ring. They telephoned Jerry and told him.

"Definitely a professional hit," said Jerry. "Clearly, an ordered hit, and one by someone who knew what he was doing. Still, I guess we should go through the routine of seeing who Nigel had contacted over the last few months. Some number or numbers may stand out. If we can get the records going back into the last year at Cambridge, that might also give us a bit more to go on."

Henry was scared. He was very sure that his conversations with the boss had led to the deaths of both Angela and Nigel. That was two of the links from Cambridge to the boss out of the way. If the boss was going to eliminate the remaining ones, the next on the list was bound to be Henry himself. He really was terrified. He did not know how to deal with it. He could phone the boss, but to do so might indicate that he was running scared and might just tip the boss's hand. He could tell the police, but to do so would guarantee him a long jail sentence, especially when his part in the Cambridge incident came out, as it would do, in court. He could try and emigrate, but, despite the earnings from the Cambridge, and now London, activities, he didn't have enough money to emigrate and hide successfully. It would need false papers, and a larger cash backup than he currently had, while he got himself established, and he didn't speak any foreign languages well enough to go somewhere non-English speaking.

He decided to make a telephone call.

"Boss. Now we have lost Nigel and Angela, I wonder whether you want me to step up a bit and do a little more to help the group?"

Be pro-active, Henry had thought to himself, *make yourself indispensable. You can easily get to Cambridge and do the pick-up from Needle, and you can stash the stuff in the flat, surprising number of hiding places in these brutalist buildings.*

"You aren't getting worried, are you?" the boss asked. "I have no intention of having you bumped off," there was a pause, "provided that you behave yourself and keep your mouth shut. I tell you what. We lost that consignment when the idiot I sent in to bump off Angela left the H in the flat. I asked him why he left it there and he said it just didn't occur to him. He did get her second phone, thank goodness. Otherwise, he was totally focussed on the job. Dope Angela's coffee and give her the overdose, then get out. If he were not so bloody good at killing people, I would take out a contract on him. If I fix up with the main man to get some more H to Needle, can you arrange to go and pick it up from Cambridge next week?"

There was a lot of bluff in that statement. The boss had no intention of taking out a contract on the hitman, and the boss was busy implying that the hitman and the drug contact were two different people. Henry believed that; the boss wanted him to continue to believe that.

"Sure," said Henry. "The only day I can't do next week is Wednesday because I am in court with one of the QCs in my chambers."

"I will let you know what day then," said the boss and rang off.

Henry decided that he was, for the moment safe. How long that would last, he just didn't know. He did not want to get in any deeper, he had always been on the periphery, a bit less involved than some of the others, and they were paying him to keep quiet. He guessed who the hitman was, and he knew him to be a homicidal psychopath. Henry thought he had better play along, however reluctantly, for a while.

****

Jerry Gregory had decided that only one of the team needed to go and look at the files. He thought it was very important to keep the pressure on Henry so he set Tommy to interviewing Henry again., Tommy went off to see Adrian Armstrong to fill him in on the details of the crime. It was a very short visit, more courtesy than necessity. Tommy then made his way back to London with instructions to put more heat on Henry. He called ahead and arranged for Henry to be picked up again and taken to the Islington Police Station. Henry could wait there in a holding cell until Tommy arrived back from his travels. Tommy was going to challenge Henry with the names of Sammy Needle and the other two student drug dealers that Arthur had told them about.

When Jerry had telephoned Marjorie Grey, the Senior Tutor at St Alfred's, she had clearly been very shocked at the news of Nigel's death, coming as it did so close on the heels of the other murder. Jerry had explained the circumstances of the murder and asked whether he might come up and see the file on Nigel in case there was anything useful there that they might have overlooked. Naturally, the college was happy to try to cooperate. Jerry had also asked if the college would mind showing him the file of Henry Castleton while he was there; the two of them seemed to be linked in London and to have been friends in Cambridge, and there could just be some commonalities that were significant. Marjorie said she believed that they had been friends before they came to Cambridge, she wasn't sure, but she thought they had attended the same school. After making the appointment for Jerry to come up that afternoon, Marjorie had got out the two files and reminded herself that, indeed, they had both been students at Brassington Hall, a minor public school in the Yorkshire countryside, somewhere between Leeds and Richmond.

Marjorie had left the files on the desk and returned to the business of the day. There was a tutors' meeting due at lunchtime and she had some papers to read before chairing the meeting.

Jerry took a taxi this time to the porters' lodge at St Alfred's. He was becoming familiar with Cambridge, and the two colleges, St Joseph's, and St Alfred's, in particular. He called in at the Senior Tutor's office and was shown into the study where Marjorie Grey was waiting for him. After the usual pleasantries, she handed over the two files.

"This is absolutely shocking, Inspector," said Marjorie.

"I'm afraid it is," said Jerry. "These two murders are definitely connected but we are struggling to find the linking factors. It always seems worse when the people involved are relatively young, such a waste of what might have been."

"Let me leave you here to look at the files," said Marjorie. "When you're done, I will be in the outer office and you can bring them out to me there."

Jerry thanked her and settled down to look at the folders in front of him.

The key observation was the one that Marjorie had already made. Nigel and Henry had been at the same school, Brassington Hall. Jerry thought it might well be important to go up to Brassington Hall and interview people who had known the two boys during their time at the school.

There was something in the references which was a little bit intriguing. Both young men had a comment that their lower sixth career had been disturbed by some difficulties with one of their study mates, but there were no details. Jerry made a note that he needed to find out about that.

Supervision reports for the three years at Cambridge were all a bit bland. It seemed, from the reports, that Nigel had been rather better at English than he was at law. Nigel had been predicted, and had obtained, a first-class result in his preliminary exams in English. The law reports indicated a rather lazy, or at least, disengaged student. The reports were mostly uninformative, they just reported attendance, and that Nigel had handed in his essays on time. Everything was middle second class in the reports. Henry's reports were a little better in the first two years, but his supervisors lost a lot of their enthusiasm for him in the final year. The reports from that third year conveyed a great deal of disappointment. There were comments such as 'if he tried, he could do well, but he seems not to be trying' and, 'Henry is wasting his considerable talent, I wonder if he is doing too much in the theatre?' Despite these reports, showing the disappointment and frustration of their teachers, the exam records of both students were more than adequate. The records had been two first class grades for Henry and a 2.1 in his final year, and Nigel had straight 2.1 results, following his first in English preliminary examinations.

The beginning and end of term tutor's notes were not very informative either. There were comments about the commitment to theatre for both men, and a comment that Henry was doing some technical stuff while Nigel was acting. There were also a couple of comments about holidays the two had taken and a note that they had been in one mooting competition. Both Henry and Nigel had joined the union but not been very active there.

Jerry closed the files having photographed the key pages of information. He took the files back out to Marjorie Grey in her outer office, thanked her again for her cooperation, and made his way back to the station.

He wanted time to think, so he walked back along Mill Road towards the station, and, almost unbelievably, he again bumped into Rowan, this time with Paige accompanying her.

"Inspector Gregory," said Rowan. "Are you stalking me?"

They both laughed, a rather strained and nervous laugh.

"This is Paige, one of my housemates," said Rowan. "Paige, this is Inspector Gregory."

"Pleased to meet you, Paige," said Jerry.

"Pleased to meet you Inspector. Rowan told me about Nigel," said Paige. "It's really shocking news."

Things of the magnitude of the stabbing are sometimes very hard to comprehend, and emotional responses to them can easily become blunted, but the sense that Nigel might have been two-timing Angela was easier to cope with and created an appropriate emotional response.

"He didn't waste much time getting a new girlfriend," said Paige. Then, she felt a little bit embarrassed.

"How is the poor girl?" She asked.

"I think she is coping," said Jerry. "As you will appreciate, it was a heck of a shock for her."

They exchanged a few more words and then Jerry went off to the railway station and Rowan and Paige went to the supermarket in the centre of the town.

The two girls talked about Nigel and Angela, and while very shocked at the second death, were genuinely upset that Nigel appeared to have dismissed the death of Angela from his mind so quickly that, within two weeks, even before the funeral, he was out on a date with another girl. They had never liked Nigel, they thought even less of him now, even if he was dead. They telephoned Meera to pass on the news.

Nigel's death was the first, and principal topic of conversation around the dinner table in Mill Road that evening. There was a lot of speculation, but all believed it was drug related. They struggled to see how the level of drug dealing that they had suspected during the undergraduate years could lead to murder. It had to be that the level of involvement had escalated with the move to London, or maybe they had only seen the tip of the iceberg here in Cambridge. Something tugged at the back of Rowan's mind as they discussed this, but it remained hidden, she could not recall what it was that she was trying to remember.

****

Later that afternoon, while Jerry was on the short journey from Cambridge to King's Cross, Tommy was talking to a visibly shaken Henry, in one of the interview rooms at Islington.

"When did you last see Nigel?" Tommy asked.

"It was the night that Judith, Nigel, Angela, and I, went to the restaurant. I hadn't seen him for at least two weeks, two weeks today."

"Had you talked to him since then?" Tommy asked.

"Yes, we usually talked regularly on the phone, but we had both been quite busy and upset since Angela's death, so I hadn't spoken to him for several days. I suppose I should have contacted him to see how he was doing, but he told me he had a new girlfriend. I need to be honest with you, Sergeant. Nigel had told me after the dinner that he was going to break up with Angela. He said it was one of those university things, and he wanted to move on. I think he was being a bit of a snob because Angela was a bit working class, and he had met this girl Samantha, who was a lawyer at a big London firm, and from UCL. I think that Nigel thought they were a better match for the long run."

Tommy listened to that and thought to himself, *what a pair of bastards*. As a policeman, he needed to treat all murders with the same detached attitude, but he couldn't help himself thinking that the death of Nigel Crofton-Jones was no great loss to the world. He stopped himself just short of thinking that it would be no disaster if Henry Castleton followed his friend into oblivion.

Tommy mentioned Needle, O'Grady, and Farrell, but Henry Castleton was good at this sort of poker face!

****

The next morning, all the national newspapers had a front-page article on the stabbing in Kentish Town. For most, it was the second story after the latest gloomy report on the political row over social care for the elderly. There was a picture of Nigel and a request for anyone who could help confirm his movement on the Monday evening to come forward. They linked the murder to the earlier death of Angela Huddleston in the block of flats in Judd Street. The CCTV pictures of the hooded man leaving the flat in Judd Street, and a similar picture of a hooded man leaving the train at Kentish Town Tube Station, were accompanied by a request to the public to come forward if they could help identify who it was.

Examination of the CCTV at the Kentish Town Underground had shown a man, in a dark grey raincoat with a hood, among a very small group of passengers who left the train at the same time as Samantha and Nigel. The man hung back a little and put some money into a chocolate machine before going out through the same exit as the two youngsters. There was no possibility of identification. He had a scarf around his neck, which would have obscured the lower half of his face anyway. He took it off and stuffed it in his pocket as he left the platform.

"Cheeky bastard," said Tommy when he saw the suspect doing this. "He's playing with us."

The police statement reported this activity and asked all passengers who got off that Northern Line train at Kentish Town, at the same time as Samantha and Nigel, to come forward for interview, just in case they could shed some light on the identity of the suspect.

There was no sign of anyone in a raincoat with a hood getting back on to the underground that evening. With nothing else to go on, the detectives decided to look at bus routes from the Kentish Town area back to King's Cross and Euston. If Samantha was right and the murderer did have a Scottish accent, albeit an acquired accent superimposed on a more basic ethnic speech pattern, these were the two stations from where he might have made his way back to safety.

They looked at the timetables of trains back to Scotland and got the team to focus on the bus stops around the stations, from the time of the murder until the last train departed, and to look at the railway station CCTV around the time of the departures.

They got lucky in a frustrating sort of way. Around 10:30 pm, a tall man in a light raincoat with a hood was seen getting off the 134 bus at Euston Road and walking in the direction of Euston Square. His face remained obscured throughout the period during which he was on camera. He must have waited in a blind spot on the station, or in the square, because he was next seen only briefly, going through the ticket barrier, and boarding the Caledonian Express. He seemed to fumble a bit going through the automatic entry point. The passenger list for the express had 153 names, including one called Charley Horse.

The transport police at every station between Euston and Inverness were asked to check the CCTV for a tall man with a hooded raincoat, getting off that train. Nobody with a hooded raincoat alighted at any station, but a reversible Macintosh with a hood was left in the first-class lavatory of a coach that ended up in Inverness. Charley Horse, apparently, lived at a non-existent address in Northamptonshire and had paid cash for his ticket on the morning of the journey. 153 passengers embarked at Euston. 153 passengers disembarked; Charley Horse disembarked at Edinburgh.

It was not much to go on, but there was at least now some evidence that the hitman who took out Nigel had come from Edinburgh. It would seem likely that he had a Scottish accent but was originally either a foreign national or someone who had been brought up in a home with a foreign language as his first language.

Acting on a hunch, Jerry asked Euston Transport Police to review the tapes from the Wednesday that was believed to be the day on which Angela had been murdered. He asked them to look for someone in a hooded raincoat boarding a train towards Edinburgh sometime in the evening. He also asked the Transport Police at King's Cross to look at their CCTV for the Edinburgh trains. It was Euston that found Charley Horse again. He caught the 22:30 train to Edinburgh and, again, he was without his raincoat when he left the train the following morning. He also again managed to hide his face from the cameras.

They were rather confident that they had identified the hitman, it was just that they did not have a clue who he might be.

Chapter 18

Rowan woke in the night sweating and shaking. She was beginning to have dreams about the day before the overdose. It was almost as if she was trying to break through to memories of what had happened that day, but it kept stalling at the point where she was walking back to her room with Angela from the Rec. Angela was saying something to her, but she couldn't make out what it was, she just had a feeling it might be important. When she awoke, she realised she must have cried out because all three house mates were gathered around comforting her. They asked what was wrong and she explained about the dream. It was apparently becoming a bit of a recurrent dream, although this was the first time it had distressed her enough to wake her.

"I keep thinking I am getting close to finding out what really happened," said Rowan. "I know that lots of people probably say this, but I don't believe I took an overdose willingly, but I cannot see how it could have been anything else. Did someone hypnotise me? I really hate not knowing, and I really do not believe that I tried to kill myself. It's not me."

Meera, ever caring and practical, went and made all four of them a small cup of cocoa each, and they sat round talking for a while.

"I wonder if the two murders are stirring something up in your head?" Meera said. "After all, Angela and Nigel were around on the day it happened. It could just be stirring you up to think about them and that day?"

"You may be right," said Rowan. "I saw Inspector Gregory yesterday and that might also have triggered my thoughts. But whatever it is, I just get so far and then the frame freezes. I get back off the Rec to the staircase and wake up sweating."

"I wonder if hypnotism might unlock your memory?" said Madeleine who had always had a thing about alternative therapies anyway.

"No thanks," said Rowan. "Not for the moment anyway. Maybe if my memory doesn't come back naturally, but I have a feeling that things are going to come back, bit by bit. I seem to get a little further into the building each time. I got to the first floor landing this time and I have never got that far before, last time I got stuck at the door."

The healing powers of cocoa are legendary, but the warm cuddles of three very close friends are even more powerful. Rowan's bedroom had a double and single bed in it, and Paige volunteered to sleep in the spare bed for the rest of the night to make sure Rowan remained safe and felt secure. They were all soon back to sleep and there were no more alarms and excursions before the morning alarm clock woke them all from their slumbers.

****

Jerry asked Tommy about the most recent interview with Henry and Tommy reported that Henry remained tight lipped and denied knowing either Sammy Needle or the two student dealers. They both agreed that they did not quite have enough levers yet to shift Henry's position.

The very next step in their odyssey would be to get in touch with people at Brassington Hall and arrange to go up and interview some of those who had taught the two young men.

It was now Wednesday morning. They arranged to take the train from King's Cross to Darlington tomorrow morning and get the local police to drive them over to the school for their lunchtime appointments.

Shortly after lunch on the Wednesday, Henry received a telephone call from the boss on the burner phone. A pick-up from Needle had been arranged for Thursday afternoon. Henry was to make that pick-up.

By a curious quirk of fate, on the Thursday morning, Henry was at King's Cross to catch the train to Cambridge at approximately the same time as the two detectives were arriving there to catch the LNER mainline train to Darlington. Fortunately for Henry, the detectives did not see him.

Detective Inspector Jerry Gregory was doing very well on the cigarette front. Marianne had stopped bringing him Gauloises and Gitanes from her trips to visit Maman in Paris. He was now using nicotine chewing gum when he got a bit of a craving, and he had not had a cigarette since the two puffs he had inhaled, just after he saw Marjorie Grey for the first time in Cambridge. That must be more than two weeks now. He was not using the nicotine gum very much either. He was conscious that his appetite had increased, and he was aware that he was going to have to be very careful not to put on weight. James, his son, had persuaded him to buy an exercise bike and he was now regularly doing 15k on the bike, at least once and often twice a day, while watching films and sport on his iPad. So far, so good. He had also bought a new bicycle for use around town and was planning to cycle to work most days. It was his birthday in a couple of weeks, and he had asked the kids to get him one of those highly luminous white cycling jackets, preferably with some fleece lining against the winter cold.

Not smoking certainly made train journeys easier. A few weeks ago, Jerry would have lit up the minute he could, after they stepped off the train, and he would have had to top up his nicotine levels in his office before even getting on the train. As it was, the two of them, Jerry, and Tommy, picked up a couple of bacon and egg sandwiches from the buffet car, and two cups of strong black filter coffee, and sat down to relax for the three hours or so it would take to get to Darlington.

Tommy, a few years older than Jerry, had been a policeman for nearly thirty years and was looking forward to retirement in five more years. He had a plan to buy a village pub on the Kent Coast, probably in a town like Whitstable. He had three grown up children, his elder son was a chef. Tommy's daughter, a primary school teacher, already lived in Whitstable, and was the deputy principal at the primary school there. She had two small children, and Tommy's wife wanted to be nearer to them, to see them grow up, and to help with the childcare. Tommy's other son, the youngest of their three children, was in the air force, training to be an engineer. The plan was for them all to eventually settle in Whitstable, and for the pub to become a gastropub, with the emphasis on good quality food using local produce and specialising in locally caught fish.

Tommy chatted about this all the way to Doncaster. Jerry pointed out all the pitfalls, the problems that new restaurants have building a client base and gaining a reputation for quality. He also teased Tommy about the dangers of publicans around alcohol.

Tommy was immune to all this. He had thought it through, he had heard it all before, and he really didn't care.

Tommy asked Jerry about his plans.

Jerry told Tommy that he and Marianne were looking to move out of London and Jerry wanted a DI or DCI post in a town not too far from London. Jerry's parents would still be living in London, and Jerry and Marianne wanted to be able to get to them quickly if they needed help. Jerry and Marianne wanted to buy a bigger house, with a decent sized garden, in which Marianne could grow her flowers, and Jerry could grow vegetables and fruit; lots and lots of vegetables and fruit.

A couple of extra coffees from the buffet car, a mid-morning Danish pastry, and the two of them were pulling into Darlington Station almost before they realised.

They were met at the station by one of the local police drivers, and after the inevitable introductions, they settled down for the 30-mile drive to Brassington Hall. It was a public school. It had been founded in 1563, by Bishop Henry Brassington, as a school for the education of the sons of clergymen. The original school building had been damaged by fire early in the 1830s, but a large portion of the chapel and cloisters had survived the fire, and a new school had been built around it. If you were to describe the architectural style of the rest of the school, it would probably be Victorian Gothic. As with much of the architecture of that time, it was draughty and impractical. With modern central heating and plumbing, it was probably fine to live in, but in the late 1800s and early 1900s, it would have been quite a spartan existence for the pupils living there.

The car approached the main building. Leading up to the main door, there was a circular carriage drive round what Lady Catherine de Bourgh, in *Pride and Prejudice*, might have described as 'a prettyish kind of a little wilderness.' The main door itself was a huge, heavy, oak door, with metal studs, like the great doors of a gothic cathedral. There was a wicket gate in the righthand door, and it was this that opened when they rang the bell. They were ushered through into the waiting area outside the head's office, and required to sign the visitors' book, for safeguarding purposes. They had an instant photograph taken and printed out. It was converted into a visitors' pass which was put into a case with a lanyard, and the lanyards were hung round their necks.

"You must keep those with you at all times," said the head's PA.

The headmaster kept them waiting about five minutes. He introduced himself to them.

"Good afternoon, gentlemen. I am Rupert Rodgers. I am the headmaster here. I apologise for having kept you waiting but I was talking to the Chair of Governors and really couldn't get rid of him. Many apologies."

"No bother, Sir," said Jerry. "I am Detective Inspector Gregory, and this is my colleague, Detective Sergeant Trinder. Its good of you to make the time to see us. If you read the papers, I am sure you know what is behind our visit today."

"I think so, Inspector. I am assuming you wanted to talk about the unfortunate Nigel Crofton-Jones. It was such a shock to hear of his death so soon after graduating from Cambridge."

"That's right," said Jerry. "If you don't mind, we would also like to ask you about Henry Castleton. He and Nigel were good friends I gather, and we are concerned to know more about Henry's time here."

"Well," said Rodgers, "Henry and Nigel were very close in the sixth form. Both boys had been here since they were 14, and both came from local prep schools. They didn't seem all that bright at first, but they were both very ambitious, and they worked hard. We have very good staff here, and they managed to get the boys to perform at a high enough level to get places at Cambridge. I believe that Nigel went to read English but converted to law in his second year. Henry read law from the start; in making that decision, he was probably influenced by his father, a local high court judge.

But I jump ahead. There were a few misdemeanours along the way before they got to that stage.

When the boys reach the lower-sixth they can choose to go into sets with three other boys. Each set has four desk areas, one for each boy, and a large bedroom with four single beds. Crofton-Jones and Castleton chose to share, and we put with them two other boys who joined just for the sixth form, Ma, and Clarke. It all seemed to be going quite well for a while, but it came to my notice, and that of several other members of staff, that someone in the school was supplying cannabis to the boys. We organised a search of the studies when the boys were in assembly one day, and we found a substantial store of cannabis in the study with the four boys I have just told you about. We questioned all four boys separately, and in the end, Jonas Clarke owned up to being the purchaser and supplier. He had to leave; he went to a school near Leeds, its only about 35 miles away, and after that, the smell of funny tobacco completely disappeared. Jonas did very well at the other school, and there was never any suggestion of drug dealing there.

If I am very honest with you, Inspector, I thought the other three boys were far more likely to have the nous to be dealers. We did find a couple of those pink ecstasy things in one of the lavatories a few months after Jonas had gone, but we could never prove that recreational drugs were being used in the school, and I suppose it is remiss of us, but we didn't really want to find that three of our star pupils were dealing in drugs. So, that is probably all I can tell you that is factual about them."

"Thank you, Headmaster," said Jerry. "I note that you said that it is all you can tell us factually about them, but I wondered if you might be prepared to go further with your thoughts about them as individuals. Completely off the record now, what did you think of those three boys as far as personality and behaviour goes?"

"Well," said Rodgers, "I thought Nigel was weak and rather subservient to the other two. I thought him easily led. There were a couple of other incidents when they got into trouble, tying cans to the exhaust of one of the teacher's cars, stealing chocolate biscuits from the kitchen stores after lights out, going into Leeds to a party that they thought we didn't know about. In each case, I am sure Nigel just tagged along. Henry is cleverer than Nigel was. I expect he had something to do with organising all these things. I did wonder if there was a bit of a protection racket going on as well. There can be quite a lot of bullying in schools like this and we cannot always keep on top of it. There was a period when the boys were in the upper sixth where some of the younger boys seemed to be trying to avoid these three, especially avoiding Charles Ma. I would imagine Henry organised the protection, if it did happen, but Charles Ma would have been the enforcer. He was about a year older than the other boys because he had re-sat some of his GCSEs at his previous school and had come to us for the sixth form. I thought that lad had a mean streak in him. He was one of those boys who did pull the wings off butterflies, and I am sure he used to fire stones from a makeshift catapult at passing cats and dogs. We had a complaint about him once from one of the neighbours, but she couldn't be sure it was young Ma. He was also obsessed with knives. We once confiscated from him a stiletto with an engineered seven-inch blade. I asked him where he got it and he said that his father had given it to him for protection when they went to Shanghai on one of his father's business trips. We returned the knife to Ma when he left but reminded him that it is illegal to carry such a knife in this country.

We have a section of the Army Cadet Force at this school. Boys usually join at 14 here when they come from prep school. Charles Ma did not join until he arrived at the beginning of the lower sixth, but he hurried through basic training and very quickly became totally engaged in it. He was a remarkable marksman; we have a small-bore shooting range and armoury at the school, and Ma was undoubtedly our best shot. The three boys also went on several courses put on by the army; they put them on to try and recruit some of the cadets. From the reports we got back about them, Henry had good leadership potential, Nigel was a real plodder and follower, but Ma was outstanding on every course he went on.

He was selected for a specialist course for commando training. I assume it was age adjusted, but he loved every minute of it and came back with glowing reports.

Of the three of them, I thought Ma was the one with the mean streak in him. Nigel was weak, Henry was scheming, but Ma could sometimes be just nasty.

Well, I've probably said too much but I am still a bit shocked about Crofton-Jones's death and I wanted to help as much as I could."

"Very helpful," said Jerry.

"Yes, sir. Thank you," said Tommy.

"Just one more thing, Sir," said Tommy, "can you give us a little more information about Charles Ma. What was he like physically? Where does he live? What is he doing now?"

"Well, Sergeant," said Rodgers, "interesting that you ask. I had thought that Ma would go into the forces; he had an aptitude and an appetite for physical activity, but he rather surprised us. Ma got a place at Edinburgh University to study Chemistry. I gather he dropped out after two years. I have no idea what happened to him after that. The home address he gave us was a place just south of Edinburgh, Peebles, if I recall correctly. He was a tall skinny boy, Chinese origin. His grandparents had escaped from China during the cultural revolution, and the family all spoke Chinese at home. Ma's father still has strong business interests in Shanghai, and when the gang of four were deposed, the whole family started to visit the People's Republic. Ma told me once that he didn't speak English until he was five years old and went to school, and he found it very hard at first at school. He said he was bullied and that was when he learnt to fight. He had a good vocabulary by the time he came to us, but he did have quite a strong Scots accent! He hasn't been in touch since he left. We write to him regularly as an old boy, but just recently, the school magazine and other letters have been returned unopened. He does seem to have vanished."

There was a bit of a look on the faces of both detectives. It was a look of interest. Tall, funny accent, Edinburgh, stiletto knife. Anything else?

"Headmaster, we would very much like a copy of his file, if you don't mind. We think he may have important information for us if we are able to find and interview him."

"I am sure you understand that we have to comply with the Data Protection Legislation," said Rodgers. "I believe there are exemptions for the detection and prevention of crime, but I am not sure how Charles Ma comes into the detection and prevention of crime under these circumstances?"

"I am not at liberty to tell you why we need to talk to Charles Ma, but we do believe he may have had some involvement in one or both of the murders we are investigating. We need to find him as soon as possible," said Sergeant Trinder.

"I'm sorry. I think I have gone as far as I can in talking to you," said the headmaster. "Will you excuse me a minute, I need to just have a word with my PA," and Rupert Rodgers left the room for a couple of minutes leaving the file open on his desk.

Charles Ma's home address and telephone number were hastily copied into a notebook. Jerry took a quick snap of the photograph of the young Charles Ma on the front of the folder.

The headmaster returned with a tray of cups, a teapot, milk, and sugar. He was gone a good five minutes.

"I thought you might like a cup of tea before you go," he said, and he buzzed for his PA.

Once the PA was in the room, Rodgers picked up all three files and said:

"Helena, would you take these three files and put them back in the archives please? I am afraid I cannot give copies to the policemen because of data protection rules."

Then, he turned to the policemen and said:

"I am sorry about that, but I hope, nevertheless, that our conversation has been helpful to you." And with considerable emphasis on the word 'All,' Rodgers added:

"I hope you got *all* the information you need."

"Chocolate biscuit, Inspector? Sergeant?"

"Thank you, Headmaster. If we do need any further information, may we call you? You have been most helpful."

The two detectives finished their teas and their chocolate biscuits and made their departure. Rogers knew he had been helpful; the detectives knew that he had meant to be.

"Decent chap, that head," said Tommy when they were back in the police car heading towards the railway station.

Then, Tommy suddenly remembered the brief attempt he had made at learning Chinese. Ma, third tone, means Horse. Charles Ma. Could it be Charley Horse? He mentioned the idea to Jerry.

By the time they got back to London, it was too late to do any more useful work that day.

Chapter 19

Jerry and Tommy went home, but not before they had asked the Inverness police to send down the carefully bagged raincoat that had remained unclaimed on the Caledonian Sleeper train; the train that they now believed the murderer had taken back to his base. They also asked Scottish Transport Police to look through the lost property log and see if they could find a raincoat abandoned on the same train line on the night of Angela Huddlestone's murder. They requested that, if they could find one, it also be sent through to London for forensics.

Jerry Gregory slept well that night. He now thought he knew for whom he was searching. He had a name; he had a history up until a couple of years ago; he might have some forensic evidence from the raincoat. More circumstantial evidence was pointing to Henry Castleton's involvement in drug dealing in Cambridge, and even before Cambridge. He needed to get the team to look at Henry's phone records and compare them with Nigel's. A shame they couldn't get hold of records from the immediate post-school years, but the law limited the requirement for storage of data to twelve months. Jerry wondered if the investigation of Nigel's laptop might provide information further back, he would check in the morning.

Henry came back to London from Cambridge with a replacement stash of heroin and stored it behind one of the roof panels in his living room. He had made a similar arrangement to the one the boss had made in the bathroom in Cambridge, with an almost invisible pair of turn catches, concealed under a piece of plaster coving above the door frame. You really would have to strip the plaster from the whole room to find the hidey-hole.

He rang the boss and reported in. The boss gave him instructions about how to distribute the heroin, and to which of the dealers it should go. There were several drops around the King's Cross and Holborn areas and Henry, over the course of the next day, would be dropping the drugs and collecting the money. This was the first time he had done the pick-up and distribution. The dealers knew the price and Henry would only leave the drugs if the money was already there. When you look carefully around a city street, there are lots of easy hiding places for small items, like stacks of notes or packets of heroin. The easiest ones to use were ones where someone might drop an item and bend to pick it up. Hiding places near street level were rather effective.

It was a relief to Henry to have completed this errand. He was slowly feeling less afraid for his life, and some of his old cockiness was returning. He rang Judith and arranged to take her out for dinner that evening. He asked her what type of food she might like, and she suggested Chinese. They settled on Zhushu, a Sichuan restaurant in Soho. Judith wanted to go home first to change out of her work clothes, so they agreed to meet there at 19:00 hours. Henry booked a table.

Henry was not quite prepared for the conversation he had with Judith that Friday evening. He was beginning to find himself looking forward more and more to seeing her, each time they went out, and he wondered how this was going to resolve itself. He was very sure that Judith would not approve of his involvement with drugs, and he was sure that she would not be prepared to turn a blind eye to it. He was amazed to find himself falling in love with such a conventional young woman.

The evening began gently enough with them ordering the Sichuan specialities recommended by the waiter. Kung pao chicken, mapo tofu, yu xiang rou si, and twice cooked pork, with dry-fried green beans were the main dishes, with a little white rice to dilute the spiciness.

Judith suddenly stopped eating and looked Henry in the eye.

"Both Angela and Nigel have been murdered. Do you have any idea why?" She asked.

Henry thought about it. The very first date he had had with Judith was with Angela and Nigel at the Greek restaurant only a few weeks ago.

"They were friends from Cambridge," he said. "I enjoyed the theatre scene with them, and I was just picking up where we left off. We had all been away for the last long vacation we were going to get, and when I came back, I naturally contacted Nigel because we were both doing law. I wanted to introduce you to them because they had been such fun in Cambridge, and I thought you might like them. It came as a real shock to me when Inspector Gregory told me that they were both mixed up with drugs. I saw nothing like that in Cambridge. I believe that Inspector Gregory thinks the murders are drug related. Beyond that, I have no idea. I cannot believe what has happened."

"Do you swear to me that you had nothing to do with drugs and whatever it is that got them into trouble?" Judith asked.

Henry reached across and took Judith's hand in his. He spoke with full theatrical sincerity:

"Believe me, I had no idea. I would never have been friends with them if I had known they were into drugs. I certainly wouldn't have introduced them to you."

And Henry gazed at Judith with the deepest insincere sincerity he could manage.

"Trust me," he said.

He was very convincing. He had never managed to act so well during his brief stage career at Cambridge. Judith was completely taken in. Henry justified himself in lying like this because, as far as he knew, he had only dealt with small quantities of marijuana and other drugs, and he convinced himself that he had certainly not condoned the venture of Nigel and others into more serious drug dealing. What he was doing now, he deluded himself, was only to try to stay alive.

"You, poor thing," said Judith. "So, you have lost two friends and had your faith in people and friendship dented. Did you have any other friends at Cambridge who you really liked and who you still might trust?"

"There was a couple," said Henry. "There was a lovely medic called Rowan Pike who was a very good friend to me. I think she is now well into her clinical medicine course. There were two other lawyers on Angela's staircase, Amanda, and Robert. They were very nice and very pleasant to me. I do remember they complained to the Senior Tutor about Angela and Nigel using cannabis, but I didn't really register that; I was too busy with the theatre and my degree course. I am in two minds about calling them. I got on rather better with the people at St Joseph's than I did with those at my own college. I think it was because I got so involved with theatre so early on in my time there, and my friends were then theatre people, 'thespies,' everyone called us."

"Tell me about the theatre then," said Judith. "I adore live theatre."

Henry's awkward moment had passed, and he could stop lying and start talking truthfully about his theatre experiences. He was brutally honest about his own relative lack of talent and Angela's theatrical genius. He was a little unkind about Nigel, describing him as a good supporting actor. It was unkind, but it was true.

Henry took Judith home by taxi to her Hampstead flat and kissed her goodnight. It was the first time they had kissed properly, and Henry's mind was in a turmoil. He really was falling in love with this girl.

They arranged to meet on Wednesday of the following week for dinner, and Henry arranged to get tickets for a play, at the Aldwych, for the following Friday.

On the way home on the bus, Henry was thinking very hard. He needed to get out of the drug scene completely. He didn't need the money and he knew that if he continued in the scene at all, he would lose Judith, and probably his career. He also knew that if he did not manage to find a fool proof way of exiting the scene, he would be likely to lose his life. He knew too much about the people who had done the serious drug things; they would almost certainly consider him to be a loose end that needed dealing with. Henry had some planning to do. He had to make it worth their while to let him leave and let him live. He thought of all those detective and spy stories he had seen where someone wants to get out of the business and arranges a form of blackmail, whereby, if they stay alive, nobody gets to see certain videos, tape recordings, documents, compromising photographs, or carefully worded confession statements, which implicate all the other crooks or spies. It always seems so easy in the films but, in practice, he was racking his brain to think what he could put into the magic safe deposit box, and to whom he could entrust the 'In the event of my death' letter. As far as he could see, the only two people he might have entrusted with that duty had been murdered by the people he wanted protection from. He had two things to do, construct the evidence that would shield him, and find some way to get that evidence safely stored. He was determined to get out and to turn his life around; he hoped it was not too late.

****

For the detectives, the Friday had been a case of simply trying to analyse some of the data they had, and plan what to do next. Charles Ma was now a priority in their minds. They set the backroom boys to trawling all the databases, births and deaths, electoral roll, everything they could think of. They needed to find Charles Ma.

The raincoats from the Caledonian Sleeper trains were down in the forensic lab. There had, indeed, been a second raincoat on the Caledonian express from the night of Angela's murder. The raincoats had arrived in the lab on the

Thursday, while Jerry and Tommy were visiting Brassington Hall. Jerry picked up the phone and rang the forensic lab.

"Any joy with those raincoats?" He asked.

"Well, Inspector," said Matthew Wilkins, the head of the laboratory. "There are a few useful things, I think. The first is that the raincoats are an identical make; they are, unfortunately, a common make. You can pick them up at almost any of the major outdoor shops. So, I don't think you are going to be able to use that to trace ownership. The other thing that is interesting, however, is that there were hairs on the collars of both coats. The hairs look identical. Black, straight hair. Fairly coarse, lots of cuticle layers, so I reckon these are Asian hairs. Probably, Chinese. I reckon we can get a DNA sample, so if we do ever find the guy, we will be able to match him to the two raincoats."

Jerry thanked him and rang off. He turned to Tommy:

"So, all we have to do now is find the bastard," he said.

The trail to Charles Ma was very straightforward until it came to the time of his drop out from Edinburgh. The home address they had obtained from his school file was confirmed, and the telephone number. Jerry called the parents and a pleasant sounding, quite elderly man, Charles Ma's father, answered. He was very apologetic that he was unable to help but they had not heard from their son in over a year. They had been unable to contact him. Charles had been left quite a sum of money by his grandfather and it seemed that he had taken all that money out of his bank account about a month before he disappeared, and his bank account had not been touched since. Charles Ma's parents had tried everything they could think of to try to contact their son but to no avail. Jerry had asked the parents to send a copy of the most recent photograph of Charles that they could find.

Charles's father had, of course, been lying. Charles was in constant contact with his father, especially over the extensive business interests that Ma Senior was building up in Shanghai and Hong Kong. It was the intention of both Charles and his father that Charles would take over the family business interests when Ma Senior decided to retire.

The Ma parents were not the only brick wall that the search for Charles came up against. All the other associations, the Old Brassingtonians, the contacts from the first two years in Edinburgh, none of them had seen hide nor hair of him. Some of the students from the dorm in which Charles had lived for the first two years were still there. Some of them were doing four-year courses and were now in their final year, others were staying on for a PhD or a master's course. Jerry and Tommy decided that another train journey might well be a good idea.

It looked very much as if Charles Ma had gone completely under the radar. He had, presumably, changed his identity, and it was going to be a much trickier task to find him than either of the policeman wanted.

They rang ahead to Edinburgh and got from the Registry the names and locations that Charles had been associated with. There were the halls of residence, his registered address when he moved into his own accommodation in the second year, the addresses, and names, of officers of any societies that he had joined, and the names of those who had taught him.

When they went to Edinburgh, they had a full two-day itinerary to keep them busy. Much to their surprise, it included meeting members of the Edinburgh University Theatre Company, which Charles had joined in his first year, at about the time that Henry, Nigel, and Angela had joined the ADC in Cambridge. It was probably a coincidence, but one worth looking at.

Henry, meanwhile, realised that he had nothing he could use to pin on the boss, or the boss's hitman, to keep them off his back if he chose to leave. He was almost sure that the hitman was Charles, and he had nothing on Charles that would be useful. He had no idea of the boss's identity because the boss always used a voice synthesiser scrambler to talk to everyone on the telephone and had communicated all messages at Cambridge through Nigel. His only chance of getting enough information was to go deeper into the organisation and start collecting video and other evidence as he went. It might be that, if he could compromise everyone he knew to be involved, it would be enough to protect himself. He could record his telephone conversations on the burner phones and be sure to include names as he talked. He would like to manipulate things so that he had a face-to-face assignation with the boss. He had not met the boss even in Cambridge; it might be very difficult to arrange. If the hitman was someone other than Charles, he had no idea who that could be. It did not matter. If he could get the whole group compromised, he ought to be safe. The first thing to do was to go back to St Joseph's and collect the apparatus that everyone had used to weigh out and distribute drugs. It would be bound to have fingerprints all over it; true it would have Henry's and Nigel's prints, because they had used it to weigh out the cannabis, but it would also have all the other's prints because they had used it to weigh out the hard stuff. Once he had the scales, he would decide what to do next. He had investigated how to make a letter of wishes which, in the event of his death, would require someone to notify the police of the evidence he had gathered. He had a family solicitor who would do that for him. His biggest problem was still getting additional concrete evidence. From now on, every phone call on the burner phone would be recorded. Once he had the evidence, he would let everyone, including the boss, know.

The trip to Edinburgh was important for the detectives. They managed to interview several students who had been in the halls of residence with Charles Ma, but nobody had been a particular friend. There were several of the students who said they were aware of Charles using marijuana, and one or two said that they thought he might have been dealing in it. Again, there was no physical evidence. A couple of students reported that Charles often disappeared at the weekends, and one said he had overheard him calling for a taxi to Waverley Station, on more than one Friday evening. He would usually come back in high spirits quite late on the Sunday evening. Someone had asked him once where he disappeared to, and he said he was going down south to see friends, but he was never more specific than that.

The meeting with the theatre company president and secretary was what made the trip interesting. Charles was, apparently, quite a good actor and a very good 'techie.' He had been stage manager for the Freshers Production in his first term and had gone on to manage several more productions, including the Edinburgh University Theatre Company production at the Edinburgh Fringe. In the first year at the festival, Charles had met up with a friend from school who was techie for one of the Cambridge University productions. They had seen very little of Charles socially after that, although he had continued to do his job in the theatre. When asked about the friend from school, the president described a tall, good looking, blond male; the description fitted Henry. Tommy showed them a photograph. They identified Henry as the person they were talking about. The two company members were shown pictures of Angela and Nigel, and these too were confirmed as part of the clique that had formed around Charles during that first Fringe Festival season. Accommodation in Edinburgh during the fringe is incredibly expensive, so several students share a room, and many of them couch surf. It appeared that Charles had arranged to move in for the summer to his second-year accommodation; he was planning to live out of halls, and he had taken his three friends to share his room. The flat was on the second floor of one of those huge tenement blocks in Newington. Charles was obviously quite well off because he had rented the flat by himself.

The two London detectives asked if anyone else was part of the group or anyone else had been involved with them in any way. There was a slightly surprising answer. Some other friends from Cambridge had visited the group and gone to the Cambridge fringe play. They had stayed for about three days and attended the play every evening. Jerry asked for a description and was told that there were three of them, a tall, slim well-dressed young man, a rather chunkier and shorter young man with a very deep voice, and a very plain young woman with thick horn-rimmed glasses. It seemed to both Jerry and Tommy that they had met these three before, in Oxford, not very long ago. These same three people had visited again the second year when Angela, Henry and Nigel had also come back for a further fringe performance. Charles had again put them up in his flat.

"Bit of a turn up for the book," said Jerry. "It really does sound as if Amanda Sayers, Robert Parker and Stefan, we never got his surname, were the visitors."

"Wonder what they were doing up at Edinburgh and especially what they were doing with those three, four if you add Charles Ma into the equation?" He added.

"That Robert Parker and Amanda Sayers made it pretty clear that they didn't like Nigel and Henry when we spoke to them that day in Oxford. And Robert was the one who complained to the Senior Tutor about the other two. What the hell is going on?" Tommy said.

"I suppose it could have been putting up a smoke screen," said Jerry. "What better way to isolate yourself from suspicion than to complain about others doing the deed you don't want discovered? I wonder if all of them on that floor were involved, and just as with the scapegoating at Brassington, Nigel and Angela were taking one for the team?"

"I don't think Freya and Rowan were involved," said Tommy. "Mind you, I didn't think Amanda and Robert were either, although now I am really not so sure."

"I think we need to ask Henry what he thought of Robert and Amanda. I assume the third student they mentioned was Robert Parker's boyfriend, Stefan?"

"Look, we are speculating but we can sort this quickly. Let's get some photos sent up and see what the officers of the Theatre Club say."

It was so frustrating for the two detectives. They had link after link but were unable to take any of it further. Maybe the locals knew something which could help to join up the dots.

They had their next meeting with the drug squad at the Police Scotland Headquarters in St Leonard's St. A couple of the Scottish Police who had been regularly on patrol at the fringe came to the meeting along with the head of the drug squad and her deputy. It turned out to be just a background information session. There had been no specific instances of trouble with either the Edinburgh or the Cambridge student presences over the past three years, and not before that either. There was a strong drug culture in the city among the non-university groups. The head of the drug squad gave a bit of the history of drug abuse in the city, starting with the big increase in heroin usage during the early 1980s. That had been fuelled by a supply of very pure heroin from Afghanistan and Iran, and this had helped to change the user profile from a small group of students and drop-outs to a much larger group of the socially deprived. With a new demographic for the dealers to target, the drug problem grew, and because it was the early 1980s, so did the HIV-AIDS problem. The commonest cause of drug related deaths in Edinburgh was still opiates in 2020. The second commonest cause of drug deaths in the city was benzodiazepines, the so-called street benzodiazepines, which include Rohypnol. The problem was not as bad as in Glasgow, but it was still much higher than in the United Kingdom as a whole. The local police had recently noted an influx of a remarkably pure heroin, thought to be from Afghanistan. It had not caused a large increase in the number of deaths, but it had greatly increased availability of the drug as it could be cut to a greater degree than the less pure stuff.

Jerry asked whether the local police thought Edinburgh was being used as a distribution centre. The answer was a definite yes. The drugs were still coming in from Afghanistan and Iran, because of the cash crop economy in those countries. Jerry asked if the Scottish Police could supply him with a sample of the local very pure heroin they were talking about, so that it could be compared chromatographically with the samples found in Angela's flat. Fortunately, they were able to do so.

There was not a lot of heroin around at the fringe. As with so many major arts festivals, there was a fair bit of marijuana smoked and probably a few of the other recreational drugs. Nevertheless, if someone wanted to obtain heroin or the street benzodiazepines, it would be relatively easy.

Jerry and Tommy got back on the train to King's Cross, a bit disappointed that they had not been able to make more progress, but they did have two new lines to follow up. The first concerned the visit to the fringe, two years in a row, by three people, at least two of whom had claimed to really dislike the three thespians. The second was a chance to see whether Edinburgh was the source of the heroin in Angela's flat

Chapter 20

Meanwhile, back in London, Henry was making his plans to collect the information he needed for protection. He had thought about it and decided that video recordings of conversations with the team would be the best way to go. He would try to get a voice recording of his next conversation with the boss and, maybe, the police could do something with the voice scrambler input, but with the other members of the group, he could do face to face and get a video. He had some technical expertise from his time working with the theatre backstage crews. Surely, it could not be too difficult to get a miniature spy camera and a recorder. It was not as if anyone would be expecting Henry to be recording conversations. At present, Henry was a valued and valuable member of the team, helping to keep the money rolling in.

The first thing to do was to decide on the best miniaturised spy camera he could find. Audio recording was easy. Lots of lapel concealed microphones available, but, because Henry wanted to have some video evidence of the person he was talking to, he had a little more work to do to make it happen.

Video evidence was particularly important because everyone else had very carefully hidden their involvement in the drug scene, and believability of the evidence would require the video footage. He settled for a camera which was built into sunglasses. It was an issue that the sun was hardly around in winter but there were times of the day, early morning, and early evening, where the low angle of the sun made it reasonable to put on sunglasses to prevent direct glare. He would have to time the meetings appropriately and make sure they were somewhere that he could legitimately be expected to be wearing these things. A shame that the targets did not play golf! He ordered the equipment from Amazon with the Amazon Prime option of next day delivery. He was going to try the recording out very carefully over the next few weeks. He had not met with most of the team since Cambridge days. The whole team had decided that there would be minimal face to face contact between them, except for the ones who were working in the same place, as Angela and Nigel had been. In a curious way, Henry was excited about his plans. He had had enough of the anxiety over being discovered, and the fact that his life would be in shreds if he were to be found out.

Collecting the scales from Cambridge should be relatively easy. He simply had to catch a train to Cambridge one evening, visit St Joseph's and wait until someone went on to the staircase, unless, as he hoped, they had not changed the lock codes, in which case he had Angela's university card that she had lent him last year. He would take his large briefcase. It should all fit in that. Wednesday night this week was dinner with Judith, Friday was the theatre, that left the Thursday evening. Henry planned to visit Cambridge on Thursday.

****

On the Wednesday morning, Jerry and Tommy got the news from the lab that the sample of heroin they had brought back from Scotland was identical to the sample from Angela's flat. It was the same strength and had an identical chromatographic profile. Jerry immediately called Josh Jacobs in Cambridge and gave him the news that the source of the drug was probably Edinburgh. They were not sure how useful that information was going to prove to be, but given that the hitman had come from Edinburgh, it was certainly worth knowing. They also sent the photographs of the three people, Amanda, Robert, and Stefan, which they lifted from their Facebook profiles. They asked the local police to show them to the Theatre Company officers for confirmation that these were, indeed, the three visitors to the fringe. That confirmation came quite quickly.

Jerry and Tommy now had to decide on their priorities. Should they interview Henry first, about his contacts with Robert and Amanda, or should they re-interview Robert and Amanda, and see what they had to say when confronted with this new evidence? They opted for talking to Henry first.

Henry had the telephone call from Tommy on the Wednesday morning, while he was at work, and arranged to meet the detectives at a coffee bar near his office. Henry was completely taken aback by the conversation that followed.

"Good afternoon, Henry," said Jerry Gregory.

"We have just come back from a very interesting trip to Edinburgh. We understand you went there a couple of times with the theatre group from Cambridge, Is that correct?"

Henry stumbled for a moment.

"Well, we were not with the University ADC group. They were mainly a mixture of Footlights and ADC; it was just the three of us, and a couple of our friends, who were putting on our own show on the fringe. Anyone can work the fringe, so we took advantage of that."

"Right. So, not part of the official group but you were there a couple of years in a row? What did you do?" Jerry continued.

"We did a spoof version of a James Bond short story '007 in New York' in which we took the mickey out of the recipes and made it sort of Fanny Craddock like. We did it two years in a row because people liked it first time round."

"Where did you stay?" Tommy asked.

"We slept on camp beds in a friend's flat."

"Oh, right. Who was that?"

"Oh, just a friend." Henry did not like where this was heading.

"Would appreciate a name, Henry," said Jerry.

"Well, he was an old school friend of mine, his name is Charles Ma," said Henry, clearly very reluctantly.

"Do you see him at all now?" Jerry asked.

"Haven't seen him since the last time we went to the fringe two years ago. No, sorry, that's not true. He came down to Cambridge a couple of times last year, but it wasn't to see me," said Henry.

"Well, who did he come to see?" Jerry asked.

Henry spluttered a bit and then he said:

"It was Amanda, I think. Anyway, he stayed with Amanda and Robert."

"Well, at the moment he seems to have disappeared from the face of the earth," said Tommy. "We are trying to contact him because we think he might know something about Angela's and Nigel's murderer. We think he might have been in London on the nights when both were killed."

All the colour drained from Henry's face. He suddenly knew what this was all about, and he also knew that it was Charles who had killed both Angela and Nigel. At school, Charles had been a bully, with a vile temper and brutally strong. He had also been the brains behind the drug supply and dealing at Brassington Hall. He had the contacts. Was he also the source of the drugs that Sammy Needles was passing on to the boss and the gang? Quite suddenly, Henry's plan to extricate himself took on a new, and much less favourable, dimension.

There was a prolonged period of silence. The detectives drank their coffees and stared, relentlessly, at Henry who clearly became more and more uncomfortable.

"I really cannot help you, Inspector," said Henry. "I just have not seen him socially at all since the summer a couple of years ago. He wanted nothing to do with me when he came to Cambridge those few times last year. Do you really think he might be involved in these murders?"

"We don't know for certain, but there is a strong possibility. And there is also a strong possibility that he is involved in the drug scene that Angela and Nigel were clearly implicated in."

Then Jerry said, "Did you have any Cambridge visitors while you were at the fringe?"

Henry could see where this was going. To lie or not to lie, that is the question? He was smart enough to know they would not have asked that question unless they already knew the answer.

"I was amazed," he said, "Robert, Stefan, and Amanda all came and visited both the years that we went to the fringe. I had no idea they were so into theatre, and I didn't think they liked Angela or Nigel, let alone me."

"So, when they came, how did you all get on?" Jerry asked.

"It was surprising," said Henry. "They seemed completely interested in the theatre stuff and we got on well. They must have known Angela and Nigel were still smoking marijuana, you could smell it everywhere in Charles's flat where we were staying, but they didn't say anything. That's why I was a bit surprised when they made the complaint to the Senior Tutor at St Joe's the following year."

"Have you seen Robert, Stefan, or Amanda since you came to London?" Tommy asked.

"No, I haven't. But I think I might just try and meet up with them again. I think they are all in Oxford doing the BCL."

"What do you think of those three?" Tommy asked.

"Oh! They're alright," said Henry. "I think they complained because they are so uptight about becoming lawyers. They don't come from legal backgrounds, and they don't have a big network of contacts, so they must be extra careful to remain squeaky clean, and they must achieve things on merit, not by influence. They all got firsts you know. If you want to know what I think of them personally, Robert is a bit pompous, but decent enough, Stefan is very quiet and difficult to get through to, but there seems to be no harm in him, and Amanda is a real bluestocking. But she is also someone who likes having a boyfriend, and although she is as plain as a pikestaff, that wasn't an issue when it came to having a social life."

"So, you were not really friends then?" Tommy asked.

"Not at all," said Henry. "You could have knocked me down with a feather when they turned up at Edinburgh."

"Why do you think they came then?" Tommy asked.

"I guess everyone wants to come to the fringe at some stage in their lives," said Henry. "Besides which I think Amanda sort of fancied Nigel. She went to see every production he was in, which, I suppose, was not all that many, when he was at Cambridge."

"Did they know your friend Charles?" Tommy asked.

"No. Not before they met him in Edinburgh," said Henry.

"So, how was it that Charles started to come to Cambridge to see Amanda and Robert?" Jerry asked.

"Well, as Pascal once said, the heart has its reasons that reason does not know. Amanda and Charles got very close. In fact, they ended up sleeping together," said Henry.

"Are they still in touch?" Jerry asked.

"No idea," said Henry. "I think you will just have to ask them."

Henry left the interview a very worried man. The carefully worked plan of isolating themselves from each other socially was beginning to come unravelled. He thought he had better telephone the boss to explain what had just happened. He got out the burner phone and did just that.

Back at headquarters, Jerry and Tommy found that Nigel's laptop was now in the department and being examined. The warrant to appropriate it had been readily given. Nigel's father had objected at first, but the warrant trumped that objection.

The police IT team quickly managed to access the system, surprisingly Nigel had been one of those who chose an incredibly simple password which took the team about five minutes to crack. It was his initials and the year of his birth.

While the rest of the team examined the email record, Terry and Jerry looked at the photographs in the photo folder. Those photographs were all date and time stamped. The interesting series was from February two years ago. It was a production of Richard III in which Nigel was taking part, and in the bar at the interval, a picture had been taken of Charles, Henry, Amanda, and Robert. Presumably, Stefan was holding the camera.

When they trawled through the photographs a little more, there were other pictures of these four, in different combinations, with Angela and Nigel. Henry had been lying to them. It was significant that Rowan and Freya never appeared in any of the photographs. The two detectives thought that they were correct in excluding these two young ladies from further consideration.

It seemed that Charles had visited Cambridge on more than a dozen occasions each year. Again, Henry had lied. One other interesting thing was that Charles was often seen in the photographs with his arm around Amanda and on more than one occasion, they were kissing.

The email search was also proving interesting. There was much email correspondence between the five students and Charles. It was all friendly. It was all arranging meetings and visits and talking about social gatherings that they had had. It was certainly not the frosty set of relationships that all of them had tried to convey to the detectives; all, that is, except Charles. They had still to meet Charles. There was a useful email address for Charles. Charley.horse@gmail.com was Mr Ma's chosen email. The two detectives immediately set the team on finding out the email history of Charley Horse.

"Right," said Jerry, "we need Charles now. I reckon there are two ways we can deal with this. We can issue his photograph to all forces, with a particular attention on London, Edinburgh, and Cambridge, or we can try and get a report of the two murders on TV. What do you think?"

"Let's do both," said Tommy. "I know the murders are old, but the news channel may take it and we could do with some help."

Fortunately, for Jerry and Tommy, the news that day was a bit thin, and so they managed to get agreement from the news team to run a three-minute slot on the murder cases. Given the lack of detail in Angela's case, the two detectives decided to concentrate on Nigel's stabbing.

It was important to get as much detail correct as they could. Angela's murder was confined to a short thirty second account, by Tommy, of the main details. It focussed on the figure in the raincoat, and his catching the Caledonian Sleeper.

For the second murder, there was a partial reconstruction, almost in the old Crimewatch style. Jerry and Tommy regretted that Crimewatch had been axed. It would have been an ideal vehicle for their purposes.

The reconstruction started at the restaurant and showed actors, representing Samantha and Nigel, walking to the tube station, catching the tube to Kentish Town, leaving the station, and retracing the route to the site of the fatal stabbing. The figure in the raincoat was again mentioned, shown conducting the stabbing, and returning to take the phones from Nigel's pockets. They filmed the actor playing the murderer catching the 134 bus, getting off at the Euston Road bus stop, and walking to Euston Station, where he caught the Caledonian Sleeper. The picture of Charles was then shown for about twenty seconds, with voice over, asking anyone who knew the whereabouts of this man, not to approach him, but to call the police immediately. A contact number was given.

The first broadcast went out at about 11 am. All the other news channels then picked up on the story, and while it was repeated hourly for the rest of the day on the BBC, the story and the photograph appeared on all the other news channels throughout the day as well.

****

In a tenement building in Edinburgh, David Fu was just settling down for the evening to watch television, with his landlord and landlady, Hamish, and Flora MacGregor. It had become a bit of a routine since David had taken the room with them about six months ago. David would come back from work, he apparently worked in IT in a start-up. They had no idea what it was he did in that start-up, but it seemed to earn him good money. Flora would cook the three of them supper and they would sit and eat it together as they chatted over the day's news. They often watched the six o'clock news together, and this evening was no exception. It was about ten minutes into the news bulletin that Angela's picture appeared on the screen. David got up and went quickly to his room. He was back just in time to see his own picture flash up, and hear Flora say, "My God. That's David."

He pressed the button on his stiletto knife, with the seven-inch blade, and struck first Flora and then Hamish with surgical precision, straight through the rib spaces on the left, straight through the ventricles. In, twist, out. Just as he had with Nigel.

Bugger, he thought to himself. *I need to find somewhere else to stay now.*

And then he wondered to himself how he was going to cover up these two murders long enough to give him time to relocate and morph into a new identity yet again. The more he thought about it, the more he thought the sensible thing would be just to get out of there as quickly as he could. It would be two or three days before anyone locally missed the MacGregors, by which time he could be long gone. His money was already in several bank accounts in a completely different name, one that he would never use for anything else. He had two more false identities set up that he could assume at a moment's notice. "Planning ahead." He thought to himself. "Always two moves ahead."

Charles Ma woke the next morning after a good night's sleep. The bodies were still in the sitting room where he had left them. Charles went to the bathroom and got out his electric clippers. He shaved his head completely and put on a blond wig that he had borrowed from the props and make up department at the University Theatre when he was still involved there. He had it in mind that someday he might need to change appearance quickly. He lightened his eyebrows. He also put in some coloured contact lenses, changing his irises from the very deep brown, almost black, natural colour, to a much lighter hazel colour. He took out a pair of plain glass, dark framed, spectacles. Once the transformation had finished, he looked nothing like the picture that had been shown around the nation the evening before.

Adam Liu, formerly Charles Ma, temporarily David Fu, boarded the train at Waverley Station, carrying a large rucksack containing all the clothes and portable possessions that he wished to take with him. He had set a timer to switch on the hob in the kitchen 36 hours after his departure from the tenement building. On the hob, he had placed three large lithium batteries that Hamish had used to power his strimmer for the grass in the yard. Next to the batteries, he had placed an open jerry can of five litres of petrol. By the time everything exploded, Adam Liu should be far away from Edinburgh. The drug supply lines were securely set up. He did not need to remain to ensure the continued supply of drugs to the gang. The last time he personally had delivered the drugs to Sammy Needle was over four months ago. The boss could organise further transfers using the telephone numbers that Charles Ma had supplied.

"I rather fancy East Anglia." Thought Charles. "I might try Felixstowe. I have never lived in a seaside town and it might be fun. I believe Edward and Mrs Simpson thought so!"

True to plan, the lithium batteries blew up and caught fire when the hob turned on. The petrol was ignited, there was a major explosion and the house, old and tinder dry, went up in flames. The fire brigade put out the flames, but not before quite a lot of damage had been done. Two bodies were found in the dining room. They were burnt but, not extensively. They were easily identified as Hamish and Flora MacGregor. Post-mortem examination showed them to have been stabbed to death with a single blow, with a long thin knife which had left cut marks on the bones in the rib space.

Chapter 21

Back in London, Henry had become panicked enough to have contacted the boss again. He told the boss that the London detectives had asked him about the links between all of them on the staircase, plus Charles and himself. He was pretty sure that they had linked all of them, except Freya and Rowan. He told the boss exactly what he had said under questioning.

It was clear to Henry that the boss was very uncomfortable. It was in the voice and persistent questioning about what Henry had said to Jerry and Tommy. It was going to be much more difficult now to create the distance Henry needed to extract himself from this mess. He began to wish with all his heart that he had turned down the easy money offer from Charles, when they sat together with Nigel and Jonas, in the study at Brassington that September, all those years ago. At first, all he had done was turn a blind eye to the dealings, then he had started to smoke the stuff himself; then he had started to act as a salesman. There had been a sense of adventure when they climbed out of the study window on Friday or Saturday evenings, and sneaked off to the garage where Charles, a little older than the other three, had stored his Golf GT. He had passed his test two months after his 17th birthday and his father had bought him the car as a birthday present, in anticipation of his passing the test, and because he had finally passed enough GCSEs to move on to sixth form.

Charles had mesmerised both Henry and Nigel. He had a lot of money, he was very street wise, he was also very domineering. Both boys, and Jonas, were frightened of him. Charles coerced them into joining his drugs enterprise. They would go to the car and all four head off for night clubs, with false ID supplied by Charles. Once there, they would buy and sell marijuana, ecstasy, and anything else they could get their hands on. All four boys made plenty of cash out of it. The excess drugs left after they left the night club would be sold to fellow pupils, not the heavy stuff but mainly the marijuana and a bit of ecstasy.

When the stash of marijuana was discovered in their study, Charles told Jonas to take the hit. He threatened to have him killed if he didn't, and Jonas believed him, and thought changing school was a much better option, especially as it would get him away from Charles. With hindsight, Henry felt that he should have realised that this was the time to get out, but neither he nor Nigel were rational about it at that stage. They enjoyed the money, and they enjoyed the adventure of the night club visits, and the challenge of concealment of the clandestine activities. The continuation of the activity when they got to Cambridge, and the recruitment of new participants, was a logical progression, but each small step down the slippery slope made it harder and harder to withdraw. There was also the escalation to harder and harder drugs, and more of it. Now, it was almost impossible to get out. The police had in their sights everyone that Henry knew to be involved. He had no illusions about loyalty. It was greed that united all the participants. It was highly likely, if it came to it, that each one of them would rat on the others, if they thought it would save their own skins, he was sure of it. His only hope was that the enterprise would remain intact as it currently stood. If that happened, he could still blackmail the remaining members into leaving him alone. If the police broke the network, then he, with everyone else, would be in trouble.

First things first. Off to Cambridge to get the scales and the other stuff hidden behind the panelling in the bathroom.

The boss called Charles.

"I am more than a bit concerned about Henry," said the boss. "It seems that the police are starting to widen their interest beyond Henry, Nigel, and Angela. They know about Edinburgh. Only Rowan and Freya are considered squeaky clean. I am expecting the police to interview everyone again. I guess everyone can say that they fell out over the drugs, after the fringe, and had no idea before that? I am tempted to think we should take out Henry, I see him as the weakest link, but for the moment, he is useful. He can do the Cambridge collection for us. So, maybe we just keep an eye on him. Are you still in Edinburgh?"

"No, I am not," said Charles. "I am afraid that bloody newscast showed my face at just the wrong time, and I had to kill my landlord and landlady. They recognised me and were just about to pick up the phone when I stuck the knife in. I gathered up my stuff, set a timed explosion in the house, and left by train. If you don't mind, I will keep my location secret. On the drug front, you don't have to worry. The numbers I gave you all still work, the network in Edinburgh and further south is intact. Just call Fergus when you want a new batch, and he will fix it with Sammy Needle. I suppose you will have to use Henry now to do the pick-up from Sammy?"

"I guess so," said the boss. "I don't like it. Henry is flaky but he is all we have. Might try to recruit someone else, do you think?"

"Stick with Henry," said Charles. "I can give him a call if you like, just to remind him what a precarious thing life is. He is absolutely terrified of me. I might just remind him of my talents."

"You do that," said the boss. "Are you far away if we need you?"

"Not as far as freezing cold Edinburgh," said Charles. "I can get to London or Cambridge in under two hours. If you need another job doing, just let me know. I intend to get a regular job, so I might need a little bit of notice, but otherwise I am, as always, at your disposal. You know we are close to having enough money to stop this game soon, especially if all of us want legitimate careers. I need to stop soon. I am needed in Shanghai to look after the Ma family business interests. Maybe we should plan just one more deal? Make it big enough and we can all retire. I would like to get out of the country and go to Shanghai. The police seem to know that I did those murders, and I am sure if they get their hands on me, they will be able to prove it."

"OK," said the boss. "One more big deal it is. And then you kill Henry?"

"Yes," said Charles. "On my way to the airport, I stop off and kill Henry."

"We still have the Cambridge problem," said the boss.

"I'll take care of that on the way to the airport too," said Charles. "I will give you as much notice as I can of my impending departure."

****

The Edinburgh police, making enquiries of the neighbours about the couple in the burnt-out house, discovered that a Chinese or mixed-race young man called David Fu had been living as a lodger with the MacGregors. The neighbours had not seen him for about two days, which was most unusual. He was a cheerful young man who always waved to and spoke to everyone as he went about his business. The officers showed them a picture of Charles Ma, all of them said that David Fu might be Charles Ma, but they were not certain. There were some highly racist comments about "how alike all Orientals looked". It was enough to trigger an alarm with the police however, and they contacted Jerry and Tommy in London to report that it was quite probable that Charles Ma had claimed a third and fourth victim on his killing spree.

In Felixstowe, Charles found a nice hotel on the seafront and booked in for a few days. He called into the local estate agents and found a flat to rent in an old convalescent home, now converted into flats, overlooking the beach. The flat was vacant, so Adam Liu arranged to move in at the weekend.

The murder made the national news, not just in Scotland. The picture was shown again. Unfortunately, Charles Ma no longer looked anything like the picture that the police had of him. Charles saw it in his new flat in Felixstowe, smiled to himself, and went for an evening stroll along the promenade, in the somewhat bracing air, confident in the belief that the police were looking for somebody who bore no resemblance to the recently created Adam Liu.

The final step of Charles's relocation was a job. He went to the local library on the High Street and looked through the classified section of the *Felixstowe Times*. He found an advert for a job as a trainee manager in a local greengrocer's shop on the High Street, applied and was given an interview. The owner could not believe his luck when someone as articulate and organised as Adam Liu applied for the post. He had impeccable references from his previous employer and was hired immediately.

Adam Liu's duties included standing in for the manager on his days off. He did all the usual things, stock taking, ordering, and cashing up, helping prepare the duty rota for the staff working in the shop. That was all quite standard. He also had a role in the delivery service. Way ahead of its time, the shop ran a delivery service for customers. Customers could order a box of mixed vegetables and fruit, and it would be delivered once or twice a week to their home. The content was not specified but would always include a large proportion of local produce in season. It was a clever system. At the end of a day, the manager and Adam would look at the stock and make up the boxes. They would start with anything that they had in excess, then they would embellish the contents with a few premium items and in the end, they ensured that what they had bought in to sell got sold. It significantly reduced wastage for the shop, but possibly increased wastage for the customers. Adam was certain that some of the items in the boxes a customer would have no idea what to do with them.

Charles, as Adam of course, was often sent to make these deliveries. He identified a couple of customers who had poor home security systems, relatively new cars, and very visible pegs on which they hung their car keys. You never knew when it might come in handy.

****

While Charles was settling into his new life in Felixstowe, Henry had made the trip to Cambridge. It was dual purpose. The boss had contacted him to go to collect another consignment of drugs from Sammy Needle. That proved to be the easy part of the trip. He left after work on the Thursday and was in Cambridge at about 6 pm. Sammy met him outside St Joe's and drugs and money were exchanged. Henry then went down to St Joe's and walked in through the main gate. One of the porters on duty recognised him, much to Henry's annoyance.

"Have you come to see young Rowan?" the porter asked. "She doesn't live in you know."

"Hello, George," said Henry. "No, I haven't. I haven't been back since we all graduated, and I went to my own college and just thought I would come and look at St Joe's as well. I spent so many happy hours here with the guys in the Cumberland Building. OK if I have a look around?"

"Well, you can," said George, and then he added something which made Henry's blood turn cold. "But they are gutting the Cumberland Building just now, putting in new wiring and plumbing and re-panelling all the rooms. Started on the top floor where all your friends used to live. In fact, I think they have completely redone that now, and are on the second floor down."

Henry recovered.

"Still like a look if that's OK by you."

Perhaps, they had not yet done the bathrooms.

"Go ahead. Don't go disturbing the fellows though."

Henry went off towards the Cumberland Building. It was empty and it was clearly being gutted. He went round the back and found an open window through which he could climb in. He went in. He took out his phone and switched on the flashlight app. He went upstairs to the top floor. He went to the bathroom, and he immediately knew that someone had beaten him to it and the drug equipment was no longer there.

In a state of shock, he climbed back out and retraced his steps.

George stopped him as he went to leave.

"You seem to be covered in plaster dust, sir. I hope you didn't get too close to the building work. It can be dangerous you know. It is a hard hat area."

"No, George. Just knocked against a few bits of rubble that were lying around. Thanks for your help. I'll come back in the spring when the ducklings are on the pond."

And with that Henry dusted himself down and went back to catch the train to London. He was not a happy bunny. He just hoped that the stuff had been destroyed by mistake. Anything else could be a problem.

The boss made sure that everyone who needed to know did know that the police suspected a wider network, including all of them, except Freya and Rowan, on the Cumberland staircase. The boss told everyone that Henry had been interviewed to discuss it and advised everyone to say that they had been friends, until the drug involvement of Henry, Nigel, and Angela had been revealed to them. It was just as well that everyone had been warned because the very next day, the Friday, Tommy and Jerry went down to Oxford to talk to Robert and Amanda.

****

They spoke to Amanda first, again at her college. She did not deny the trips to Edinburgh but said very clearly that she had gone there in the first two years and had only realised about Nigel and Angela being involved in drugs during that second visit to Edinburgh. Jerry asked her about Charles.

"He seemed really nice, and I confess, I rather fell for him. In fact, we had a bit of a fling for a while, starting in that first summer and on and off through until I graduated in June. I only found out he had dropped out of Edinburgh when he told me, around graduation, that he couldn't see me anymore. I admit I was a bit upset."

"Drugs? Charles? Surely not?" Amanda said in answer to the questions. "I admit we got drunk a bit, but what student doesn't, and yes, we were lovers. He was very gentle and loving with me. I would take him back like a shot."

Jerry explained that they genuinely believed that Charles was responsible for four murders, including Nigel and Angela.

"Surely, not Charles," said Amanda. "He was much too gentle for that."

The policemen pushed her a little harder.

"His former headmaster said that he was a bully. What was his relationship like with the others?"

"Well, he wasn't there much, and when he was, he was often with me. But from what I did see, there was no bullying going on. He was always perfectly decent with them, even Angela and Nigel when the drug thing started."

"Did Henry do drugs?" Jerry asked.

"I can't say for certain, but I don't think so. I think it was Nigel and Angela."

"What about Freya, Rowan, and Robert?" Tommy asked.

"Oh, come on, Sergeant. Those three little goody two-shoes? You must be joking."

"Did you ever do drugs?" Jerry asked.

Amanda coloured bright pink.

"Once, Inspector. By mistake, I tried a cigarette. I don't smoke, and it turned out to be a reefer. I just didn't like the way it messed with my head."

And that was about it as far as information from Amanda was concerned. Amanda Sayers had batted away and explained every element of the story the detectives had picked up in Edinburgh. The detectives were not sure how much they believed her, but everything she had said was entirely consistent with every element of the information they had to date. They still recalled that first impressive interview with her when they both thought of her as a potential high court judge. The next thing to do was to interview Robert again and see how he handled the suggestion of friendship before that final year.

"I wonder if Robert will sing to the same hymn sheet as Amanda," said Jerry. "I cannot believe that there were only two people on that staircase using drugs and that Charles was squeaky clean, and if Charles wasn't squeaky clean then, do we believe Amanda now?"

"I don't," said Tommy. "But we can't prove a bloody thing about them and drugs. And if we do believe that Amanda, Robert, and Henry are involved in the drug scene, then we also believe that they are involved in the murders, at least indirectly."

They went back into town and found Robert, as last time, at his college, and, as last time, Stefan was in close attendance. As last time, Stefan walked off out of earshot as Robert began to talk to the two policemen.

"Would you like a cup of coffee gentlemen?" Robert asked. "We can go and sit in the middle common room if you like. There is nobody there at this time of day and there is a half decent coffee machine"

Jerry, who, now that he had given up smoking, had developed rather a strong caffeine habit, grabbed at the chance.

"Yes please, Robert," he said. "I was beginning to feel caffeine deprived!"

They went into the middle common room, a spacious old room, seventeenth century, with a very high ceiling and exposed wooden roof beams. There was, indeed, a coffee machine. One that grinds the beans fresh for each cup and offers you a bewildering choice of different strengths and styles.

They went and sat over by a leaded glass window in an alcove, in rather splendid leather armchairs of the sort that you associate with retired generals, and senior politicians, in a London Club.

Robert brought over Jerry's double espresso, with a small glass of chilled water, rather in the Italian style. He went back and fetched Tommy's latte, and then he made himself a simple café Lungo to which he added cold milk.

With the beverages distributed, the conversation could begin.

Tommy led this time.

"We know that you complained about the drugs in the Cumberland Building, but we are a bit puzzled because we have several witnesses saying that you, Stefan, and Amanda, went to visit Nigel, Angela, and that chap called Henry, up at the Edinburgh Fringe. They said you went two years in a row and seemed to be very good friends."

"We were, Sergeant," said Robert. "But that was before Angela and Nigel started using marijuana on our staircase. Once that happened, and it was so strong that I started to feel light-headed and even a bit stoned some days, I just couldn't afford to stay friends with them any longer. A police caution would put a serious dent in my career plans, and I just couldn't risk that. I did try to warn Angela and Nigel, but they just laughed at me. Amanda was the same as I. She couldn't afford a caution either and we were both afraid that, if we didn't do something, we might get implicated. That was what caused the big bust up between the four of us. I suppose I should include Henry too. I never liked Henry, he hung around a lot, but I don't think he did drugs. I think he just had a big crush on Angela, even though Nigel was going out with her. I didn't like him, he never seemed to have a bath, I probably described him as smelly to you once before."

"Well," said Tommy, "that seems to explain things. There was something else we wanted to ask you about. In Edinburgh, you met a friend of Henry Castleton, Charles Ma. What was your relationship to him and what did you think of him?"

Robert answered, "I never really got to know him well. As Pascal once said, *the heart has its reasons that reason knows nothing of...* and this Charles chap seemed to fall head over heels for Amanda. They quickly became an item, so whenever he visited Cambridge, which he did probably a dozen times a year, he spent the whole time with her. I would be hard put to give an opinion of him. I don't think I particularly liked him, but he was kind enough to show us around Edinburgh when we were there, I think he was a student there."

Jerry thought to himself:

That Pascal quote, I've heard that before. Henry used it about Amanda and Charles. I think two people have been talking together here.

Tommy then asked, "Someone has suggested to us that this Charles person was a bit intimidating and rather a bully. Did you see any evidence of that in your dealings with him in Edinburgh or Cambridge?"

"Absolutely not," said Robert. "He struck me as a bit wet actually."

They finished their coffees, and after a little small talk, the detectives left Robert and headed back to the Station and their London train.

"Why do I feel that this is all like the misdirect in a conjuring trick?" Jerry said.

"Because everything is just too pat," said Tommy. "You could have taken a voice synthesiser and fed Amanda's lines through, and it would have come out in Robert's voice, and vice versa. And did you notice that both Henry and Robert quoted Pascal? What is more, Robert suggesting that Charles was 'wet' flies in the face of everything else we have been told by very reliable witnesses like the Head at Brassington?"

"There's another thing that puzzles me," said Jerry. "Looking at Nigel's phone records, there is not a single telephone call to any of the group except Angela. No call to Robert, Amanda, Henry, or Charles, and looking at Nigel's laptop records, there is no email to any of them either, even going back through his archived emails for the two sessions up in Edinburgh. Samantha said that when Nigel was murdered, the murderer took two objects from Nigel's pockets, one was his iPhone. I reckon the other must have been a second phone, and I bet that all these guys have second phones too, exclusively for communicating with each other."

"We didn't find a second phone in Angela Huddlestone's room," said Jerry. "Have they cracked the password yet on her iPhone?"

"No," said Tommy.

"Let's get her phone records for the past year to see if the same people are missing from her iPhone call list, and also let's have another look at her emails to see the same thing, does she email these guys or are we talking about pay as you go messaging?"

It is one thing to look through every email message that someone has sent for three years and quite another to look for something specific. Now that they had some idea of what they were looking for the trawl of Angela's and Nigel's emails might be more useful.

****

Rowan and her housemates had got into the habit of using the food shop at the railway station for picking up some items for supper, especially on occasions when all four had been on placement. On the Thursday evening that Henry went to Cambridge, Rowan happened to be in the station food shop at about 8 pm, picking up some milk and two large M&S lasagnes. She happened to look through the window into the station foyer, and she happened to see Henry, going through the ticket barrier to catch the 8:15 train back to London. Whether it was because she was tired and some of her mental barriers were down, or maybe her subconscious had been working on it anyway, the sight of Henry triggered a further flashback to the day of the overdose. She remembered that Henry was involved in whatever it was she was trying to recall. Going with Angela up the staircase was now very clear in her mind; she knew that she had then seen Henry, and she knew that was important, but she could not remember the context.

"Excuse me, Miss," said the man behind her in the queue. "Are you going to buy those items, or may I come past?"

"So sorry," said Rowan. "Daydreaming. Tough day," and she gave him a smile. She paid for her goods and off she went home.

That evening over the microwaved lasagne, and the fresh green salad with the Paul Newman's balsamic dressing, Rowan told the others that she thought she had seen Henry, she couldn't be sure, but it had triggered a response in her memory.

"Do you think he was something to do with your overdose?" Paige asked.

"I really don't know. I think he might know something about what happened. I'm very tempted to go and talk to him. It hadn't occurred to me before that Henry, after all he was at St Alfred's, might have been involved, but now I think he might know something. I am going to think about this. I might arrange to meet him. I am sure Amanda or Robert will know how to get in touch with him. I might just give them a call."

After supper that night, Rowan sent an email to both Robert and Amanda asking if they had a contact number for Henry Castleton. She explained that she thought she had seen him in Cambridge at the station that evening, and that it had prompted her to try to get in touch with him, to see if he could shed any light on what had happened that day back in June. She also asked them if they would mind having another conversation with her; she was beginning to get some recollection of events, and she thought that talking about it with others might trigger further recollections and allow her to achieve closure on the incident. Having tried to put the incident out of her mind for a few months, she was finding herself more and more anxious to find out what really happened. As she had told the others, she did not believe that she had attempted suicide. An accidental overdose perhaps, although it was hard to see how that might have happened.

She had become particularly concerned to know how she had managed to access so many paracetamol tablets. She rarely had headaches and almost never took painkillers. In the past, if she needed a paracetamol, like the time she got freshers flu, she had used cold and flu capsules, containing paracetamol, but never just paracetamol by itself. She had gone back through her credit card transactions looking for purchases at a chemist, but she could find nothing for the month before the overdose. She always bought her tampons and toiletries at the supermarket in town, it has a chemist shop in store. There was the obvious purchase of a few months' supply of these toiletries in late April, at the start of term, and then nothing else that could have included paracetamol. Where did the paracetamol then come from? It was a long email, and she was not really expecting much of a reply, just contact details for Henry.

Rowan went to bed at about 11:30 that evening, but she lay awake turning things over and over in her mind. The thoughts were going round and round in her head. It just wouldn't compute. Seeing Henry had disturbed her greatly. She decided to call her brother Tom, now in his final year, and just run a few thoughts past him.

Tom answered the phone, even though it was well past midnight when he got the call. "Hi, Rowan, it's a bit late you know," said Tom.

"I know," said Rowan. "I just have to run something by you and ask you a couple of questions. It is about the overdose. I still do not believe I willingly took an overdose, and it occurs to me, I never bought paracetamol in my life, only ever as cold and flu, but never pure paracetamol tablets. So, where did they come from? Tom, do you remember or were you ever told anything about the packets that the paracetamol came in? How many empty packets were there? Did they have any labels indicating which shop they had been bought in? I've started to get some recollection of the day of the overdose and there is nothing about feeling down or being depressed or anything like that. Up until early afternoon, which is as far as my recall has gone, I was studying and happy and the sun was shining. I have been through my credit card records and I can't see that I made any purchases in chemists in the Easter term, other than my usual toiletries and tampons. I also saw that I bought some stuff from that Chinese supermarket in the morning, and I do remember that. I was going to make wonton soup and I bought those nice frozen wontons. So where did the paracetamol come from?"

"I don't know," said Tom. "These are good questions. I don't know why we didn't think about all this before. I think the porter who came and found you was George. Maybe George will remember? And wasn't Meera the one who went and got George. Perhaps, Meera remembers what the packets were."

"I guess we were all too shocked and just grateful that I pulled through," said Rowan. "I just wanted to put it behind me. But now, I don't. I want to know what really happened. How did I come to take an overdose? It is so not me. I'll ask Meera in the morning at breakfast. Good idea about George. I am going into college on Saturday to see Adrian about the project. I'll see if George is on duty and if not, I'll find out when he is."

"If I can help at all, let me know," said Tom. "I need to get some sleep now but let's meet on Saturday after you have seen Adrian. I fancy a coffee and a chat with my little sister. I'll buy you a couple of those amoretti."

"You're on," said Rowan. "Sorry, I rang so late, but I saw that bloke Henry Castleton at the station this evening and it has stirred something up. I don't quite know what, but it set my mind racing. I'll try and get some sleep now. See you on Saturday, say 11:30?"

They agreed to meet and Rowan, finally, settled down to sleep.

Rowan's email to Amanda and Robert led to some interesting outcomes. Amanda sent a telephone number and email address for Henry to Rowan. Robert said he did not have the telephone number but that the email address he was using was the "@cantab.org" address given to all Cambridge graduates.

****

Robert and Amanda arranged to meet at the Law Faculty in Oxford.

"A bit of a turn up for the books," said Robert.

"Unfortunately, yes," said Amanda. "I thought Rowan Pike had moved on, but it appears that an accidental sighting of Henry has triggered a bit of memory recall. I wonder how long before that recall leads to trouble for all of us? I wonder if the boss needs to contact Charles to get him to take some action?"

"I wonder too. Might be a bit previous at this stage? What do you think Charles would do? Kill Rowan or kill Henry? I am really not sure how that would help," said Robert.

"Getting rid of Rowan would permanently deal with the problem," said Amanda. "Getting rid of Henry would just back it up one more stage, there would still be Rowan sitting there like a ticking time bomb. If Charles does anything, it has to be that he takes out Rowan. I am not sure Charles would be up for that. The boss says Charles is simply waiting to collect a bit more cash and then disappear to China. He must be quite close to having enough for that already. This last consignment that Henry brought back from Cambridge should bring in about £3,000,000 and Charles's cut will take him well into the range where he can afford to disappear. Let's suggest that we shift the goods and slightly up Charles's share on condition he bumps off Rowan before he goes. I'll contact the boss and put that suggestion forward. We could give him a bonus payment if he takes out Henry too. But I think we are going to have to call time on this little business anyway. We can't keep on dealing when we are the only two left from the group of friends in Cambridge. I am sure the boss will understand. Neither you nor I have any reason to visit Cambridge regularly, and with Charles gone, the link to the Edinburgh suppliers also goes. The boss has all the numbers, but contacts do fade away after a time."

"Well. I think the boss will have to spend some time planning exactly what to do. I reckon it will take a month to shift and launder the cash on this latest deal. Will you call the boss then?" Robert asked.

"Leave it to me," said Amanda. "I think a warning telephone call to Henry is probably in order too. Why did the stupid bastard get himself seen? I suppose it was just bad luck that Rowan was at the station at that precise time. If she mentions it to anyone, and it gets back to the police, Henry is going to have a lot of explaining to do. They will have CCTV at the station and around the town.

They are bound to get that he arrived early evening, went down to the bus station, picked up the package, and came back pretty much immediately. The more I think about it, the more I think Henry is done. The more I think about it, the more I think Henry needs to be gone. At this moment, they know we were all friends, but they have Nigel and Angela and Charles on the drug scene and the rest of us just sometime friends with these three junkies. I don't trust Henry. Henry was always weak, and I think he is going to crack under questioning. I think I might arrange a meeting between Henry and the boss to get a final idea of how he is holding up, and if the boss is not happy, then Charles will have another job to do."

Chapter 22

Rowan did not catch Meera that morning because she slightly overslept and Meera had already left for Stevenage.

Henry had a telephone call from Rowan just as he left the office to go out to lunch. He was meeting Judith that evening to go to the theatre, so he had to find time to make his drop-offs of the drug haul, as discretely and quickly as he could. He thought that getting some of the nearer drops organised during the lunch hour was a sensible approach. He could use the darkness after work to make some of the drops in the slightly more populated areas. He estimated it would take about two hours to make the rounds, so an hour at lunch time would buy him a good bit more time that evening. He answered the call, although it came up as an unknown number because he and Rowan had never exchanged mobile numbers. There just had not been that sort of contact between them.

"Hello," said Henry.

"Rowan Pike here," said Rowan. "I got your number from Amanda. I hope you don't mind. I think I saw you in Cambridge last night and it reminded me that I wanted to have a chat to you about that day when I got taken to hospital."

Henry was nervous. This did not sound promising. The events of that day were etched in his memory, but he was rather counting on the fact that, so far, they seemed not to have been etched, even faintly, on Rowan's memory. Did this call now mean that she was beginning to remember? If it did, then a lot of people, except the two who were already dead, were going to be in a lot of trouble soon. He went theatrical and started to play his part.

"Oh, delighted to hear from you. Yes, popped up to Cambridge on business. My firm often gets briefs for the Crown Court there. How are you these days?"

"I'm fine, thanks. I still can't remember much about the stuff that happened but when I saw you, it triggered something and I seemed to remember, through a bit of a fog, that I saw you that afternoon, the one before the overdose I mean. So, I wanted to ask you if you could tell me anything about my behaviour that afternoon that might help me to sort this through in my head. Do you know what happened early in the afternoon? It's important to me. Can you tell me anything that might help me remember something? You see, I don't believe I took that overdose deliberately, but how it happened, well that is still a huge mystery."

Henry moved the phone away from his ear so that Rowan did not hear the sudden sharp intake of breath. This was all getting a bit too near the mark for comfort. A phone call to the boss was certainly needed after this. When he had recovered his poise, he put the phone back to his ear and said, "Sorry. Just thinking."

And in the belief that truthful lies are easier to manage, he said, "I did meet you that afternoon and you, Amanda Sayers, Angela, and I had a cup of coffee together. You had been working in the library. I think we just chatted for a bit and then you went back to your room and the rest of us got on with the day. I think you were the only one who still had exams. Our law exams and Angela's English exams had finished ages earlier. Do you remember that at all?"

"I do. But weren't we playing a game or something? I seem to remember small silver and gold counters and some money."

A little more memory was coming back. In her mind, she could see real money. And these funny little pieces of silver and gold coloured metal. But as soon as things started to come into focus, they blurred again.

"No. No," laughed Henry. "The only silver and gold things were the wrappings on the chocolate biscuits. Mind you, you knocked back the biscuits, and the coffee."

Then a diversionary tactic. "Let me see. You have black with the tiniest splash of milk. Have I remembered correctly?"

Rowan laughed too.

"That's right. Black with a splash of milk."

The diversionary tactic had backfired. Rowan remembered something else about that afternoon.

"But there was no milk that day, was there? We had all run out. And one of you put some powdered milk in my coffee for me. Who was it that did that?"

"I don't remember which of us made the coffee. I certainly handed out the biscuits," said Henry, now sweating profusely.

Then a bit more thinking happened.

"Was there someone else there? Were Robert, and that bloke Nigel from your college; were they there too? And was there a tall guy that used to come up sometimes? What was his name? Chris or something? No, Charles?"

"They were around, but it was just the four of us having coffee. I hadn't got enough chocolate biscuits for more than that."

"OK. Things are starting to come back to me. Do you mind if I call you again if I have any more questions? This is most helpful. I really feel as if I might just get to the bottom of it all."

"No problem," said Henry, thinking to himself anything *but* no problem. "Call me anytime."

"Thanks," said Rowan. "Have a nice day. Bye."

The minds of both Rowan and Henry were in turmoil, but for different reasons. Rowan was frustrated that she had got so far and no further. Henry was scared that Rowan was getting too close to the truth. He immediately reached for the second phone and called the boss. As always, the boss's voice was disguised. Henry often wondered why that was. He felt it had to be because he knew the boss and the boss didn't want to be recognised, but he couldn't think who it might be. At one time, he had been convinced it was Nigel, so he tried ringing Nigel and then the boss, while he was still on the line to Nigel, but the second call went through, so that meant Nigel was not the boss. He did the same for Charles. Charles was not the boss. He had given up trying to find out who the boss was. In his plan to get out of the drug scene, he needed to identify the boss so that they could meet, and Henry could make a recording. That was why he had bought the spy cam and microphone. It was not going to happen. Plan B, meet Amanda, and Robert, and get recordings. Better fix that up. Better than nothing. Perhaps, one of them knew who the boss was? He could ask during his meetings with them.

Henry told the boss what had just happened with Rowan, and the boss brought him up to speed with what was intended.

"Amanda and Robert had a meeting and they decided it was time to quit the drugs racket. Are you happy with that?"

Henry could have bitten the boss's hand off.

"That suits me well," said Henry. "I have more than enough money put by, and the risks are increasing all the time. Those policemen are convinced I am involved in the drugs and that Robert and Amanda are too. I just know it."

"OK, well you realise we may need to finish what we tried to do in Cambridge that day?"

"I do. How we manage to complete that without detection this time, I just don't know?"

"Charles will do it on his way out of the country," said the boss. "They will know it was Charles, but he will be long gone before they realise."

Henry went back to work. He was less than efficient that afternoon. And he still had most of the drug drops to do before he could go home to get ready for the theatre.

When he left the office that evening, he called both Robert and Amanda and told them about his conversation with Rowan. He asked whether they wanted to meet, and they suggested that he come down on Saturday morning to Oxford, and all three of them meet at Robert's college, to talk about what might be done.

Henry met Judith that evening, as arranged, and they went to the theatre to see 'Tina,' the musical about Tina Turner. Henry took Judith home to Hampstead and then went back to his own flat for the night.

****

In Felixstowe, Adam Liu, a.k.a. Charles Ma, was enjoying a rather untroubled existence. He was working at the greengrocer's serving customers and being the 'charming self' he was always capable of being. The money was irrelevant, he had so much already that this was just occupational therapy. He quite liked to fill his day with activity. He also kept very fit. Running on the shingle beach was hard work, and he enjoyed open air swimming, even in the cold water of the North Sea. He kept in touch with the supply chain from Edinburgh. He had arranged the shipment that Henry had collected on the Thursday evening.

He was running along the promenade, just going past the Pavilion, when the telephone rang. It was the boss. Charles was updated on the situation, especially as it related to Rowan and Henry.

"I can take Henry out on the way to Heathrow when I leave," he said. "What do we want to do about Rowan?"

The boss didn't hesitate.

"I don't think we can risk letting this run too much longer. She is clearly getting some of her memory back. It might not be long before she gets it all back. How could you take her out?"

"I'll need to find out exactly where she lives. I think, from what she said when I was last in Cambridge, just before the overdose, she was planning to live with the three other girls. I need to see how secure that house is. Do you think I should go and check it out or can it wait until I leave?"

"Up to you," said the boss.

"I am just going to have to get my timing right, as usual," said Charles. "The other thing I could do is to wait until the Christmas vacation and take her out on her way home to, where was it her parents live?"

"Cornwall, Truro," said the boss.

"Ought to be easy to pick her off down there," said Charles. "Especially as she goes for those cross country runs every day."

"We have a plan then?" The boss asked.

"I have a plan," said Charles. "How is the money collection for this round going?"

"Only just distributed the drugs," said the boss. "I'll let you know when money is ready. Which account do you want it put into?"

Charles gave the details.

"If you solve our two problems there will be a bonus," said the boss.

"Thank you. I need to finish my fitness training now."

And Charles hung up.

****

Jerry and Tommy were not at all surprised to find that the phone and email accounts of both Angela and Nigel had no contact details for any of the group. It was almost certain that all these students, and Charles, were communicating by using a separate set of mobiles that were pay as you go and with no record of calls attributable to any of them.

Jerry said, "I think our only chance of finding anything now is to go with surveillance. I think we need to put someone on Henry, and I wouldn't mind asking the Oxford police to keep a bit of an eye on Robert and Amanda. I would particularly like to know if they ever come up to town, and what they do if they do come here."

The tail they put on Henry started that evening. He picked Henry up at his flat and followed him to the theatre where Henry met Judith. The tail had no chance of getting a ticket at this late hour, so he simply sat in a café across the road and waited for nearly three hours while the cast of Tina sang their way through the musical. When Henry came out, the detective followed him as he took Judith home, and then again as he returned to his flat. It was a boring evening. The night shift took over at midnight. This tail was going to be round the clock. If, as they suspected, Henry was involved in the drug scene, something would turn up. What a pity they had not put the tail on earlier in the week. Hindsight is a wonderful thing.

On the Saturday morning at about 6 am, Henry woke, had a very quick coffee, got his recording equipment ready, and left the flat. The detective watching his flat missed Henry's departure. He had just gone for a quick pee and thought that 6:30 am would be an OK time to do that. It was very bad technique, but it gave Henry a break he did not deserve.

Henry was able to get the tube and head for Paddington and the Oxford train. He had his sunglasses and recording system with him. This was going to be the first part of his video protection.

He had a leisurely breakfast at Paddington Station. He was beginning to run to seed a bit and a full English breakfast was not going to help him combat that.

At Oxford, he went to Robert's College, where all three had agreed to meet, and Robert took them both to the privacy of his own room.

"Coffee folks?" Robert asked. "Quite like old times this, isn't it?"

Robert made them all an instant coffee and they sat in the three chairs in the room, Robert at the desk and the other two in easy chairs beside the fireplace.

"I wanted to talk to you," said Henry, "because I had that disturbing phone call from Rowan. I told you the gist of it but what I couldn't really tell you was that she is very close to remembering why she ended up having an overdose. Robert and Amanda, you and I know, we were all dealing in heroin and cocaine, benzodiazepines, and other stuff, as well as the marijuana and ecstasy, don't we?"

Henry looked at Robert, to make sure he was on camera.

"Yes," said Robert, "it was us three and Charles, and Nigel a bit. Angela hadn't got a clue really, had she?"

Henry looked at Amanda, once more on camera.

"No," said Amanda. "Poor naïve, Angela. Thought a little pot and ecstasy was bringing in all that money when all the time it was the heroin and other stuff that we were taking down to London on the train. By the way, did you use the same distribution network when you dropped off the drugs yesterday?"

"Sure did," said Henry.

"How much have you got stashed away now guys?" Henry asked. "I've got about eight hundred thousand."

"Well, you did join in a bit late on the hard stuff," said Amanda. "I reckon I have over a million. How about you Robert?"

"About the same as you," said Robert. "I really don't need to carry on risking discovery. I think it is probably time to pack up for all of us. We can have legit careers now with a bit of a financial leg-up. I bought a flat in Bloomsbury, in Stefan's name too. He doesn't know where the money came from. He thinks I have a rich aunt, now deceased."

All the while, Henry was turning his head to make sure everything was caught on camera. It was all going far better than he could have hoped.

The conversation then took a serious turn.

"Does anyone know who the boss is?" Henry asked.

Nobody did.

"I told the boss about Rowan," said Henry. "The boss said it would be taken care of."

"Amanda, I think that means that your friendly thug, Charles, will be sent down to deal with her. That's my guess," said Robert.

"He is not a thug," said Amanda.

"Just because you were in love with him, and sleeping with him, doesn't mean he isn't a thug," said Robert.

"Well, I miss him," said Amanda. "So, no more nastiness about Charles, please."

Robert couldn't resist it.

"Wonder why he is called horse?" he said.

Amanda hit him, playfully but quite hard.

"Shut up," she said.

The rest of the conversation was small talk, until at the end, Amanda said, "We are none of us going to be safe until Rowan is dead. You know that don't you?"

"It doesn't seem fair," said Henry. "If she hadn't had that bloody viva the next day, we would all be home and dry."

"If the boss hadn't ordered the hit on Angela, we might be," said Robert. "In hindsight, that was a mistake."

"But Nigel caused that by planning to chuck her and by letting her see the heroin he had brought back from Cambridge," said Amanda.

"I suppose so," said Henry.

"Ah, well," said Robert. "Let's hope Charles gets Rowan before Rowan gets her memory back. Now, this college does an amazing brunch on a Saturday, instead of breakfast or lunch. Anyone want to join me in Hall for brunch?"

Henry switched off his recording, praying that it had worked, and went for his second enormous full English of the day, this time with black pudding, a small piece of steak, a chop, and lots of fried eggs and hash browns.

In the Hall, Henry told the other two just one more highly relevant thing. He explained that he had, while collecting the drugs from Sammy Needle, taken the opportunity to go and try to recover the drug equipment from St Joseph's, but it had gone. That produced a bit of consternation among the other two lawyers, but they agreed that the most likely explanation was that it had been thrown on a skip during the clearing process of the Cumberland Building refurbishment.

****

On the Saturday morning, Rowan and her housemates got up a little later than usual and Meera, who loved America, cooked them all a stack of American pancakes, with bacon, and maple syrup, and lashings of butter. Rowan asked Meera about the paracetamol packets. She couldn't quite remember but she thought they were an own brand packet, very plain. That meant that Rowan was probably correct in thinking that she could not have bought them. She explained to the others that she had checked her records and could find no record of purchasing them. She had another question for Meera. Rowan asked whether Meera had seen anyone else on the staircase when she made the visit on which she found Rowan unconscious. Meera tried very hard to think about this, but she couldn't recall seeing anyone at all on her way to Rowan's room, let alone anyone who shouldn't have been there.

"Thanks anyway," said Rowan. "I may be clutching at straws, but I really think there is something else I am missing about this. I know people will be thinking I want to deny what happened, but it isn't that. You all know me. Why would I buy wontons and stuff at lunch time and attempt suicide at just after teatime?"

There were nods all round and a general agreement that it did not make sense.

"Oh, blast," said Rowan. "I am going to be late if I don't get a move on. See you later, folks."

She rushed to put on her hi-vis jacket, grabbed her helmet and bike keys and off she went. She arrived a good twenty minutes before her appointment with Adrian and locked her bike up in the rack outside the college.

She was in luck. George was on duty.

"Hi, George," said Rowan. "I have to go and see the Senior Tutor this morning, but are you around afterwards for a chat? I want to ask you a couple of questions about the day I was taken to hospital."

"For you, Rowan P, anything. Yes, I'm on until 5 today so come and have a cup of coffee afterwards. I tell you what. Let me know what your poison is, and I'll get Ben to nip out and get a couple of take away coffees from Savino's."

"Americano with a little cold milk please, George. And I'll pay."

Rowan was about to go off to see the Senior Tutor when George said, "Did that friend of yours, what's his name, Henry or something, did he find you on Thursday evening?"

"What?" Rowan said. "Henry was here looking for me?"

"Well, that's what he said," said George.

"No, didn't find me, George, and he isn't really a friend. Did he do anything else while he was here?"

"Yes," said George. "He went and had a look at the Cumberland Building. They're doing it up you know. Came back covered in dust. I reckon, he sneaked inside the staircase for a look, but he just said he had brushed against some rubble. Look, you run along and see his nibs and when you're done, we'll have that coffee. How long do you reckon you'll be?"

"About an hour, George. See you then. By the way, my brother Tom will be here at 11:30. Can you look after him for me?"

And Rowan went off to the Senior Tutor's Office.

They talked for about an hour. The first thing was to go through the paper that was being sent off to the Journal of Developmental Paediatrics. This was almost exactly word for word as Rowan had written it up for her project. There were a couple of decisions about what sort of statistics to use for some of the data, would it be reasonable to use parametric or non-parametric data analysis. They concluded that they could not be confident the data were normally distributed, so settled for non-parametric tests. The results were highly significant either way, but Adrian was a bit of a purist when it came to analysis, and Rowan was learning to follow suit.

The next bit of their conversation was about the analysis that Rowan was going to do over the Student Selected Component period coming up in a couple of weeks. Adrian knew that Rowan was very good technically and he wanted her to do as much practical work in that period as she could. He pointed out that it would mean her having to do the analysis later, in her own time, and he was reluctant to overburden her, but she was quite happy to do that. It was clear that she wanted an academic route during her training and was going to be an academic clinician with a strong research programme.

As they wound up the conversation, Adrian said, "I really don't want to overload you. I should hate to see another episode like that last summer."

Rowan's reply was quite sharp.

"There is no danger of that. I am absolutely convinced that I did not take an overdose of paracetamol knowingly. I have been through my credit card records and I never bought any paracetamol in the Easter term, and I never bought any paracetamol in my life before that. The only paracetamol I ever took was in cold and flu capsules. It must have been an accident, and I am not going to have another accident I can assure you. I would like to know where the paracetamol packets they found next to me came from, but Meera can't remember. She says they were a sort of blue colour, and had a chemist's name on, but she cannot remember what it was. I am going to ask George in a minute if he can remember. He's kindly getting me a coffee by the way."

Adrian thought for a minute and then said, "I saw the packets. We scooped them up and put them in a bag to go with you to the hospital. They were capsules, by the way, not tablets. I expect they were gelatine capsules containing paracetamol in powder form. What I remember is that the packets were blue and white, and I think they had a flower, or something printed on them. Anyway, you go and ask George if he remembers. I am really looking forward to seeing you in the lab again. So, apparently is James."

Rowan smiled. James was the PhD student who had acted as her lab mentor during her project. They were quite good friends but not in a romantic sense, for now, and maybe, for always.

George had the cup of coffee waiting and Tom Pike, Rowan's brother, was sitting there waiting too. Rowan went behind the counter of the Porter's Lodge and sat with Tom and George by the nice open fire that was always kept burning there in the winter. George produced some homemade oatmeal cookies.

"An Aussie recipe I got off the internet," he said. George was famous among the students for two things, his delightful little dog, Patch, a border collie with a white patch over one eye, and his amazing cookies and cakes, which he generously dealt out to anyone who needed a shoulder to cry on late at night, or a bit of home comfort during the day, or just because he was generous and liked the student.

"George," said Rowan. "You know the night you came and helped save my life. Can you remember what the paracetamol packets I was lying next to looked like? You see I just don't have any record of ever having bought any paracetamol, and I wonder where they came from."

"Well, it's funny you should ask that," said George. "One of the bedders was cleaning out the rooms on your old staircase just before the maintenance team moved in, to strip and do the place up, and she found one of the packets that we hadn't picked up when we sent you off to hospital with them. I put it on one side in case I saw you again. I think it sounds daft, but I thought you might like a souvenir."

"George," teased Rowan. "What on earth made you think I would want a souvenir of nearly dying?"

George got all flustered and started muttering and spluttering, so Rowan went over and gave him a hug.

"Just teasing you, George. Have you still got it?"

And George went out to the back room of the lodge and came back with a plastic bag containing a packet of paracetamol capsules and a couple of loose tablets.

"This is what she brought in," said George.

The packet was blue and white. The flower on it was a thistle and the name on the packet was Lindsay and Gilmour, Edinburgh.

"I could hug you, George," said Rowan. "This proves I could not have purchased those paracetamol tablets."

Rowan took the plastic bag, and without opening it or touching the contents, she looked at the white tablets, they had FM1 printed on one side and Roche 2 printed on the other. Rowan had seen a tablet like that before. As part of their pharmacology lectures in the second year of pre-clinical study, they had talked about the benzodiazepine drugs, including this one. It was Rohypnol. She felt a shiver run down her spine.

I wonder, she thought to herself, *could someone have slipped me some Rohypnol?*

"George," said Rowan. "Would you mind ringing the Senior Tutor to see if he is still there? I think I need to go and see him."

Tom looked on. He was astounded by what had just happened. At last, things could be beginning to make a bit of sense.

So, about half an hour after the morning meeting, Rowan was back in there talking to Adrian. Tom came in too.

Rowan gave the packet containing the two sorts of drug to Adrian and explained that one of them was Rohypnol. Adrian rang the police and asked to speak to Inspector Josh Jacobs. They were fortunate. Josh was working this weekend and came over straight away to collect the drugs and to talk to Rowan.

"Yep," said Josh. "That's Rohypnol alright."

Rowan explained her position, that she had been found with an overdose but had never bought any paracetamol in her life. She had certainly never been to Scotland let alone bought paracetamol there. She said she had never had any suicidal inclination, and this was all puzzling to her. She asked Inspector Jacobs, "Could I have been given Rohypnol and then been made to drink paracetamol without realising it?"

"Certainly," said Josh. "I wish this stuff had turned up at the time. We could have looked for Rohypnol in your blood at the same time as doing the paracetamol analysis. If they had stored a sample of your blood at minus twenty, we could probably still find traces of it or traces of its metabolites, but I don't suppose they did. I would like, if you will allow me, to take the packet and have it looked at for fingerprints. I expect there will be ones from the bed maker and maybe that will be it, but you never know."

"Take it by all means," said Rowan. "I strongly suspect I was doped but there are one or two things that bother me. I know I never went near a bar, so how did someone slip me a Rohypnol. I wasn't raped or sexually assaulted as far as we can tell, so why was I doped? The third thing is that I think whoever did it must have meant to kill me; I survived so are they going to try again?"

Inspector Jacobs said, "People don't realise that you can put Rohypnol in tea or coffee, and it is just as effective as slipping it into an alcoholic drink. It is just because the commonest way people think about it is as a date rape drug, and people looking on see someone drinking and attribute the drowsiness and lack of co-ordination to alcohol. That lets the rapist get away with it. But it could have been slipped to you in anything you drank that day. It is colourless and odourless. You ask will they try again? I fear they may do. It depends on why they did it in the first place. The other thing I wonder is, why haven't they tried to kill you again yet?"

"I think the answer to why it happened is in the part of the day I cannot remember," said Rowan. "I keep getting a bit more recall every now and again. I am sure that Henry Castleton is involved somehow, and he says Amanda and Angela were involved. I just can't break through to what happened."

She put her face in her hands and muttered a frustrated growl.

"I suppose that the reason why they have not tried again is simply that they are relying on my not recovering my memory. Unfortunately, people now know that I am getting it back, slowly. I may be a bit vulnerable again. I told Henry, for example, because I saw him in Cambridge the other day, and it triggered something, but he said it was just having a tea party with chocolate biscuits. But if he is involved, then I bet everyone else involved knows I am recovering."

"This Edinburgh thing," said Rowan. "Angela, her friend Nigel, and his friend Henry, went to Edinburgh to the Fringe festival a couple of times, and I think Robert and Amanda went and visited them. Then, there was this other friend of Henry and Nigel, someone called Charles. I think he lived in Edinburgh. I guess any one of them could have brought that paracetamol down here. Oh, and another thing, Sergeant, George, the porter, tells me Henry was in college on Thursday, and that is when I caught sight of him at the station that evening. He said he came here on business to do with the Crown Court, but he was here very late in the evening, and I cannot think the legal offices were open at that hour. I thought you might like to know."

"That's very interesting," said Inspector Jacobs. "I know a couple of policemen in London who will be very interested in what you have just told me."

Then, Joshua Jacobs emphasised something that Rowan had not realised.

"Remember, Rowan, if you think back and you remember having any drinks at all on that day, the Rohypnol could have been in anything you drank. It is colourless, odourless, and tasteless and it is stable in hot coffee or tea. So, any drink Rowan, any drink at all."

"By the way," he went on. "Street versions of Rohypnol and other benzodiazepines are pretty common in Edinburgh, so it is highly possible that the same person slipped you the old date rape drug, and the paracetamol."

He paused for a minute and then he said, "Be very careful. Try not to go anywhere alone after dark. Always make sure that people know where you are and vary your routines. I would not be surprised if you are still in danger. Those two little white pills make me think that your overdose was not an accident. So, bloody frustrating."

"The other thing you need to know because it will make you more careful, is that Angela was slipped a Rohypnol in her coffee before she was given an overdose. Her overdose was heroin, and it was lethal. The same people could be involved perhaps?"

It was all very frightening, but Rowan, Tom, and Adrian, were now firmly of the opinion that Rowan was 'done unto' rather than doing.

They all chatted a little longer, Adrian made them all another cup of coffee in his espresso machine, and then Josh Jacobs went back, with his forensic specimen, to the police station. He also sent a long email to Jerry and Tommy at the Islington Police Station, and he asked the Railway Police to look at the station CCTV. Acting on a hunch, he got the team to look at the CCTV around Emmanuel Street and the bus station. Dealing was still going on around the public lavatories there and they had set up a permanent camera, in place of the temporary surveillance camera they had used earlier in the year. It did not take long for the report to come through that Henry Castleton had somehow managed to bump into Sammy Needle in Drummer Street and a bag swap had taken place. Josh sent the good news to London.

Rowan and Tom went and had a brief lunch in Hall. It was so nice to chat about anything and everything. Tom Pike was so relieved that something was beginning to emerge which might help to explain something that had always before seemed completely inexplicable. He was, however, very aware that his sister might still be in danger.

"Put my number on quick dial," said Tom. "I will run as soon as you call me if you need me. And be very careful."

Rowan went home and brought the other girls up to date. It was still early afternoon so there was a bit of daylight left. Paige and Rowan often ran together, and this time, they went out and ran down through the town, round the Backs, and across Lammas land to Brookland Avenue and then home. Running with Paige allowed Rowan to relax but she knew that, following Inspector Jacobs warnings, she was going to be very nervous about running by herself for a while. She realised that the Grantchester, Coton footpath, and Baits Bite loch runs, out into the countryside, were out until further notice, unless Paige was going with her.

Chapter 23

"So," said Jerry. "I wonder if the drug team has a new courier. Did they send Henry Castleton to collect the drugs now that Nigel is dead? Let's see if the Super reckons the CCTV footage is enough evidence to get a warrant to search young Castleton's flat. Of course, we may be too late. It's Saturday now and he got the drugs on Thursday, but we might find traces. Let's get the sniffer dogs and see what we can find."

The tail they had out on Henry was still watching and following and he reported that he had seen no sign of Henry dealing out drugs or receiving money. He omitted to mention that he had not seen Henry at all during the whole of the morning, because he had missed him leaving. Henry had come home at about 2:30 pm, from somewhere. That was also not reported. All the tail reported was that Henry had gone out to a late lunch and met his girlfriend on the embankment. He had escorted her home and he was still at her place in Hampstead. The search warrant was quickly granted but Jerry decided that they should wait until Henry returned home before executing it. He would give Henry the chance to allow a voluntary search first and then present the warrant if permission was refused. The policemen sat there all day and all night, and it was not until the Sunday morning that Henry returned home and the search took place. Henry agreed to a voluntary search telling the detectives that he had nothing to hide.

The sniffer dogs were interested in a couple of places in the flat but there was no obvious stash of drugs or, for that matter, no large sums of money sitting there. One of the dogs stood under the doorway barking but there was nothing obvious. Brutalist buildings like the Barbican flats have relatively few hiding places. Jerry was tempted to start removing the ceiling and wall panelling, but he decided against it.

He looked at the panelling around the door, but it all seemed perfectly smoothly joined, no obvious seams or cracks in the plastering. In concrete terms, the search proved fruitless. It did, however, rock the boat.

"Mr Castleton," said Jerry, "you told us that you went to Cambridge to deliver a brief to another firm. If we contact your office, will they tell us the same thing? We have reason to believe that, while you were in Cambridge, you met a known drug dealer at the bus station. Is that correct? And why did you go to St Joseph's? It was not your college I believe."

Henry looked shaken. It was quite a while before he replied.

"I did tell a bit of a fib about why I went. The real reason was that I have this new girlfriend, Judith, and I wanted to go to get her something from Cambridge to give her as a Christmas present. I guess I was a bit too embarrassed to tell you guys that. I was going to get her a St Alfred's College scarf and a university charm bracelet, but I got there too late. I shall have to go another time or order it online."

"OK," said Tommy, "but you haven't answered the other questions. Why St Joseph's, and what about Mr Needle?"

"You know, I suddenly realised that I have been missing one of my favourite Radiohead t-shirts, and I seemed to remember having hung it up in one of the gyp room cupboards on the Cumberland Building staircase, so I went back to have a look and George, the porter told me they were refurbishing the building, so that was a waste of time too."

"And Mr Needle?" Tommy said.

"I have no idea who Mr Needle is," said Henry. "I certainly didn't meet any drug dealers. I told you several times, I don't do drugs. Angela and Nigel did. Nobody else on the staircase or among our friends did drugs."

"I'm sorry," said Jerry. "We know you are lying. We have you on CCTV swapping briefcases with Mr Needle. You both put your identical briefcases down, you had a cup of coffee and a chat, and then you picked up each other's cases and left."

"Oh, my God," said Henry. "I did chat to some bloke at the bus station, he seemed a nice bloke, bit of a Cambridge accent, you know the one with a mix of cockney and fenland, but he seemed OK. Has he complained I stole his briefcase, because I must have his briefcase here, and he must have mine? It's lucky I didn't buy the scarf and the bracelet because they would have been in there. I haven't opened my briefcase since I got home late on Thursday. I didn't take it to work on Friday, so it is still here. Would you like to see it? I wonder what he had in it."

And with that, Henry went into the bedroom and came out with the briefcase. He passed it over to the two policemen, told them the combination for the lock, and they tried to open it. The combination did not work.

"That cannot be my briefcase," said Henry. "Can you get my briefcase back for me from this bloke? It has a few papers in it, nothing too confidential, but it will be embarrassing if the firm finds out."

"Let's try three zeroes," said Tommy.

The case opened.

It contained two teddy bears and four packets of sweets.

It was all Henry could do to keep a smirk off his face. The looks on the policemen's faces were priceless. He thought to himself, *Thank you, boss, for the telephone call.*

"I expect Mr Needle will want his toys and sweets back," said Henry.

Sammy Needle had noticed the new CCTV camera on the junction of Emmanuel Street and Parker Street. He had called Charles, who was his go between, to warn him that the exchange might have been noted on CCTV. Charles had called the boss, and as they say in these circles, the rest was history. Henry had bought the two teddy bears on Friday morning, and the packets of sweets, at King's Cross, on his arrival back in London. He had put the items in his spare briefcase and set the combination to triple zero. He had taken the briefcase, with the drugs, in his rucksack to work, along with his laptop. The policemen were just not getting any breaks at all. They were doing nothing wrong, they were doing everything right, but lady luck was running hot with the gang.

"Thank you, Mr Castleton. We will see if we can get your briefcase back for you. In the meantime, we will gladly return this briefcase to Mr Needle."

It was all Jerry and Tommy could do to contain their anger. They knew this had been a set up. The first suspicion was that there had been a leak from either the Cambridge end or the Islington Station, but they quickly dismissed that idea. They came to the correct conclusion that street-smart Needle had spotted the new CCTV camera and that had triggered alarm bells. They wondered what the line of communication was, but then, if they knew that, they would probably have the whole gang in their sights.

The air was blue in the police car on the way back to Islington. There is nothing worse for a detective than knowing what is going on, who is doing it, and not having enough evidence; in this case, nothing other than circumstantial evidence, to prove what you know.

"We'll get them, Jerry," said Tommy. "They can't keep on getting so lucky. Let's test this briefcase for drugs anyway, might have been used previously you know, or he might even have used it this time and substituted those bloody teddy bears before we got to him."

****

Charles telephoned the boss.

"We really need to wind up this operation," he said. "I have a few million stashed away, how about you?"

"Yep," was the response. "Three years' worth of effort at just over a million a year. The others have a bit less than that, but I have about three million. I have enough for my mortgage free house and a cushion to let me follow any career path I choose. I find flying by the seat of my pants like this far too stressful. Time to get out. Shall we plan on your leaving at Christmas?"

"That's too late," said Charles, "Henry could crack any time and Rowan could get her memory back at any moment. I reckon it needs to be early in December if we are going to get away scot-free. And to protect you, both need to be dead before I leave. I think I will book my flight now. I shall miss the gang, but they can always visit in the vacations. When do you want me to take out Henry and that girl?"

"You've got to realise that when you do take him out, the heat will rise. I suggest you stick to the original plan and take him out the night before you get on the plane. Book an evening flight and take him out early evening. You'll be halfway round the world before they even find him if you do it right. As for Rowan Pike, we need to work out exactly what she saw. Henry, Nigel, and Angela are very much the front facing part of our enterprise, and you, of course. Robert and Amanda are much more in the background. Make sure that your route to Heathrow, via London, goes through Cambridge. I suggest you have a busy evening. If my calculations are correct, Rowan Pike will be working in the laboratories during the last few days of November and the first week of December, so given how it is already dark in the evenings, you should have plenty of opportunity. Take them both out then."

"OK, I'll plan it. I have already moved most of my money to Shanghai. I have contacts. I reckon I can disappear there easily. I have my Chinese passport. Good thing my parents brought me up speaking Mandarin."

The die was cast. As far as the boss and Charles were concerned, Henry's and Rowan's days were numbered.

Amanda and Robert had a conversation.

"The boss is closing down the operation," said Robert.

"Probably for the best," said Amanda. "You should have a few million put aside by now."

"I do," said Robert. "Despite what we said to Henry, we always sold him short, and I suppose the money that Nigel got from the operation is lost now. Stefan knows nothing about it, of course. He really does believe I had this rich aunt who died and left me money, so that I could buy that property outright. If I need to explain the rest of my money, do you have any more 'rich aunts' you can lend me?"

"It's a good time to pack up, I think," said Amanda. "We are going to complete our BCLs and then have distinguished careers in law. The financial kick start is all that either of us really needed."

"Henry is a bit of a worry, and Rowan; he is liable to crack, and she might just remember what she saw."

"I bet the boss has that under control," said Amanda.

****

Henry was doing some thinking. He still had no idea who the boss was. He tried calling each person's number in turn and then, while still on the call, the boss, but it produced no result. He had hoped that he would get the engaged tone when he called the boss after calling the first number. It did not happen.

Who was the boss? It certainly seemed as if it was not one of the regulars from the gang. He had suspected Charles, simply because of the previous history, but that didn't seem to compute now. So, how was he going to get his insurance policy, and what was going to happen if Rowan suddenly got her memory back. The boss said it was under control but Rowan spotting him in Cambridge had already caused a lot of trouble, and she had clearly decided that he, Henry, was connected in some way with the events of the day of the overdose. There was something bothering him about the conversation he had had with Amanda and Robert. He couldn't put his finger on it, but it worried him.

He had downloaded the film from the hidden cameras onto a couple of memory sticks and put one of them in an envelope. It clearly implicated both Amanda and Robert in hard drug dealing, and he got Charles Ma thrown in for good measure.

He sealed the envelope and got ready to send it to his solicitor with the 'in the event of my death' statement.

Henry had stayed the night with Judith for the first time over the weekend. He was now even more sure that he was in love with her. He sat down on the Monday morning at work and ordered the scarf and the charm bracelet. He used his iPhone as no personal emails were allowed on the work system. He rang Judith, and when she answered he said, "I love you."

"I love you too," she replied.

"Are you free for dinner, or the theatre, or the cinema, every night this week?" Henry asked.

"What shall we do tonight?" Judith asked.

"There's one of those Picture Houses," said Henry, "it's showing 'Closely Observed Trains.' We could grab some supper and go to the late showing."

"That would be wonderful," said Judith.

"7 o'clock at 'Le Bistro'?" said Henry.

"7 o'clock," said Judith.

That night, and every night that week, the detective tailing Henry was treated to seeing Judith and Henry enjoying a meal and going to a different play or film. At the end of the week, Jerry called off the tail. No drugs in the flat, no sign of any contact with known drug dealers. Henry must have got rid of the drugs very quickly after bringing them back. That meant it had to be distributed very close to his office or his flat. He hadn't been anywhere else in the interval between getting back from Cambridge and having the tail put on him on the Saturday.

Towards the end of the week, there was still no sign of Henry passing on drugs or collecting money.

Chapter 24

On the Thursday of that week, Sammy Needle had a job to do. He woke very early and cycled to Cambridge Station. He caught the 05:57 train to Peterborough. Unfortunately, for Sammy an off-duty, narcotics squad, policeman was just arriving from Littleport for the day shift and recognised him. The policeman called Josh Jacobs and Josh asked him to get straight on the train and follow Sammy to Peterborough. Josh rang ahead to Peterborough and arranged for someone to take over the job of following Sammy to wherever he was going. Between the Cambridge and Peterborough narcotics teams, they arranged coverage at Ely, Manea, March, and Whittlesea. Sergeant Bronowski in Peterborough promised to make sure that all stops on the next train that Sammy took would also be covered. He also arranged to double up on the tail, one to always stay on the train and one to get off if Sammy got off. They were determined not to lose him. This could be important. Sammy was carrying a green holdall, and a small briefcase which contained his iPad.

At Peterborough, Sammy left the train and went to the café on the platform between the mainline tracks. It was not clear at that point whether he would be heading south or north, so two policemen waited, one on the north bound main line route and the other on the south bound. There was no way they could tell where Sammy's intended destination was because he had collected his ticket at the station from one of the pre-paid machines and there had been no time to chase things up through the train line booking systems.

As it turned out, Sammy drank his coffee, put the cup diligently in the recycling, and caught the mainline train towards Scotland. Two detectives got on the same train. One in the same carriage and one in the next carriage behind. Jacobs rang ahead and arranged for someone to be on watch at each stop on the route as far as Edinburgh. As he said, "If he goes beyond Edinburgh, we can make a few more telephone calls."

Sammy did not go beyond Edinburgh. The train arrived a few minutes late at around 11:20. Sammy got off, looked around to check that he was not being followed, and went out through the ticket barrier. He headed for the taxi rank where, by a miracle, the first taxi in the rank was being driven by an undercover policeman.

"MacDonald Road Library in Leith, please," said Sammy.

"That'll be fine," said the driver.

They drove to the Library Building and Sammy asked the taxi driver to wait for him. The policeman couldn't believe his luck. Talk about making it easy to follow someone.

Sammy walked about fifty metres along the road to a tenement block, knocked on the door, and disappeared into the building. He was gone about fifteen minutes and when he came out, he no longer had the green holdall with him, but he was carrying a briefcase, identical in make and design, to the one that he had swapped with Henry that day in Cambridge.

"Can you take me back to Waverley, please?" Sammy asked.

Back they went, Sammy caught the 2 pm train back towards Peterborough. The driver radioed the station and reported on the address in the tenements. Within twenty minutes, the tenement was surrounded, and a very successful raid took place. They recovered drugs, and money in a green holdall.

Sammy was followed all the way home. He became a little suspicious that he was being followed so, when he reached York, he got off the train, taking both bags with him, as if he was going to stop there. He noticed a man who he had seen in Edinburgh also get off the train. At the last possible minute, he got back on the train; the other man turned quickly, but too late to get back on board.

Sammy felt rather smug about this, he was convinced he had been tailed and that he had slipped the tail and was now home and dry. He decided that the relatively small amounts of Class A drugs he was carrying on this trip were not worth the risk, so he went to the lavatory and flushed about £50,000 worth of heroin down the loo. He was wrong about having lost the tail. After another short coffee break at Peterborough, and the forty-minute journey on the Cambridge train, Sammy came off to a reception committee of Josh Jacobs and a few of his team. Sammy Needle was nicked!

****

That Friday, Jerry and Tommy were reviewing the week. Henry had done nothing except pursue his love life.

"I give up," said Tommy. "We need another shipment before we have any chance of finding anything out about the distribution network. It doesn't look as if that is going to happen in a hurry."

Jerry agreed.

"I guess we have several other crimes to think about. I am disappointed our photo of Charley Horse didn't bring in any news. Is there some way we can stir that up again?"

Things were at a bit of a low ebb.

Just then, the telephone rang in the office. It was Josh Jacobs from Cambridge. He sounded very excited, and by the time he had finished talking, the mood of both Jerry and Tommy had lifted appreciably.

"I'm going to put you on speaker phone," said Jerry. "Both Tommy and I are here. You OK with that?"

"Of course," said Josh. "I think you are both going to like this."

"We think our surveillance and undercover exercise with Arthur is coming to its natural end. We know pretty much everything we are ever going to know about the drug scene here in the town and Arthur needs to go back to normal policing. He is a rare talent, and he has done a great job, but I think it is getting very dangerous for him now. The last piece of the jigsaw fell into place yesterday when Sammy Needle took a day return trip to Edinburgh and one of our guys at the Cambridge Station saw him go. We got in touch with the Peterborough and the Edinburgh police and we tracked him all the way. The clever lot in Edinburgh managed to get some of their guys in taxis to the front of the rank and one of their drivers took Sammy from Waverley Station to some tenements in Leith. They saw him go into one of the tenements and come out with a briefcase, like the one he swapped with Henry Castleton. They let him leave and then they went in and arrested everyone in the house."

In the house, they found a big stash of Class A drugs, loads of diazepines, opiates, cocaine, marijuana, you name it, it was there. They also found one million English pounds in used £50 notes in a green holdall. It had Sammy's fingerprints all over it. The guy with the money is still talking but so far, he has said that this was a regular arrangement, and his name is Fergal Cameron, and he was a classmate of your Charles Ma. In fact, he lodged in Ma's flat during their second year in Edinburgh. He dropped out of the same chemistry course at the same time as Charles did. They are still questioning him. It seems he saw your Charles Ma a few weeks ago, just before you put the poster on the news.

He said Charles was living in a very nice tenement in the centre of Edinburgh with a couple of elderly Scots. The place where he was living had a serious fire on the night the picture went on the news. The old couple had each been stabbed to death with a single stab wound to the chest, right through the heart. Charles Ma had disappeared. The local police said that the Chinese student living there had called himself David Fu and he had disappeared without trace a few days before the fire. They said the fire was deliberate. The forensic experts say it was set using a couple of lithium batteries, a can of petrol and a timer switch which was used to turn on the hob under the batteries and cause them to catch fire. Whatever, Fu was long gone before the bodies were discovered. The police showed your Charles Ma pictures to the locals and most of them said it could be him, but an awful lot of them said "all Orientals look alike."

"Blooming heck," said Jerry, who was trying to give up swearing. "More circumstantial evidence linking Henry, via Sammy Needle, particularly, to the Edinburgh scene and to Charley Horse, and to the murders. I am beginning to wonder even more whether our lovely lawyers in Oxford are as 'squeaky clean' as they would like us to believe."

Then Jerry asked Josh what had happened with the tail.

"The tail lost him. He got off at York and the tail got off too, but just as the train was pulling out, at the last possible minute, Sammy Needle got back on and our man was left fuming on the platform."

"Bugger," said Tommy. Who was not trying as hard as Jerry to give up swearing.

Josh laughed:

"No worries," said Josh. "We do belt and braces in Cambridge. We had someone at every station waiting for Sammy to get off, and someone on the train as well. They tag teamed him all the way back to Cambridge. When he got off at Cambridge, we picked him up and brought him in for questioning. He is refusing to say anything. My guess is that he will not sing at all. He knows the rules. He had somehow managed to get rid of the class A drugs between Peterborough and Cambridge. I reckon he knew exactly what he was doing in York, I think he must have 'made' the tail. He probably has a huge amount of money in the bank somewhere, probably in Spain by now. He is looking at a five to ten stretch for Class B drugs and probably a £50–100K fine. My bet is that his UK bank balance will show enough to cover the fine, but not much more than that. He was wearing gloves, so even if we do find packets of heroin scattered along the railway line, needle in a haystack job, if you forgive the pun, we won't nail him for Class A. My guess is he did make the tail and he probably flushed the heroin down the lavatory.

Sammy Needle will not give you Henry Castleton, but at least you now know you are genuinely on the right lines."

Josh continued, "I'm going to debrief Arthur on Monday. If you want to come up and sit in on the debrief, you would be very welcome. There might be something you can use. Otherwise, I'll call you tomorrow after I talk to Arthur and let you know what he had to say. At this moment, he is sitting in a bathtub, soaking in the most expensive bath salts he could get. He came back from his squat with a rucksack full of clothes that could probably have walked here by themselves. He put all his clothes in a bag and threw it in the incinerator. One of my staff went out and bought him fresh socks and underwear, a pair of clean jeans, a couple of shirts and jumpers, and a nice warm jacket. There is a museum in America which has smelly trainers in it, the ones Arthur took off would not be out of place there, they stank. He has a barber in there cutting his hair while he soaks. He has a book in one hand and a whiskey in the other. I treated him to a bottle of 30-year-old single malt! I think my wife and I are taking him out to dinner at Midsummer House tonight. It will be £500 on expenses, but he has earned it.

Do you want to come for the debrief?"

"I'll be there," said Jerry. "What time do you want me?"

"I'm starting at 8 o'clock," said Josh. "A bit of an early start I'm afraid."

"OK. We'll be there," said Jerry. "I could join you for the dinner, but I don't think our expenses will stand it. Tommy and I will probably stay overnight on the Sunday to make sure of joining you for the debrief. Any suggestions?"

"Try the De Freville. It overlooks Parker's Piece and is five minutes' walk from the police station. The other hotel nearby probably won't be allowed on police level expenses!"

When he hung up, Jerry asked Tommy again if he had any ideas about how to get Charles Ma into the public domain again. They decided that they would try and get one of the news channels to talk about a serial killer connected to the drug scene. They now had four murders to lay at Charles's door.

"There is a girl I was at school with," said Tommy. "She works for the Capital News Agency. Let me give her a call."

Helena Chilvers proved to be very willing to try to work up a news item on this serial killer. The three of them, Jerry, Tommy, and Helena, sat down to work out exactly how to push this. They were obviously going to put out the original photograph again, but Jerry thought it unlikely that Charles would have done nothing to disguise his appearance. They sat and thought about the most likely disguises he might have adopted. Facial hair was high on the list, so they got the photoshop expert from the police department to work up a few facial hair photos.

"He might have gone blond," said Jerry.

They tried that too with photoshop.

"Coloured contacts?" Tommy said. "My niece has sparkly ones she puts in for special evenings out!"

They came up with a short 40-second clip with transition from the original photo through all the possible variations and back to the original photo.

"That's bloody impressive!" Tommy said. He still hadn't given up swearing.

And the forty-second clip was impressive; it was planned to go out on the evening news bulletin on the following Wednesday.

Charles, meanwhile, was packing and clearing out his junk. He had things down to the barest minimum for travel to Shanghai. He was flying Virgin Upper Class, direct. He was flying in the name of Shaun Chung, the name on his Chinese passport. He threw out a lot of clothes, but he could not bring himself to throw out his Radiohead t-shirt from his school days at Brassington. It had been almost a cult thing for himself, Nigel, and Henry. He was planning to wear it onto the plane, as a sort of final anti-establishment gesture. Upper class with a Radiohead t-shirt rather appealed to him. No doubt many modern teenagers would think that a bit pathetic, not cool at all, but Charles thought it cool, and for him, that was all that mattered. He gazed lovingly at his seven-inch stiletto knife. It had one more job to do, possibly two. He hadn't quite worked out yet how he was going to kill Henry. He certainly was not going to do anything too elaborate, but he was thinking whether he might do something which would prove once and for all that Henry was the boss of the drug gang. More thinking to do. But it must be quick. The flight was the following Tuesday, 2 December. It was the evening flight, around 10:30 pm.

Charles decided. He would have to kill both Rowan and Henry on the Monday evening. He would have to do it in such a way that the bodies would not be discovered until he was comfortably on the plane. He suddenly knew exactly how he was going to manage it.

Chapter 25

It was the last week of November now. The days were really drawing in. The cold east wind from the Ural Mountains was hitting the east coast and making everyone get out their thermal underwear and their padded puffer jackets. The Christmas posters for the pantomime at the pavilion were plastered all over the town, on every lamppost in the main street, and pretty much anywhere that had a flat vertical surface. The stringy lights along the promenade and across the main street had been dug out of the store cupboard and were waiting for a local celebrity to throw the switch. A typical seaside town preparing for the depths of winter.

It might have remained that, a typical seaside town waiting for Christmas, had the Wednesday news bulletin not gone out with the updated photofit pictures of Charles Ma. What the team had done was to facially morph Charles Ma into Adam Liu. Adam Liu worked in the town and had a face that was well known to dozens of people.

The showing of the 40-second clip on prime-time news threw all Charles's carefully prepared plans into turmoil. Charles's exit from Britain would probably have gone smoothly if it hadn't been for that Wednesday evening news bulletin. The clip, with the fade in and fade out to Charles's picture, created a remarkable likeness to a trainee manager in the greengrocer's store on the Felixstowe High Street. Adam saw the bulletin as he was walking back to his flat past one of the High Street electrical appliance shops. He had no doubt that the owner of the greengrocer's and many of the customers would recognise him and call the police. He had to move fast.

He cut through to one of the back streets and ran as fast as he could back to the flat on Sea Road. The fact that he had already been preparing for departure helped him no end. He simply added a few more things to the case and rucksack he had packed over the past few days, grabbed his travel documents and wallet, and went out of the back door of the block of flats as quickly as he could. He now needed a car.

He had two possible addresses from where he could steal a vehicle and he chose the nearest one on Hamilton Gardens. He had noted these addresses during his delivery rounds for the greengrocer's. It was so simple. He left the bags in a safe place hidden behind the fence. He opened the kitchen door, it was not locked and there was no alarm system, he took the spare key off the peg. He walked through to the sitting room where Josiah Derby, the 79-year-old owner of the car, was sitting watching television. Josiah Derby did not deserve to die; even Charles recognised that, and knowing that nobody would come to visit Josiah until meals-on-wheels called tomorrow lunch time, there was no need to do anything other than tie him up. The house was sufficiently isolated that it was not even necessary to gag him. Charles marched Josiah through to the kitchen at knife point and tied him to a chair at the kitchen table, he did not gag him.

It was only twenty minutes between noticing his image through the shop window and getting into the car to drive out of town.

The car was a three-year-old Ford Focus. Charles threw his bags into the back of the vehicle and drove off. He was only just in time. He was beyond the roundabout to the docks and well on the way towards Ipswich before he saw the first of many police cars. As he drove along the stretch of road between Kirton and Ipswich, he saw police car after police car heading in the opposite direction, sirens blaring and lights flashing. They were clearly going to lock down Felixstowe. Had Charles thought a bit more about Felixstowe, he would have known that there was only one significant road in and out, the A14, and there was no way he would have chosen it as somewhere to hide away. It was probably the reason that the town had such a low crime rate. It was very easy to pick off crooks heading back to London when there was effectively only one road to block. Had he been five minutes late, they might well have stopped Charles, and it was impossible to believe that they would have ignored a Chinese male, by himself, in a car heading out of town. They would have checked the number plates and known that he was not Josiah Derby, aged 79.

Charles was out of Felixstowe and beyond Ipswich before the police had time to set up a roadblock on the A14. At most times of the year and at most times of the day, the A14 is a very quick road. Getting out of the area was the first problem solved. The more serious problem was what to do now until he could begin his exit strategy. Where on earth could he hole up for five nights without attracting attention.

He took off his blond wig and went into the supermarket off the roundabout where the A12 and A14 met. He topped the car up with petrol, paying cash. He purchased enough food and drink of various sorts to last him for four or five days.

He bought himself a coffee at the drive-through MacDonald's and moved into the parking area. He took out the phone he used to contact the boss and called the number.

"Charles here," he said. "I have a problem. I was planning to leave next Tuesday on the 10:30 pm flight but this bloody news bulletin meant I had to get out of my flat immediately. I am clear of the area, but I need somewhere to hole up for a few days. I plan to take out Rowan and Henry next Monday night and be at Heathrow and away the next morning. Any thoughts on how and where I can hide up for the time being?"

The boss thought for a moment and then said, "How about somewhere in Cambridge. You could call Sammy Needle and see if he has anything, and if not, there are plenty of cheap hotels. There are not many people staying in Cambridge this time of the year; it is more a summer tourism spot. You might want to go to one of the cheap hotels in one of the villages to be on the safe side. Have you got a car?"

"I stole one," said Charles. "I'm driving it now. I reckon I have until at least tomorrow lunch time because the old boy I took it from is tied up and the next visitor he is likely to get is meals-on-wheels tomorrow lunchtime."

"Can you get some false plates for it?" The boss asked.

"Well, I drive past that big garage on the outskirts of Cambridge. I guess I can try to swap number plates with one of the old wrecks up the back of the parking lot. It should probably be OK for a couple of days and maybe I can get some more plates for over the weekend."

"Be careful," said the boss. "It would be a pity to blow things now, so close to getting away and starting over with all that money. Besides which, what are we all going to do for our summer holidays if you don't get away. I, for one, really do want to see Xi'an and the terracotta army."

The take-away Thai food shop next to the MacDonald's had a television running to entertain the customers while they waited for their food to be cooked. Charles had half an eye on that while he was talking on the telephone. He caught sight of the photograph they showed of him on the later news bulletins. It was Adam Liu. Blond, and with the hazel-coloured contacts.

The wig and the contacts had to go. They ended up in a trash can behind the MacDonald's in the shopping complex. Charles had kept his hair very close cropped under his blond wig, it had grown back a bit since he shaved his head completely on leaving Edinburgh, but it was still short enough that it made him look very different from any of the photographs the police had so far shown. He had a beanie hat which he could wear, and some plain glass spectacles. He set about making that transformation.

After talking to the boss, Charles was still undecided about where to stay. Cambridge was a possibility, but he knew that the police had connected him with the drug scene there, and they might be a bit more alert to him than in some other towns and cities. He reasoned that he should get to London as quickly as possible. It is always easier to hide in a big city. He reasoned that they might expect him to head back to Edinburgh. The obvious misdirection plan would be to head for Peterborough and leave the car in the car park there. Did he need a car? Probably not if he could manage his disguise well enough. He could get from Peterborough to London or Cambridge very easily by train.

He wondered if any of his drug contacts might help him out. The obvious person to telephone was Sammy Needle. Needle knew people in London, although recently many of his deals with London had been through Charles, Nigel, and the boss.

Sammy Needle's telephone rang in the police station. Inspector Jacobs had kept the phone charged and was monitoring any calls that might come through to it. He answered:

"Hello!"

The caller hung up immediately, but he had left his number on the recent call list. Just for once, Charles had not thought ahead, or he would have gone for number withheld. Josh got the number and called back. There was no answer to the call back, and it was cut off by the person he was calling before it could go through to voice mail. Josh tried again, but this time his number was blocked.

Charles went back into the supermarket and went to the section selling pay as you go phones. He bought another phone, with some calling credit, and took it back with him to the car.

Charles called the boss again on the burner phone.

"Sammy Needle is not answering his phone. I rang the number and I think I got a policeman. I wonder what has happened. The copper rang me back, so he now has my number. That means they can trace where it goes. I need to ditch it and I will not use this phone again. I'll get back to you, but I thought you ought to know. I have a new phone."

He gave the boss the number.

"It should be activated in about two hours which is about how long it is going to take me to get to Cambridge. I will ditch the other one as soon as I hang up and I will completely trash it. I will see if I can find out from Fergal, my contact in Edinburgh, what has happened to Sammy."

"OK," said the boss. "I'll see what I can find out if anything. Let me know if you get any information."

Charles called Fergal Cameron. He got no answer. It was still only about 9:00 pm. Fergal would have been working, selling to the punters. He had never failed to answer a call from Charles. Charles was beginning to be decidedly nervous. He switched his phone to airplane mode to try to stop it being located. They would be able to tell that he had been in this carpark near Ipswich, but it would be much more difficult to tell where he went next.

He headed for Cambridge. That was the first thing to do. Whatever plan he was going to use would involve his going through Cambridge. That was where the A14 went, and, from Cambridge, Peterborough, Edinburgh, and London, were all available.

By the time he got to Cambridge, he had decided that getting rid of the car was a sensible thing to do. He decided to apply a little more misdirection. He pulled up in a lay-by, about 100 metres from the large garage and used car lot on the outskirts of the city and turned off the lights. He took a Phillips screwdriver out of his bag and headed off through a hedgerow into the field beside the parking lot. It was dark and he made sure that nobody saw him. He identified the position of the CCTV cameras watching over the parking lot and made sure that he was not in their field of view. He found two cars with similar size and shape number plates to the ones on the car he had stolen, and he removed them from the vehicles. He took them with him back to his car in the lay-by. He took out the jack and jacked up his car so that it looked as if he were replacing a wheel, just for the benefit of passing traffic. He also put his red triangle at a suitable distance. He worked as quickly as he could and replaced one set of plates on the stolen car. He now had two sets of plates. One from the stolen car and one from the parking lot. They were going to help the misdirection.

He lowered the car to the ground, put away the jack and got back in. He then set off towards the centre of Cambridge. He came to a large housing estate on the left of the road and turned onto the ring road which passed through it. It was one of those estates, built immediately after the Second World War, with houses that had no significant front gardens, and no garages. There were a few garages in a block somewhere buried in the centre of the estate. Car ownership immediately post war was very low in the less well-off sector living on these estates, and the planners, prescient as always, didn't bother about parking. The roadways through the estate had been modified so that cars were parked all the way along the grass verges either side of the main road, on grass reinforced with that plastic mesh material that prevents the cars churning the grass up into mud tracks.

Charles turned into one of the entrance roads to the estate and found a very quiet cul-de-sac. He removed one set of number plates on a Ford Focus in one cul-de-sac and then found another quiet road and removed a second set of number plates. He was counting on the drivers simply getting into the vehicles and riving off, not noticing the lack of plates. Although it didn't really matter. The police would now have at least five different number plates to be looking for. They would also know that he was in or had been in Cambridge.

He headed back towards the centre of the city and then towards the westbound A14. He pulled off the road into a quiet village at about midnight and slept for a few hours. He drank one of his cold 'energy drinks,' with plenty of caffeine, and ate a pain-aux-raisins which he had bought the night before in the supermarket near Ipswich. At about 6 am, while it was still dark, he drove to Peterborough and parked in the station car park. He wiped down everything he thought he might have touched, put on his reversible anorak, removed his bags, and went to the station ticket office. He paid cash for a day return to Edinburgh. He booked a day return to London online, his Shaun Chung account was still uncompromised, and collected it from the machine. Taking his bags, he went through to the platform and made sure that the CCTV picked him up on camera waiting on the Edinburgh platform.

He also made sure that the camera saw him walking towards the carriages when the train pulled in, but he quickly moved down the train and emerged a little further down, behind the bulky catering trolley that was being used to refill the restaurant car. He went into the toilet, reversed the anorak so that the bright yellow side was outermost, and went out of the gentlemen's lavatory block door on the other side of the platform. He sat to wait for the London train.

Twenty minutes later, he was on his way to London. It was still only Thursday morning. A long time to go before Charles could get on that airplane.

****

The placements were temporarily finished in Cambridge and the students were on a week of what was known as formative review. It basically meant a set of lectures and seminars and tests, the inevitable tests. All four girls were well prepared. They were a well-matched group of students who all worked hard, all had a good work life balance, all took exams in their stride. It meant that they had time to go and sit in college and have a coffee in the MCR, the middle common room, and go up to the attic in which the medical students had a dedicated study room full of anatomical models, imaging videos, and procedural equipment, which they could use for private study. It made surgery so much easier to understand when you could see the anatomy in three dimensions and even remove layer upon layer to reveal the hidden secrets. Some of the models were like those matryoshka dolls that the Russians are so fond of.

Rowan and Paige had their SSC starting immediately after this 'formative review' week. It meant that the three-week holiday period was embedded within the SSC, and apart from a week of review, Rowan and Paige could effectively have nine weeks to complete a good project. The other two girls had surgery, with a holiday sandwiched between work on the wards and in the operating theatre. That was one of the reasons they were all there working in the medical room. Rowan and Paige were doing some final preparation for the SSC; Meera and Madeleine were trying to remember some anatomy.

Adrian kept bumping into Rowan and the others as they wandered around college. Towards the end of the week, Adrian said to Rowan, "I've got some slightly obscure journals and reprints that might be useful for you before you start in the lab next week. I am using my study all day and every day this week, and I am afraid I am in there until Saturday lunchtime, but if you like you can use my outer room on Saturday afternoon and have a look at them. I will leave them on the shelf behind the desk for you."

"OK," said Rowan. "That suits me fine because we have a couple more tests to do, and I'm playing college soccer on Saturday morning, and mixed netball on Sunday morning, followed by a lunch at our place. I have a date on Saturday night, so Saturday afternoon will be perfect. Shall I ask the porters for a key?"

"I'll arrange it," said Adrian. "It's nice to see you and the others back in college. We all quite miss you. By the way, do you want to do some supervision for us next term? I thought the four of you between you could cover the second-year biologists on physiology, and, perhaps, the second-year medics on reproductive biology?"

"My answer is yes," said Rowan. "Shall I consult the team? And do you want any neuro supervision? Meera came top of the year in neuro."

"My neuro is so out of date that I worry about my teaching," said Adrian. "Can you ask Meera if she wants to do it? She can share it with someone if she likes."

Rowan went back to the team with the information that they had the chance to bolster their curricula vitae with some teaching, and at the same time earn a bit of pocket money. They went and had lunch in Hall and got back to their studies for the OSCE (Objectively Structured Clinical Examination) the next day.

Chapter 26

Charles arrived at King's Cross. He had again reversed his anorak. It was almost a habit to start and finish activities with the jacket turned the opposite side out. He didn't know if it really made a difference, but he did it anyway. He put up the hood and hid his face from the cameras. His Asian appearance meant that he was able to wear a face mask without attracting too much attention. Ever since the SARS outbreak, many visitors to London had worn face masks. He was not the only one wearing a mask who exited the station after getting off the Peterborough train.

Where to stay? He rang Henry on the drug network phone.

Henry went out of the office to the toilets. Then he answered.

"Henry, old chap," said Charles. "I'm here in London and I need to hide from the police for a couple of days before I leave the country. Any suggestions?"

Henry thought for a moment:

"My girlfriend, Judith, dog walks a couple of dogs in Hampstead for an elderly couple. They happen to be away for December and January. They always go away in the winter to Thailand. I think they have a place there. The dogs are in kennels for the duration, but Judith still has the keys and she goes in on a regular basis to check everything for them. I know where they keep their spare keys and I know the code for their burglar alarm. I went with Judith last weekend when she went there, and she had forgotten to take her keys. The keys are under a flowerpot on the back patio and the burglar alarm code is 313131. You press hash tag, then the numbers, and then enter. The alarm is a white box on the wall opposite the door. You have twenty seconds from entering to disable the alarm. I expect we will go on Sunday again to look at the place, but I think you might be able to hide there in the meantime. The back garden is surrounded by high leylandii. The couple have put those switches in which randomly turn on and off the lights, so the place looks occupied. That frees you up to use the lights as you wish. Just don't damage anything. I am sure Judith would notice if anything was out of place. How long do you need it for?"

"Until Sunday night," said Charles.

"Then that should be OK. I think there is a cleaning lady who comes in on Monday and Thursday morning so, as long as you are gone by then, no one will ever know you were there"

"Don't worry," said Charles, smiling to himself. "By Monday morning, I will not be a complication in your life."

And Charles thought to himself:

You will not be a complication in my life. That might be more what I mean!

Henry gave Charles the address and then rang off. He called the boss immediately and said what he had done. The boss seemed relieved. Henry, on the other hand was far from relieved. He feared Charles, and much preferred it when Charles was a long way away.

Charles took a bus to Hampstead, one change at Baker Street, and went to the address he had been given by Henry. The house was one of those big detached houses, with burglar alarms, a big front garden and drive, with a double garage attached to the house. There was an unlocked side gate to the back garden, and as promised, Charles found the keys to the house under the flowerpot on the patio. He let himself in by the front door and switched off the burglar alarm. He went through to the back of the house and set up camp in the kitchen and the garden room. The garden room had double doors opening onto the garden, and a pleasant south facing aspect. He thought it best not to stray too far. There was a bathroom off the hall, and he could use that for his toilet needs. He had a slight concern that, should Judith and Henry visit on Sunday, as Henry had suggested they would, they might find something out of place and be suspicious of an intruder. He really did not want to have to kill yet another innocent. Henry was fair game but Judith, the girlfriend, that just seemed unfair. Still, if it meant survival, he would do it.

He looked in the cupboards and found all sorts of goodies, like chocolate and crisps. They would help to keep him going. He had had to abandon most of the supplies he had bought near Ipswich when he changed his plan and decided to come to London. He made a sort of camp bed up on the couch in the garden room using blankets he found in the airing cupboard outside the large bathroom on the first floor. He thought it ironic that his sheets and pillowcases had bright red poppies all over them.

He got out his iPad and looked for the router for the Wi-Fi. As he had hoped the passcode for the network was printed on the router itself and for good measure, the owners had written it out in large characters on a piece of paper which sat beside it on the telephone stand. Charles was back in contact with the cyberworld.

By early afternoon, he was all over the BBC news feed. Pictures of him in multiple guises, the clip of him morphing from one facial feature to another, the story of his masquerading as a trainee greengrocer for a few weeks, the theft of the car, these made quite a website story, all clickable for further information. Charles was surprised to find himself relieved that Josiah had not suffered from the period of being tied to the chair. There was an interview with Josiah who said that he had recognised Adam Liu as the person who had delivered his fruit and vegetables. He had no idea just how dangerous the man could be. When they asked Josiah, what had been the hardest thing about being tied to the chair he simply said:

"I was bored, and I got a numb bum!"

They asked him if he had been afraid.

His reply was again simple.

"No," he said. "I was in the army for many years and had quite a few scary moments. A tin pot crook like that wasn't going to scare me."

Charles found that comment very annoying. His ego was bruised. He should have got his stiletto knife out and seen whether that made a difference.

The report on the news said that the police had been informed immediately after the news bulletin the night before, by several customers and the manager of the greengrocer's shop, that Adam Liu and this Charles Ma were one and the same person. The roadblock out of Felixstowe had been put in place within thirty minutes of the first telephone call but somehow the fugitive had escaped. The train station and all the buses had been carefully watched. The website gave details of Josiah's car, make, model, colour, and number. People were asked to report if they saw it and not to approach the driver.

During the afternoon, the story was updated.

The first additional piece of news was that some cars in a used car lot in Cambridge had had their number plates taken. These number plates were also included on the webpage and people were asked to watch out for them.

The second additional piece of news was that Charles Ma might be in the Peterborough area since the stolen car had been found in the car park at Peterborough Railway Station.

The next update was that a man possibly fitting Charles Ma's description, had been seen boarding the 7:19 Peterborough to Edinburgh train. It was thought that he might have alighted at any of the stations en route to Edinburgh, or since he had previously resided in the city, might be back in Edinburgh itself.

Charles was very pleased with himself, the misdirection seemed to have worked, at least for now.

He cooked himself a supper of spaghetti and some meat sauce he had found in the freezer. No point in passing up that opportunity. He would be long gone before the owners missed it.

Chapter 27

It was Thursday evening and that was the night that Rowan went to the pantomime at the ADC theatre in Park Street. It is the oldest student theatre club in the country, founded in 1855. At the end of every Michaelmas Term it is host to a student written and student performed pantomime. It is always a curious mixture of traditional panto: *He's behind you, Oh no he didn't, oh yes, he did*, and much more topical material, and more adult jokes. There is also an original musical score and original songs. Rowan's new boyfriend, Thomas, was the pantomime dame. A brilliant actor with a good singing voice, he was the perfect choice for the part which held the show together. All four of the girls, and the partners of the other three, had booked tickets very early in term. They sat in the best seats in the house. Row C seats 1–7. Whenever they went, the girls would try and get that row. It was far enough back not to get soaked when the pantomime stage action started, the water pistols and the shaving foam sprays, but it was near enough to be able to see and enjoy every detail. It was also near enough to the front exit door that, when the stewards came in at the interval to sell ice creams, the girls could grab an ice cream and sit on the stage to eat it, before half the audience had even got out of their seats.

The seven of them met early in the evening and had supper in Hall. The cafeteria system was good at St Joe's. There was always plenty of variety and the food was served at what was effectively the cost price of the ingredients, plus a tiny mark up. Cambridge students are spoilt!

They went to the Theatre Bar before the show, it opened at about 7:15, and they booked their interval drinks. There was always a cocktail and a mocktail (an alcohol-free cocktail), with a theme based around the pantomime. The pantomime was 'Beauty and the Beast.' This week's cocktail was called Belle-Gin-Chocolate, and the mocktail was called Gastonberry Soup. The girls usually just had a coffee before the show.

The house lights went out. Rowan had never been to a performance at the ADC which started on time, and this was no exception. Always five minutes late, always, always, always.

Rowan reminded herself that Row C was safe. She had forgotten that Thomas was such a major character in the panto and that he had been going out with her now for a couple of months. It was scene two, the forest, when the cast began dragging audience members up on stage. Thomas made a beeline for Rowan. She should have guessed it would happen.

The script took a lot of liberty with the original story of Beauty and the Beast, and this sketch involved bringing up members of the audience and getting people to categorise them as either beauty or beast. It was done in a very good humoured and cheeky way and was not capable of giving offence, but Rowan, and each one of the seven in the Row C seats 1–7, was dragged up on stage. As might have been expected, all four girls were described as beasts and the three lads as beauties. They were dressed up accordingly and put through various theatrical paces, including singing. To everyone's surprise, including Rowan herself, she turned out to be a huge hit. She had to sing a version of *I am Beautiful*, the Christina Aguilera song, with new lyrics. Rowan's version brought the roof down. Thomas looked astounded. As he ushered her off stage he whispered:

"Where did that come from?"

"Belle-Gin-Chocolate," Rowan said. And they all sat down to enjoy the rest of the show.

At the interval, the others just couldn't stop talking about that performance, and several other members of the audience asked her whether it was a put-up job.

"No," said Rowan. "My wretched boyfriend grabbed me. I am really a medical student and I have never been on stage before in my life, except in school."

After the show, the producer came over to find Rowan specially, and she said that she was casting the Lent Term musical. It was going to be 'Grease.' Please, please, would Rowan come and audition? Rowan promised to think it over.

It was Thursday night, not the night to get hammered when you had an OSCE (Objectively Structured Clinical Examination) the next day, so around midnight, Rowan and the others went back home and to bed. All four girls believed that last minute cramming was not the way to go. Having thoroughly enjoyed the play, they all slept soundly and woke the next morning ready for the fray. For Rowan especially it was a great relief. She had been having the recurrent dreams about the day of the overdose, but this morning she woke up having slept dreamlessly through the night. It felt good.

****

That same Thursday evening, Judith and Henry had gone out to dinner at a Japanese restaurant. They had had a simple meal, sushi, and sashimi; it was basically an excuse to get together. They were in love and they were beginning to spend every moment that they could together. The phone call from Charles earlier in the day had disturbed Henry deeply. He knew that they were so close to finishing the drug involvement and he was desperately hoping to get out before Judith found out about him. He had the feeling that all he had to do was to get through the Sunday visit to the house in Hampstead, and the road to salvation would be his. For one thing, Charles would be out of the country and he was certain that Charles had killed Angela and Nigel. He did not trust Charles as far as he could throw him. For as long as Charles was in this country, Henry thought none of the gang were safe.

For the first time in his life, he was beginning to feel remorse. He wondered how many people's lives he had ruined by selling them drugs. He knew for certain that Angela and Nigel would still be alive if the drug dealing had not started, and he began to think about that awful thing that had happened to Rowan. He just had to put it out of his mind.

Henry and Judith went back, as was now their habit, to Henry's flat. They were sleeping together every night now.

"So much to lose," thought Henry. In fear of Charles, he was extra diligent about locking the door and setting the burglar alarm.

****

After a couple of nights in the cells on remand, Sammy Needle was beginning to think how much he could safely divulge without being labelled as a copper's nark. He was taken into the interview room early on the Friday morning for a further period of questioning. There were two things that knocked him off his perch.

The first was that the line of questioning was not so much about drug dealing as his relationship with this fugitive murderer, Charles Ma. The second was that the two people interviewing him were Inspector Jacobs and someone Sammy recognised as a regular drug user, cleaned up perhaps, but someone to whom Sammy had regularly sold drugs. He had known the guy as Arthur.

"Good morning, Mr Needle. I am Detective Sergeant Edward Lyons."

"Oh shit," thought Sammy.

"I think you know Inspector Jacobs," said Edward. "We want to ask you about your relationship with Charles Ma, the fugitive we are trying to trace in connection with four murders. My first question for you is how do you know Charles Ma?"

Sammy thought about it. Did he know Charles Ma? How did they know he knew Charles Ma? It had to be that little Scottish git, Fergal Cameron. They would know he knew Ma.

"Right, before I talk to you, I want to know that you are only going to do me for the drugs that you caught me with this last time. Anything else I tell you is off the record and not going to be used against me. Is that agreed?"

Inspector Jacobs looked at Sammy.

"You know I can't promise anything like that."

"Yes, you can, because you don't have any other physical evidence against me, only circumstantial and a few video clips of me with people you say are drug pushers. Do we have a deal?"

"We'll see what we can do."

"Not good enough. Do we have a deal?"

"Alright. We will leave it at what we got on you this time. I reckon it will get you five to ten anyway. You know that, don't you?"

"I know. OK, if we have a deal here goes," and Sammy began to give information.

"He used to telephone me when he wanted drugs for his group. I never met him. It was always a deal over the phone. The guy I handed drugs over to was someone called Nigel. I guess you know the person in Edinburgh I got them from, it was that guy, Fergal Cameron. I want to make it clear I never touched heroin. It was only the Class B drugs and marijuana, but the Scots had wonderful marijuana, I think they grew it by hydroponics, like in that film, what was it called? Oh yes, 'Saving Grace'."

"Come off it, Sammy," said Edward. "I saw you sell heroin, in fact you sold some to me because you thought I was a junkie. We are getting a warrant to search your house anyway. When did you first get contact from this Charles Ma?"

"You won't find anything in the house, mate. You must think I am stupid if you think I would keep stuff there. And you said we have a deal, so I will tell you things but not for evidence."

"It started a couple of years ago," continued Sammy. "I was supplying some marijuana and a bit of ecstasy to a couple of students and a couple of them were friends of this Charles Ma. Anyway, this Nigel person, one of Ma's friends as it turned out, asked me for some contact details so that a friend of his could get in touch with me because he wanted to do some dealing and he had big money for buying. He said the bloke's dad was a Chinese businessman and had a lot of money to stake drug deals. I thought this was bullshit, but I gave him the details anyway. First deal the bloke goes for was a hundred thousand pounds. I thought, rubbish, but, sure enough the money came in £50 notes in a briefcase. I swapped it for some drugs and the trade started. That friend of Nigel's was Charles Ma."

"What were the names of the students you handed drugs to?" Edward asked.

"There were three main kids who took marijuana. There was this bloke Nigel, there was a girl called Justine and another lad called Michael. Nigel was the only one who took the heavy stuff and that only started after I heard from Charles."

"Did you come across a girl called Angela, or a lad called Henry?"

"I think I saw them. I got the impression they were just hangers on, did a bit of pot but nothing more. I think that Angela was Nigel's girlfriend."

"We have a bit of video of you swapping briefcases with Henry a few days ago. What was that about?"

"The Charles guy rang me and said that Nigel had met with an accident and there would be a new courier. He said they had 'persuaded' Henry to do this last pick up for them. He said this was going to be the last pick up because they were shutting up shop and he, that is Charles, was going abroad.

Henry certainly seemed really uncomfortable when we met in Cambridge that day."

"Anything else you want to tell us?" Inspector Jacobs asked.

"Yeh," said Sammy. "I don't think Charles was the brains behind the outfit. I think there was someone else running things. Charles would say to me on the phone that someone he called 'the boss' wanted another shipment. It was always 'the boss.' I think this bunch of students was supplying locally, but I also think they were making a lot of money in London. The thing is, they were spending big sums of money. At one stage, I reckon they were doing a million pounds worth of business every month. I would take a rucksack with the money up to

Scotland and bring back the goods. What that got them in the marketplace I dread to think. I reckon they must have made twenty million over the time I dealt with them. This recent deal was the biggest ever, and they said it was going to be their last. The thing is, it is dead easy to get from Cambridge to King's Cross, and a lot of drug dealing goes on around there."

"What about this Michael and this Justine?" Edward asked.

"Small stuff," said Sammy. "Originally, they got it from the guy on the Market Square but when they found I could let them have it cheaper, they came to me. Only marijuana and ecstasy."

"Any idea who this boss person might be?" Josh asked.

"No," said Sammy. "But I reckon they were pretty smart because nobody had an inkling what was going on and who was behind it."

"So, you never saw this Charles Ma?" Edward asked.

"No, never," said Sammy. "I tell you one thing though; he had a dead weird accent. It was almost like a Chinese person speaking Scottish, but a bit posh too. I sometimes had to ask him to repeat himself."

"Did you ever see Nigel with anyone else when he came to pick up the drugs?"

"Only that Angela girl. Oh, no, wait a minute. There was one time when he came with a couple of other students, a boy, and a girl. It was last summer, I think. Yes. Probably around May or June time. I remember because they were all a bit drunk and one of them had an open bottle of bubbly in her hand. Might have been just after they finished their exams or something, they often get a bit sozzled then."

"Could you describe them at all?" Josh asked.

"Not really. The girl was a bit funny looking, with buck teeth. I remember thinking it was a pity her parents hadn't got her to an orthodontist."

All this didn't mean much to Edward Lyons or Josh Jacobs, but it would certainly ring a bell with Jerry and Tommy.

Sammy went back to his cell. Edward and Josh decided to call Jerry with the information they had got about Charles, Henry, and Nigel.

Jerry answered the phone and Edward reported on the recent conversation with Sammy.

"So, Henry was very much a passive partner in this enterprise then?" Jerry asked.

"Maybe," said Edward. "Looks as if he might have been bullied into doing this recent pick-up. But there were a couple of other students that Sammy mentioned, and I don't know if you have come across them. There was a bloke called Michael and a girl called Justine. Does that ring a bell?"

"No," said Jerry. "Except I think you mentioned them yourself when we saw you that time in Cambridge."

"That's right," said Edward. "So, I did. Forgot about that. They were very small beer. But he mentioned that Nigel was the courier for the London end of the enterprise, and he said it was always Nigel that turned up to collect the drugs when they were in Cambridge. The deal was always done with this Charles who had a weird accent. Sammy described it as a Chinese Scottish and posh mixture. He also said that Nigel turned up once, just after their exams, with a boy and a girl. He said the girl had buck teeth. He said they were all a bit drunk, probably just finished their exams. That ring any bells?"

"We've got two bells clanging here," said Jerry. "The poor girl Samantha who was with Nigel when he was stabbed said the murderer had a weird accent, she thought Scottish and Chinese came into it. And Amanda Sayers, the girl who lived on the same staircase as Angela Huddlestone, has buck teeth. I feel a few extra interviews coming on here.

Look, thanks for all this. Do you think Sammy would be able to identify the girl from a photo if we got one and sent it to you?"

"I don't know. You can ask him yourself on Monday. He isn't going anywhere. He has been remanded in custody for a fortnight until his case comes up at the Crown Court."

"OK. Thanks for all this. See you Monday," and Jerry rang off.

Tommy, who had been listening in on the speaker phone said, "So, it could be that Henry was just a stupid schoolkid who got into small amounts of marijuana, but he did go and pick up the drugs that day in Cambridge, so I have an open mind on that. Angela was collateral damage, Nigel was quite central to the operation as a courier and distributor, Charles was the go-between, between the supplier and the gang, and someone else was the boss. Want to bet that that Amanda girl and Robert thing in Oxford were involved in some way?"

"I wouldn't bet against it," said Jerry. "But we do not have any proof. Just living on the same staircase is not proof of complicity. So far, all we have is a dead drugs courier and a fugitive go-between and hitman. Wonder what more we can get on Monday morning? Can you arrange to get a photo of Amanda, and while you are at it, Robert as well. You never know, the boy with Nigel and Amanda might have been Robert. They were all doing the same exams, so they might well have been celebrating together. We can take the photos with us and show Mr Needle on Monday."

And with that, the pair of them went off duty for the weekend. They were still on call if any sight or sound of Charles Ma turned up but, otherwise, they could get a bit of a rest.

"See you at the station on Sunday evening," said Tommy. "I hope they are running trains and not one of these bloody replacement bus services. They seem to always be repairing and servicing the lines at weekends."

Chapter 28

This Friday evening was a big event for Henry. Judith's parents had insisted that Judith go home for supper on the Friday and bring her new young man with her. Judith's family lived a short train ride out of London at Digswell, near Welwyn Garden City. It was too soon to suggest that he stayed overnight, so they planned an early supper. He could get back to London on several different trains, the last one left at half past midnight.

Since his delivery of the drugs after the Cambridge trip and knowing that that was the last shipment the gang was going to organise, Henry was beginning to feel more confident about his future. Once Charles was out of the country, Henry would feel much more relaxed. It was only a matter of days now. He was still very afraid of Charles, he always had been, ever since school. The thing he had to do now was to choose his time to let the boss know that he had the incriminating evidence in the event of his death. Given the recent phone call he thought he might do that sooner, rather than later.

Henry met Judith at King's Cross Station and they travelled together on the train to Welwyn North. Welwyn North is a peculiar little station. The reason it is there at all is that Queen Victoria refused to stay on the train as it went on the Digswell Viaduct. Despite Victoria opening the viaduct in the mid-1850s, she was terrified of its height and refused to remain on the train when it crossed over the viaduct. She alighted from the carriage at Welwyn and travelled the length of the viaduct by horse drawn carriage before reboarding the train at Welwyn North. Judith's parents, and many others have benefitted from that odd quirk of history.

It was well and truly dark when Judith and Henry arrived at the station. They walked down the hill through the tree-lined streets to New Road and then turned left. A little way up the road on the right was the Blackett's house. It was large, set in about an acre of grounds, surrounded by mature hedges and with a well-tended garden. The structure was mock-Tudor. It had been built by a master builder, sometime in the 1940s, for his own residence, and had changed hands a few times since, every time being modernised, in terms of plumbing and electrical utilities.

Judge Matthew Blackett and his wife, Sarah, known to her friends as Sally, greeted Henry at the door. They were charm itself. The fact that the person he hoped was to become his father-in-law was a high court judge had done nothing to ease Henry's anxiety about his student indiscretions with marijuana, and drug dealing, being discovered.

The evening meal went very well. Sally Blackett was an excellent cook and had produced a delicious meal of chilled watercress soup, with homemade wholemeal rolls, a mild lemon and coconut chicken curry, and a dessert of homemade mango ice cream. They had Cobra beer with the curry, the beer first produced by Baron Bilimoria to offer a less gassy lager for people to consume with Indian food. Judge Blackett asked Henry about his career plans and was pleasantly surprised to find that Henry was interested in becoming a solicitor with a specialisation in family law.

"Not enough good lawyers going into family law," said Blackett. "If you apply yourself, you could do well in that field. I guess you do a lot of conveyancing, and all that other more boring stuff, as you work yourself into the practice, but a specialist in family law, in the long run, should give you plenty of work and plenty of interest. Mind you, I hope you like divorce and money squabbles!"

They all laughed.

"I read that long marriages without divorce are probably inherited," said Judith.

"You're kidding us," said Henry.

"No, I can show you the article if you like. It seems that people whose parents have a long and stable marriage are a lot more likely to have one themselves than people whose parents are divorced."

"Tell us about your parents, Henry," said Sally Blackett.

No pressure, thought Henry.

But what he said was, "My father is a high court judge up in Leeds and my mother is a principal at a local private school there. She is a linguist, very useful when we travel abroad. I have two sisters, both younger than me. One is about to graduate from the Courtauld Institute with a degree in Art History, that is Agnes. She wants to go into gallery work. The other is in her first year at Cambridge doing medicine. The folks tried to put her off, but Phoebe was not for turning."

The looks on the family faces said it all, you pass!

"My family all had long marriages," said Judge Blackett. "My parents were married for 69 years. I have two brothers and a sister, all married for more than twenty-five years and still going strong. Same sort of thing on Sally's side of the family. I think Judith's article must be right."

At about 11:15, Henry said his goodbyes and went out to the porch with Judith. The Blacketts were sensitive enough to allow the two younger people a moment or two together to say goodbye and exchange a long and passionate kiss.

"They like you," said Judith.

"I like them," said Henry.

"I have to stay the weekend," said Judith. "Can you do me a really big favour? Can you go to the Silver's house in Hampstead and just check up on it for me? The one we went to last weekend. At least you don't have to walk their dogs. I still do it because they used to live here in the village and I walked their dogs for pocket money when I was still at school and it seemed rude not to do it when I lived near enough to them in Hampstead."

Henry trembled at the thought that he might bump into Charles; but then he thought his luck must be changing. He would go and check on the house and there would be no danger of Judith finding out about Charles. Henry would get brownie points with Judith, and Charles would be gone soon.

"It would be my pleasure, my love. I will go tomorrow morning. And I will see you next Monday after work."

Henry made his way alone to the station and caught the train back to King's Cross. He decided to walk back to his flat in the Barbican. His mind was racing too much to go straight to sleep.

****

The girls in Cambridge, that evening, had sat down and conducted their usual post-exam post-mortem. It went:

"That was OK," said separately by each of them.

It was usually followed by, and this was no exception:

"Whose turn is it to cook supper?"

For the three years that they had known each other, they had adopted a policy of no post-exam post-mortems. Exams were done and dusted when you came out of the exam room. Life began anew. It would, no doubt, have been different if one or other of them had had a disaster, everyone would have gathered round and offered comfort, but, so far, there had been no disasters, and if you looked at it objectively, more than their share of triumphs. All four were scholars; all four had a string of first-class results behind them.

The convenient location of the house in Mill Road meant that, this evening, the post exam party for the whole year was going to be held there. It was going to be the usual bring a bottle party that happens in student digs. Paige was good at putting together play lists, and they had good speakers. They had been round to all the neighbours and warned them. Most of the folk in that part of Mill Road were quite young and they were invited. There was one slightly older couple that lived opposite, but they assured Madeleine, when she went to speak to them, that they had been young once, and provided it was not every night, they could handle the odd party like this. They could always sleep in late tomorrow.

The girls had supper first. A quick take-away fish and chips from the chippy down the road. It had, deservedly, been a regional winner in the fish and chip shop of the year competition.

They put up a few decorations, adjusted the lights, and sat back to await company.

Rowan was a little sad that Thomas was still in the pantomime and would not be able to get there until 11:30. She hadn't quite realised how much she was beginning to like him. For a while she had kidded herself that it was going to the theatre that she liked, but she was now recognising that slight butterfly feeling in the stomach when he came into a room. One of her friends, who was a good friend of Thomas's, told her that Thomas was also 'rather interested.' It was nice for Rowan. After Vincent left the scene, she had been a little wary about new boyfriends, mainly because of the overdose scenario. Now that she was convinced that something had happened to her, she was beginning to open up more, and Thomas was just what she needed.

The place began to fill up around 10 pm, Paige was playing the tracks and people were dancing and drinking, and generally unwinding from the exam and the first few weeks of the medical course. Proper medics know how to party. There had been a series on television called 'Tomorrow's Doctors' filmed at one of the London medical schools. Both Patti and Matthew Pike had suggested that the doctors in it were much too well behaved. Rowan's grandpa, James, had trained in the 60s. His comment was:

"In my day, we worked a full 36-hour shift, came off duty, threw up, and went out for the evening."

Rowan was never quite sure whether he was saying that was a good thing or a bad thing. Knowing grandpa, he was probably bragging.

It was not long before someone who had been at the theatre on the Thursday night started talking about Rowan's singing of the Christina Aguilera song, and someone begged her to repeat the performance. She did, and just as she finished singing it, Thomas came in from his theatre show and grabbed her and kissed her.

The rest of the evening was a bit of a blur, but around 1 am, Rowan headed off to bed. She was playing football in the morning and wanted to do reasonably well. The party broke up around 2 am and the other girls cleared up most of the mess.

****

In Hampstead, Charles was going over his plan. He realised he did not know Henry's exact address in the Barbican, so he texted the boss to ask for it. It came back almost immediately. He decided to call the boss, his new phone was now active, and they had a bit of a chat.

"Henry was a good organiser and for a while he really liked the money, but rumour has it he is in love," said the boss. "I think he is a bit of a weak link. If anyone arrested him, put pressure on him and offered him a deal, I am sure he would crack. He only suspects that Rowan's suicide attempt was a bit fishy. He doesn't know what really happened. Amanda and Robert say he wasn't there that afternoon, after the tea party. You just must take him out I'm afraid."

Charles said, "When I get back to China, you all have to wait at least six months before you get in touch again. And use a VPN. Also use WeChat. They don't let WhatsApp calls happen because of Facebook."

They chatted a bit longer and then both hung up and went to sleep.

****

The next morning, Rowan woke a bit before the others and had a breakfast of shredded wheat with some mixed berries. She always had wholewheat cereal before a game. It gave a nice long sugar release, and it didn't sit on the stomach. She was not averse to a full English breakfast, but not before exercise.

She packed her kit in her sports bag, including her boots which, just for once, she had cleaned properly. They were always teasing her about her muddy boots, but she always claimed it was because she tackled and ran more than the others. That was probably true, she was a good player, but she had always been a bit lazy about cleaning her boots. She had the number 8 shirt, the creative midfielder shirt. The team played 3, 4, 3 formation and Rowan was a creative central midfielder. She was actually good enough to play for the university and had got a blue in the first two years, but she had decided to follow other sports in the third year, and now that she was a clinical student, time constraints meant that the occasional game in term time was all she could play. There was also a rule that blues could not play in the leagues, only in the cup competitions, so Rowan was using this, and some other friendly games, to get ready for the cup competition next term.

She unlocked her bicycle from the rack at the back of the house and put her kit on the pannier rack. She fastened it on with the hooked elastic straps that she always used. She got her bike helmet and her cycle jacket and headed off for the sports ground up near the university athletics track. It was about a 5 km cycle ride to the ground, just enough to warm up nicely.

Kick off was at 10:30 and Rowan arrived at the ground at about 10:00 for a bit of a kick around. The college had an arrangement with a couple of American Ivy League Universities for the exchange of students, and one of the girls in the college team was a very good player who had been a university team member in the States. She was easily the best player in the team; Rowan was a reasonable second best. They spent fifteen minutes or so passing the ball to each other before the rest of the team arrived to play. The opposition turned up five minutes later. The referee, a lad from St Peter's College, turned up five minutes before the game.

It was a cold typical late autumn, early winter day in Cambridge. Fortunately, the early mist had cleared, and the sun was beginning to peep through. It had little warmth, but the lightness was welcome.

The other three girls at Rowan's house had finally dragged themselves from their beds and piled into Paige's car. They arrived just as the opposition goalie was picking the ball out of the net after the first goal. It was only ten minutes late. Afterwards, they explained that they were late because they had called round and collected Thomas, who wanted to see Rowan play football.

There was not exactly a big crowd, maybe about forty or so friends, boyfriends and girlfriends, and a couple of parents who were visiting for the weekend. The main thing was that there were enough spectators to act as ball boys and girls when the ball went out of play. Thomas, forgetting to protect his voice for the pantomime, shouted rather loudly every time Rowan got the ball.

St Joe's won comfortably, 7-0. Thomas was suitably impressed, and the three girls and Thomas drove back to college to wait for Rowan. Rowan had a quick shower, changed into her warm clothing, and cycled back to St Joe's. The five of them went for a coffee at Savino's. Rowan had arranged to, and Thomas insisted on, buying each of them a slice of carrot cake. They all knew that Rowan was going over to the Senior Tutor's room to work and Thomas and Rowan agreed to meet at the Theatre at 7:00. Thomas told Rowan to ask the girl at the front desk to let her through to the club room. He said he would make sure that some of the take-away pizza was saved for her.

Rowan finished her cake and her coffee and went over to the Senior Tutor's room to start work.

****

Adrian Armstrong's room was a typical fellow's room at St Joe's. Situated in one of the seventeenth century buildings, it had wooden panelling, a relatively high ceiling, and very small windows. It did, however, have one of the best views of any room in the college. It looked out over the duck pond and the 'Rec,' the large grass area around the perimeter of which were most of the college buildings.

Rowan was not there to admire the view, she had come to work, but she did pause a moment to look at the sun shining on the grass and glistening on the pond. She went over to the shelf where Adrian had laid out several reprints for her to look at. They included some more obscure journals like Pflügers Archiv and the Japanese Journal of Physiology. He had also left her a list of papers that she could find online. Pflügers Archiv is the oldest Physiology Journal in the world, founded in 1868, but most authors in Adrian's area of research publish in the American Journal of Physiology, or The Journal of Physiology itself.

Rowan got out her laptop, plugged it into the mains and connected to the university wireless network. She started to read through several of the papers and systematically made useful notes in her reference database. She worked solidly for about two hours and decided it was time for another coffee. George was on duty again, so it was a case of a coffee and a homemade biscuit with George, yet again.

"So, young Rowan," said George. "Those tablets we found were useful then?"

"Absolutely, George," said Rowan. "They convinced me and the Senior Tutor that there was something funny that went on that day. I am quite sure I am going to get there soon and know what really happened."

"How was your football game this morning, Rowan? The girls were saying that with you and the American girl in the team they might just win Cuppers this year."

"It was good, George," said Rowan. "We thrashed them 7-0 and they are supposed to be one of the top two teams in the league."

"A little bird tells me you have a new boyfriend, Rowan. The same little bird tells me you sing like an angel, or at least like Christina Aguilera."

"George, you are a right blooming gossip," said Rowan. "If we all didn't love you so much, you might get a serious telling off!" and they both laughed.

"OK," said Rowan. "Just to satisfy your curiosity, I have a new boyfriend. He is very nice, he is an amazing actor, and he is called Thomas, and you are quite likely to see him around a fair bit. Now keep it to yourself."

"Want to take another biscuit and cup of coffee with you back to that room? Isn't your brother called Tom?" George asked.

"Please to the coffee and yes to my brother's name, as you well know," said Rowan.

Rowan had no idea what was about to happen. Nobody could have predicted it. It came right out of the blue.

Rowan went back to Adrian's room and sat down at the desk again. When she was ready to do some individual writing, something a bit more creative than writing notes, Rowan found it easier to think with a fountain pen and lined A4 note paper. She took her silver Cross fountain pen out of her bag and filled it with ink and started to write the introduction to her Student Selected Component research project.

She had written about a dozen lines when she remembered that she had spotted something in one of the papers she had put back on the shelf behind her; so she got up to go and collect it, and as she did so, she knocked her pen off the desk onto the floor. It rolled under the desk. She went and got the paper, put it on the desk and bent down to pick up the pen.

In front of her, on the bottom shelf of the bookcase, behind the desk, she saw an object.

It was a polished wooden case, probably walnut, with brass hinges. It was about 30 cm long, 25 cm wide, and 12 cm deep.

On the shelf above it was a length of rubber tubing, a filter funnel and a pestle and mortar.

She started to breathe deeply; she knew it was important; she had seen the box before. For the moment, she could not think where she had seen it.

Rowan pulled it out and lifted it onto the desk in front of her. She opened the lid of the box and began to assemble the balance inside.

The more complete her assembly, the more distressed became her breathing. There was a pounding in her head. Suddenly, she was back on the afternoon of the overdose.

She knew.

She knew what had happened.

In her mind's eye, she left the library, and she met Angela on the Rec. She went back with Angela to the college and into Angela's room. Henry was there, and Amanda Sayers, not Nigel, just Henry and Amanda Sayers. They all had a coffee together and some chocolate biscuits, she remembered the chocolate biscuits. She remembered going back to her room after the coffee and biscuits.

Then she remembered that she had done a little more reading and made herself a cup of coffee but, having realised that she had no milk, she had gone back to Angela's room to ask her for some milk.

When she walked into Angela's room, she had seen Nigel, Amanda, Robert, and the friend of Henry and Nigel, called Charles, all sitting on the floor with the balance in front of them, weighing out packets of white powder. She remembered saying, "What the hell are you lot doing?"

She remembered sitting down and the five of them telling her some story about weighing out flour for flour bombs as a post-exam joke. She knew that was a lie, but she was scared and outnumbered.

They suggested she sit down and have a cup of coffee with them and talk things over. She sat down and they gave her a coffee. Amanda made the coffee and brought it over to her. And that was the last thing she remembered.

Rowan left things as they were, locked the door to Adrian's study, and went back to the Porter's Lodge.

"George," said Rowan. "Can you get the Senior Tutor here for me, please? It's urgent."

Adrian Armstrong lived in a college house in a road very nearby. It took him less than ten minutes to turn up.

Rowan told him what she had now remembered and who she believed had drugged her with the Rohypnol. She explained that she had seen all four of the people weighing out what was obviously heroin, or something similar, and that is why they had drugged her and tried to kill her. Angela and Henry were not there, presumably Angela was at a rehearsal for one of the May Week plays, and Henry may well have been doing techie stuff.

Rowan said, "I would lay odds that fingerprints of some or all of those people are on the balance, and the weights, and on the funnel and tubing, and pestle and mortar. Thinking about the Lindsay and Gilmour capsules that the bedders found, I think they almost certainly force fed me the paracetamol down that rubber tube and funnel. I think they meant to kill me."

"Right," said Adrian. "Nobody else must touch the apparatus. Nobody has touched the weights. Only you, me and Andrew, the head of maintenance, have touched any of it since it was fished out of the hiding place in the Cumberland Building.

You sit there, Rowan. I am going to get George to bring you another cup of coffee and I am going to go into my inner study and call the police."

Rowan was suddenly overwhelmed by emotion and she started to sob, deep sobs. By the time Adrian came back, she had composed herself again, and although a little red eyed, she was back in control.

The knowledge that she had been attacked rather than that she had, inexplicably, tried to kill herself, was, strangely, a relief.

George came in with the coffee and half a dozen of his Aussie oatmeal cookies.

They sat there for about half an hour. It was dark by the time that Inspector Jacobs and Sergeant Lyons arrived. They came with a couple of crime scene people who carefully bagged all the evidence and took it away.

Josh Jacobs and Edward Lyons looked at Rowan.

"I am so sorry," said Josh. "It must have been awful living under the stigma of attempted suicide when you knew in your heart that it could not have been. I am so glad that you have found out what was happening here. You gave us the Rohypnol tablets before, but you now know who gave them to you. Is that correct?"

"Yes," said Rowan. "It was Amanda Sayers who brought me the coffee."

"We still don't know who gave you the paracetamol," said Edward Lyons.

"I don't think it matters," said Josh, "you said they were all there. That makes them all accessories."

"It might be hard to prove. We don't have a lot of concrete evidence. We need to get lucky with the forensics," said Edward.

"I reckon they were dealing for quite a long time and they have still been dealing since they left Cambridge. Their bank balances may be worth a look."

"I think we need to move very quickly now," said Josh. "We need to pull in Robert, Amanda, and Henry, and to find that Charles Ma. I am a bit worried for you, Miss Pike. Charles Ma has disappeared; you are the only significant witness to what went on. Nigel and Angela are dead. I would not be surprised if Charles comes looking for you to tie up yet another loose end. I am going to get a lady detective to come and stay with you tonight. She has just been seconded here from London. Her name is Sergeant Jenny Patel. You can do whatever you would normally do but she will be there too, all the time."

"OK," said Rowan. "If Sergeant Patel needs to stay overnight, there is a spare bed in my room and she can sleep there. I am supposed to be going to the theatre tonight to see my boyfriend in the pantomime. It is sold out and I will be in seat C1. We can arrange for your police lady to sit on the steward's seat at the side of the theatre. Very conveniently, it is right next to C1. Thanks for arranging it, Sergeant. I must admit I am a bit scared. I am also concerned for my house mates. We are all very similar height and build and I wonder if Charles might just mistake one of them for me in the dark. Do you know if he is in Cambridge?"

"We don't think so, but he is a slippery customer, and he may well be coming here just to get you."

Josh rang Islington Police Station and talked to Jerry Gregory. Jerry immediately rang the Oxford Police. Robert and Amanda were picked up within the hour and taken, by police car, to the Islington Station. They arrived there shortly after 8:00 pm.

Finding Henry was not as easy. The police went round to Henry's flat in the Barbican, but he just was not there.

Chapter 29

On the Saturday morning, about the time that Rowan headed off for the football match, Henry had woken up around 10 am and begun a leisurely morning. He telephoned Judith and had a long conversation and told her he was going to the Silver's house in Hampstead that morning.

"Call me when you finish there. You need to check the bedrooms to make sure there are no water leaks. It has been cold and the one thing that house lacks is proper loft insulation, so there might just have been a frozen pipe. I doubt any pipes have frozen, it hasn't been that cold, but that is one of the things I am supposed to do. Can you also check their garden shed? The key for that is on a hook just inside the kitchen. They have a lot of freezers in there. The Silvers have a big kitchen garden, and they keep a lot of frozen veg in the freezers in that huge garden shed. Just need to be sure that nothing is defrosting. I think Mr Silver put the wiring in himself and he is not that great at DIY, so you need to check."

There was quite a long list by the time Judith had finished. Henry thought to himself that surely the cleaning lady would be checking these things too. He had no intention of spending hours at the place. There was a rugby match on television that afternoon and he wanted to be back to watch it. He already had several beers in the fridge.

Since college, and since giving up marijuana and smoking, Henry had begun to put on weight. Food had replaced the cigarettes and alcohol had replaced the marijuana. His appetite had increased greatly. He made himself a full English breakfast with two sausages, three rashers of bacon, mushrooms, two eggs, black pudding, and two slices of fried bread. A rack of sourdough toast accompanied all this, and he washed it down with a glass of orange juice, his nod towards healthy living, and several cups of strong black coffee. It was only at weekends, he indulged so heavily in artery blocking breakfasts, but it was symptomatic of the problems he was having maintaining healthy eating after stopping smoking. Last weekend, when he went to Oxford, he had eaten two full English breakfasts on the Saturday before going out to lunch with Judith. He had also stopped regular exercise almost completely. In Cambridge, he had gone to the gym and walked around quite a lot. Cambridge is a walking and cycling town, especially for the students. In London, he walked much less.

At about midday, he went down to the bus stop and started his journey to Hampstead. He walked the short distance to St Bartholomew's Hospital and caught the Number 46 bus to Hampstead, getting off at the Royal Free Hospital.

It was another short walk to the Silvers' house.

Henry went to the back of the house and found the key under the flowerpot where Charles had replaced it. He went into the kitchen and got the key to the garden shed off the hook where Judith had said it would be. He checked the massive garden shed; Mr Silver's DIY wiring was intact, and all four chest freezers showed green lights, indicating that they were working and at temperature.

Henry went back into the kitchen, hung up his coat on the peg on the back door, and decided that, despite several black coffees, he was still caffeine deficient; he put the kettle on.

He heard a noise behind him and turned round. There was Charles, looking very different from the Charles that he had known at school and during their university days, but, still, unmistakably Charles, full of menace. He realised, with horror, that he had become so wrapped up in trying to please Judith that he had rather forgotten that Charles would still be there.

"Hello, Charles," said Henry.

"Hello, Henry," said Charles, in that unmistakeable odd accent of his. "Long time, no see."

Coming from Charles that last phrase sounded like a Chinese mantra, or a description of some obscure Mandarin deity.

"How are you?" Henry asked.

"Delighted to be going home," said Charles. "I have been on the run for many weeks now and I am leaving on Monday evening for Shanghai. My father has business interests there and I shall be helping to run them. I expect that you, like me, have plenty of money for the future?"

"I do," said Henry. "A few million actually. Hidden away of course. I shall have to be careful how I use it."

It was obvious to Charles that Henry was extremely nervous; Charles could understand why.

"Are you making coffee?" Charles asked.

"I am," said Henry. "Would you like some?"

"I do not like black coffee," said Charles. "I have run out of milk."

"I could go and get some," said Henry.

"Yes, I suppose you could," said Charles.

And then he added:

"Would you like to do that for me? There is a small grocer's just around the corner. I am sure they will sell milk."

"OK," said Henry. "I've got some more checking to do when I come back, but it would be good to have a coffee and talk about old times. I have a checklist from my girlfriend of things I have to do, and I have to call her when I have finished it."

If I let him know that someone knows I am here it should protect me, thought Henry.

"Off you go then," said Charles.

So, someone knows he is here, thought Charles. *I had better let him make his telephone call before I kill him.*

Henry went back out to the kitchen and took his coat off the peg. He left through the back door. He knew he had to decide on a course of action. He could go back with the milk, he could inform the police, or he could run like hell and try to hide until Charles had left the country. Not going back was a no brainer, as the rather vulgar idiom goes. He was certain that, if he went back, Charles would kill him. If he called the police, would Charles rat on the whole group of them? He rather suspected that Charles would implicate all of them. However, without concrete evidence, Henry thought he stood a good chance of getting away with it. He did not know that Amanda and Robert had already been apprehended, nor that Rowan had finally recovered her memory. He thought getting away with it would depend only on Amanda and Robert keeping quiet, and they had as much to lose as Henry did.

Once upon a time, public call boxes had been everywhere in London, but with the advent of mobile phones, they were now much less common. He found a payphone at Hampstead Underground Station. Henry took out the card that Detective Inspector Gregory had given him all those weeks ago. He rang the mobile number; he had several twenty pence pieces if he needed them. Jerry Gregory answered:

"Hello, Inspector Gregory here."

Henry put a handkerchief over the mouthpiece, not great at disguising voices, but better than nothing.

"Charles Ma is in the house at 79, Prince Caspian Road."

And Henry immediately rang off and headed for the tube.

When Henry was not back within ten minutes, Charles knew what had happened. He felt foolish at having let Henry go. He had been arrogant; he had thought that he had control of Henry. He had thought that, by letting Henry leave and return, he would have quieted Henry's fears and could have killed him at his leisure. Ah, well. Another flight. Charles was getting good at this.

Bags all ready. No need to tidy up. Off to the station.

It took less than ten minutes from the telephone call for a squad car to be roaring up outside number 79. Two detectives in stab vests leapt out of the car, one went round the back, one went round the front of the house. Their bird had flown.

Inspector Gregory got to the house before Sergeant Trinder. The place had obviously been occupied. The kettle in the kitchen was still hot. There were dirty dishes in the sink. There was a sort of camp bed made up on the sofa in the garden room, sheets and blankets obviously taken from the airing cupboard on the first floor.

Once they were certain that their fugitive had got away, the two policemen left the scene and the forensic chaps moved in.

In the car, Jerry said to Tommy, "Sorry to have been a bit thick but do we still have the briefcase we were supposed to be returning to Sammy Needle on Monday?"

"We do," said Tommy.

"It's got Henry's prints all over it," said Jerry.

"Oh my," said Tommy. "What a stroke of luck!"

He winked at Jerry.

"Get onto the forensic boys at the house we have just left and ask them to check if Henry has been in the house," said Jerry.

Policemen all over London were alerted to the possibility that Charles Ma was in the capital. All the road, rail, and air terminals were alerted to watch out for him.

Jerry also rang Josh Jacobs in Cambridge and was interested to learn that Josh was already arranging for Rowan to have extra police protection. Josh explained to Jerry why he had instigated this extra security. Now that they knew that Charles was in the south rather than up in Edinburgh, this extra protection seemed even more necessary. By the end of the conversation, both London and Cambridge were fully briefed.

Jerry was now very worried for Henry, and for Rowan, particularly Rowan. Rowan was the total innocent in all this. Jerry was becoming less and less convinced that Henry was innocent. Nevertheless, he did not want another murder on his hands.

Jerry asked for extra police to be put on duty at King's Cross, Finsbury Park, Tottenham Hale, Liverpool Street, and Cambridge Stations. He also arranged for a watch on Henry's flat at the Barbican.

Henry, meanwhile, had found a cheap hotel in South Croydon where he booked himself in until Tuesday morning. He called Judith and told her all was OK and then said that he was having to go to Wales for a meeting on Monday but would be back on Tuesday. He had an elaborate conversation about it, full of fabrication. His mind was so scrambled that he forgot what he had said almost as soon as he said it. He promised to call when he got there and every evening while he was there. He hoped like mad that Judith would not call him back and ask questions like, "How is it going?" How the heck is what going? *What tangled webs we mortals weave...*

That evening, after the nine o'clock news, Henry decided that he ought to phone the boss and ask the boss to let Amanda and Robert know to be careful. He called the boss's number on the network phone. As he got through to the boss, he remembered what it was about the conversations in Oxford that had puzzled him. When Amanda said that Nigel had caused Angela's death by planning to chuck her and showing her the heroin, he knew that the only person he had had that conversation with was the boss. Could Amanda be the boss? Whatever.

On the desk of the custody officer, a mobile phone rang. There was a choice of four mobiles on the desk in front of the custody sergeant. He called Jerry out of the interview room and Jerry picked up the phone.

"Hello," said Jerry. "The voice synthesiser did its job, it scrambled Jerry's voice nicely."

"Boss," said Henry. "Henry here. Charles is on the loose in London and I think he is trying to kill me. Could you let Robert and Amanda know to be extra careful? He may come after them. He is planning to leave the country on Monday. He says he is going back to Shanghai to look after his father's business interests there. I went to see him in this house he was hiding in and I am sure he was going to kill me, but he sort of lost it, and sent me out for some milk for his coffee, and I just ran. I rang the police from a payphone, but I think, he must have got away. If they do get him, he might well squeal but if we all stick to our stories, we should be alright. Tell them please."

"OK, Henry," said 'the boss.' "Where are you now? Are you safe?"

It was a clever move by Jerry, 'Are you safe?' sounded really concerned; it did the trick.

"I'm in a cheap hotel in South Croydon," said Henry.

"Stay put," said 'the boss.' "I will let Amanda and Robert know."

Jerry went back into the interview suite where Amanda and Robert were in separate rooms. He went to Robert first.

"Henry just called me," he said. "He asked me to let you know that Charles is loose in London and planning to kill people before he leaves the country."

Robert turned pale.

"Will you catch him?" Robert asked.

"Sooner rather than later, I hope," said Jerry.

"Now, tell me about the attempted murder of Rowan Pike," said Jerry.

"It was nothing to do with me," said Robert. "When Rowan surprised us in Angie's room, we all surrounded her and persuaded her to sit down and have a coffee and talk it over. Amanda slipped the roofies into Rowan's coffee and when Rowan passed out, the others decided that she had to die. It was Amanda who suggested we might try and make it look like an overdose. Charles had been buying large doses of paracetamol for acute back pain he had in Edinburgh when he injured himself playing football. He still had a load of them with him. He mixed them all up in a cocktail with some water but he said it wasn't enough and so he went and got some more from Boots. He ground the tablets up in the pestle and mortar thing we had and then he added them to the mix. He stuffed the tube down Rowan's throat; she was so far out, she didn't even gag at all, and then he poured the stuff into her down the funnel.

Charles and Nigel carried Rowan to her room, put her on the bed and shut the door. We all stood guard, but when it was Amanda's turn, quite late in the evening her period started, and she went to the loo to sort herself out, and when she came back, Meera had called in and found Rowan unconscious on the bed. I didn't do anything. It was Amanda and Charles."

"But you knew what was going on and you could have stopped it," said Jerry.

"It would have meant the end of my career," said Robert.

"Well, I think that is where you are now," said Jerry. "The end of your career."

Robert put his head in his hands.

"How much money did you make and where is it?" Tommy asked.

"I am not going to say anything more until I have a solicitor here," said Robert.

"Just tell me one more thing. Was Angela involved?" Jerry asked.

"Not in that," said Robert. "Angela only ever did marijuana and ecstasy. She was doing a play when Rowan came and found us, so was Henry. It was Amanda and Charles who masterminded the overdose."

"OK," said Tommy.

"Robert Jones, you are under arrest on suspicion of the attempted murder of Rowan Pike. You do not have to say anything, but it may harm your defence if you do not mention when questioned something which you later rely on in court. Anything you do say may be given in evidence."

"Do you wish to call a solicitor? If you do not have a solicitor, we can arrange for the court to appoint one for you."

Robert mentioned the name of a solicitor and she was duly called to assist him.

The team turned its attention next to Amanda Sayers.

"Henry just called me," said Jerry. "He asked me to let you know that Charles is loose in London and planning to kill people before he leaves the country. He thinks you may be one of the people Charles plans to kill."

Amanda looked at Jerry.

"I want a solicitor," she said.

"OK, boss!" said Jerry.

There was a flicker of anger across Amanda's face.

"What did you call me?" She asked.

"Boss," said Jerry. "You are the boss, aren't you? This is your phone, isn't it?"

There was no response.

"My guess," said Jerry, "is that Henry doesn't know you are 'the boss.' I think you use that voice synthesiser to disguise from him the fact that you are the boss. Does Robert know? Does Charles know?"

"I have nothing to say until my solicitor is here," said Amanda.

"Amanda Sayers, you are under arrest on suspicion of the attempted murder of Rowan Pike. You do not have to say anything, but it may harm your defence if you do not mention when questioned something which you later rely on in court. Anything you do say may be given in evidence."

Jerry finished speaking and left the room.

Chapter 30

Charles took the underground to Tottenham Hale and caught the slow train to Cambridge North. He was missed by the surveillance at the London Station. At Cambridge North, Charles left the train and walked towards Milton Road. Just off Milton Road is an industrial estate and Charles decided that one of the storerooms on this estate might be quite a good place to find shelter for the night. He still had tomorrow to finish off Rowan Pike. It wasn't important to hush her up about the drugs because Charles was sure that Henry was going to talk to the police, and the whole drug thing would come tumbling down, but if Rowan remembered what had happened that day back in June, then attempted murder might carry a much longer sentence. Charles did not know that Rowan had already remembered the events of that afternoon.

Charles was angry that Rowan had managed to avoid death on the last occasion, and he rather wanted to finish the job he had started with Amanda. Besides which, it might give Amanda some satisfaction as she sat there serving what was undoubtedly going to be a long prison sentence, to know that Rowan Pike, who had inadvertently stuck her nose in and caused a lot of trouble, had been eliminated.

Rowan's trip to the theatre that evening was completely uneventful. Jenny Patel accompanied her and sat on the steward's seat. Jenny reflected that this assignment was one she would gladly have repeated every Saturday evening.

After the show, the 'last night' party took place in the Theatre Bar. Everyone pressed Rowan to reprise her Christina performance, and then someone sat at the piano, and lots of people gave spontaneous performances of their favourite songs. Thomas was very attentive to Rowan. Rowan was equally attentive to Thomas. It was a typical theatre party. There was a lot of performing of party pieces, there were lots of spontaneous duets, and trios, and choruses, and there was general theatrical fooling about. It was very entertaining.

The party went on until 3 am. It was a huge release of tension and excitement from a two-week production of the pantomime. Those who do not participate in theatre probably do not recognise the tension and nervous energy soaked up by nightly performances, with four matinees a week thrown in. At each performance, there are so many things that can go wrong. It is partly people; it is partly technical equipment; it is partly audiences. A student written show like the pantomime evolves through the weeks. Some things work, some things do not work. You drop the ones that do not work, and you amplify the ones that do. That soaks up creative energy. It makes it an evolving, living thing, it is almost parasitic.

At 3 am, Rowan and Jenny Patel got a taxi back to Mill Road. They crept quietly into the house so not to disturb the sleeping housemates. Rowan's room had the extra bed in it, the one that Paige had slept in the night that Rowan first had nightmares about the day of the overdose. Jenny Patel was very happy to sleep there for the night. She knew how dangerous Charles Ma could be and it was Jenny's job to keep Rowan safe.

They slept late the next morning and Meera brought both Jenny and Rowan a cup of tea at about midday. Sergeant Patel luxuriated in the longest lie-in she had had for weeks; Rowan just woke up happy, knowing that the nightmare of the not knowing had finally been laid to rest.

****

At the Islington Police Station, nobody had managed much sleep. It was a whole night of questioning, about the drug dealing in Cambridge, about the drug dealing in London, about suppliers and distribution, and about money. There were no reports of any sightings of Charles Ma.

The police now had five phones. They had both Robert's and Amanda's standard phones and the additional phones that they used only for network contacts. Amanda had two such phones, one as Amanda, and one as the boss. The two iPhones were not going to be easy to get into, in fact, as far as Jerry and Tommy knew, the iPhones were a dead loss. The only thing is that they were able to get the numbers, because they were able to check on the account holders with the phone company and find the numbers from them. From that, they could get the past three months' call lists. Those lists were, in the end, completely unhelpful. Just routine friends and business calls. It was going to take a long time to find out from the internet service providers which websites the two had visited. It was certainly not going to help in the hunt for either Henry or Charles.

The detectives would hand the other three phones over to the specialist teams. They needed to find out the numbers. Even if the phones were held anonymously, the numbers dialled from each one would have been recorded. The phones were not iPhone encrypted, so there was a good chance that the information from these phones would be available before too long.

Finding Henry was going to depend on whether he had his iPhone with him. The police contacted his phone service provider and asked them to notify the Islington Station as soon as the phone was switched on. Henry kept his phone on airplane mode for all of Sunday.

The overnight questioning of the two law students had been persistent and aggressive. The lawyers for each had arrived and had mainly told their clients not to answer the questions.

They stopped denying that they had been involved in drug dealing and simply answered, "No Comment," to every question they were asked. At about, 3 am they had been put into the cells, their shoes, and any possible articles of clothing they could use to harm themselves, were removed and they were left to sleep, under careful watch, until morning.

****

Charles did not know where Rowan Pike lived. All he knew was that she had been at St Joseph's College and that she was still there as a medical student. He didn't know how that worked. He didn't know whether it meant that Rowan would live in college or spend a fair bit of time there, but he remembered that she had been a popular member of the college, and he surmised that she would have a lot of friends still studying, and they might well meet up in college on a Sunday. He knew where the dining hall was, and the middle common room, and he wondered if Rowan had a pigeonhole still.

He took a gamble that nobody would be watching any of the downtown CCTV. It would just be recording for scrutiny if needed. He woke from his sleep and climbed rather stiffly out of the window of the storeroom. The storeroom window had been alarmed, but it was ridiculously easy to slip a credit card between the window and the frame and lock down the release button that triggered the bell. After he opened the window, he used some chewing gum to stick down the button and just pulled the window to gently. The alarm system was useless.

He walked the short distance down Milton Road and went into the Co-Op shop near Mitcham's Corner. He was pleasantly surprised to find that it sold warm freshly baked pastries as well as the usual groceries. He stocked up for the day. He had been forced to abandon his supplies at the house in London when he left in such a hurry. It was getting to be a habit of his, buying food and then having to abandon it.

He went downtown and walked in through the open gates of St Joseph's, careful to make sure that the porter was looking the other way when he passed through the gates. He went to the pigeonhole room and looked at the names to see if Rowan did still have a pigeonhole, she did; it was full of notices and correspondence. It was very likely that Rowan would be calling to collect her mail at some time during the day. If he was going to kill her tonight, he had to know where to find her. He was not usually a patient man, but this was a little different from usual; he would wait patiently to see if she came and then follow her home. He hung around all day until late afternoon.

****

Rowan wanted to go for a walk in the afternoon on the Sunday and Jenny Patel accompanied her. They walked into town and sat for a while on the benches on Parker's Piece, then Rowan took Jenny to 'George's Café' in St Joseph's. She called at her pigeonhole to collect notices and any correspondence, and then went back to the Porter's Lodge. True to form, George made them both a cup of coffee and provided homemade biscuits, this time ginger snaps.

"Are you still in danger, Rowan?" George asked.

"I'm afraid I am," said Rowan.

George turned to Sergeant Patel.

"You look after her, Sergeant. I need her to sort my arthritis out when I get just a little bit older!"

"Don't worry, George," said Jenny Patel. "I intend to make sure that Rowan gets to put the people that tried to kill her behind bars, for a very long time."

They wandered back to the house and joined the others in the sitting room watching a rubbish movie on the television.

Charles was watching when Jenny Patel and Rowan called on George, and he followed them as they walked home to Mill Road. They called, first, at the police station on Parkside and were there for about half an hour. Charles felt a little conspicuous sitting on a bench on Parker's Piece on a cold and dark evening, but he really didn't have much choice. He sat there for about ten minutes, decided that was long enough to begin to be suspicious, walked over to Warkworth Street, and started walking in a pattern that brought him back every five minutes or so to his starting point. He was on one of the outward loops when Rowan and Jenny left the police station, and he very nearly missed them, but he turned and saw them heading off towards Mill Road. He hurried and caught up to a reasonable distance from them by the time they had passed the swimming pool and the road leading to Hughes Hall. From there, it was a long but straightforward walk to the house in Mill Road. He noted what Rowan was wearing. It might be important if she went out later. She had a green anorak, camouflage trousers, and a pair of dark brown boots. She also wore a beanie in St Joseph's College colours. The girl she was with had a blue anorak, black trousers, black boots, and a pink beanie. The other girl looked a little older than Rowan, but they were chatting animatedly all the way along Mill Road, so Charles assumed it was a flat mate.

Charles noted that some of the houses along Mill Road had put their recycling bins out on the pavement. He wondered if that might mean that an opportunity would arise tonight if Rowan were to be the one putting out the recycling bins for her own household. If not, he might just have to be a little patient and wait until she left to go to work in the morning. That would involve more risk, and she might be with another girl. He had managed before. It was what he had done with Nigel. It would be a case of walking up behind her, stabbing her and walking on and away before she or the other girl realised what had happened. If necessary, he would kill the other girl too.

Charles walked along to another of the many cafes and take-aways in Mill Road and got himself a coffee and a kebab. He found somewhere to put his bag that was on the route from Mill Road to the station. He put his rucksack on his back and settled down to wait.

It was about 7:30 pm when the two girls, one in a blue anorak and one in a green one, came out of the front door and opened the side passage to the back garden. They were clearly going to be coming back with the recycling bins. The blue bin for plastic and the green bin for garden waste and compostable material. They came out colour co-ordinated. The girl in the green anorak with the green bin, the girl in blue had the blue bin.

Charles was waiting for them as they came out. He stepped forward and stabbed, right over the heart, first the girl in the green anorak, Rowan, then the girl in the blue anorak. He did not wait to see the result; he knew his skill and that they would be dead. He simply turned and ran. The two girls fell to the ground.

It was all over before either of them could see where Charles had gone.

They sat there on the ground, eyes open, staring at each other.

When it was obvious that Charles was not coming back, Jenny Patel sat up in the green anorak she had borrowed from Rowan and phoned in the details of the attack. Josh, at the Parkside Station, immediately sent out an alert to the railway and bus stations. Roadblocks were set up on all the main roads out of the city within about ten minutes of the attack. Jenny asked for an ambulance or a squad car to be sent to take them to A and E.

"Bugger. That hurt," said Jenny, sitting there in Rowan's green Anorak.

"You're telling me," said Rowan with great feeling. Rowan was wearing blue and pink.

"How far do you think the knife went in?" Rowan asked. "I am sure, it cut me because it stings."

"Well, they say these spike-proof vests limit penetration to 7mm," said Jenny.

"It's a good thing I've put on a bit of muscle with all that gym work lately," said Rowan.

"And it's a good thing I am a bit chunky, at least that's how my boyfriend describes it," said Jenny.

The trip to the police station had been worth it. Knowing how Nigel had been killed, with a long stiletto blade, had made it easier to prepare for a likely attack on Rowan. They had wondered if Charles might try to identify Rowan's address by following her, so the whole day had been choreographed.

There were a lot of policemen deployed around the Mill Road area, waiting to pounce in the event of an attack, but somehow Charles managed to avoid them. He climbed over garden walls and fences and hid up in a potting shed while he decided what to do next. He assumed he had killed Rowan and the other girl; he had no reason not to; he was an expert with a knife.

At Accident and Emergency, the girls removed their vests, and the wounds were examined. They did, both, have a cut about half a centimetre deep, but only a matter of ten or twelve millimetres long, over the fourth rib space on the left-hand side. There was no doubt that, had they not been wearing spike proof vests, Charles would have added two more to his list as a serial killer.

The task now, for the police, was to find Charles.

Charles, giving up on the idea of killing Henry, simply wanted to get out of the country. Like Henry, he still did not know that Rowan had finally remembered, and that Amanda and Robert were now in custody.

He made one final call to the boss. The boss didn't answer, so he left a voice message:

"I didn't manage to get Henry. I am sorry. I hope he keeps his mouth shut. Amanda and Robert should be alright. I am pretty sure I finally silenced Rowan Pike. I hope you all make it to join me in China. I am off tomorrow night. I will wait for you in Shanghai."

****

Charles got out of Cambridge on the Monday morning by finding a lorry parked at the railway station car park. It belonged to a firm in Chigwell, Essex, and Charles hid under some sacking in the back of it. When the driver drove off that following morning, he headed for the A10. The lorry was stopped at one of the check points on the A10, but not seriously looked at, and it reached Chigwell at about 10 am. Charles got off the lorry when it stopped in its depot and managed to exit from the depot without being seen.

Chigwell Station, on the central line, provided him with access to London. He went to the Greek restaurant in Soho from which he had followed Samantha and Nigel on the night he had stabbed Nigel. He enjoyed a delicious lunch and tipped generously. He then caught the tube to Heathrow.

Just in time, he remembered that he still had the stiletto with him and managed to drop it down a drain on the way into the airport. He was sad to see his old friend go, but it would have been an issue going through security.

He checked his bag in at a Virgin upper-class desk, went through passport control, and went through security, all with no difficulty, in the Virgin Atlantic Upper-Class Lounge.

He had just ordered a supper of a beef burger and a pint of lager, he planned to have an undisturbed sleep on the plane, when his phone rang.

It was the pay-as-you-go phone.

It had taken the experts until about breakfast time on the Monday to finally unlock all the pay-as-you-go phones. The call that Jerry, masquerading as the boss, had received from Henry, was the give-away. Coupled with Charles's final message, it had confirmed that Charles was on his way to Shanghai. They assumed that he would be taking a direct flight. Given the number of Chinese looking people on each of these flights, it was going to be very intrusive to question every single passenger on every single flight to China on that Monday night, but they had a presence at every check-in desk and were doing their best to cover all the angles. Jerry believed that Charles did not know that Amanda and Robert had been picked up. He decided to make sure that there were no reports of their arrest in any newspapers or news feeds anywhere.

Jerry and Josh decided to publicise the knife attack, but to go easy on the detail, and report only that a very serious knife attack had taken place in Cambridge, and police were looking for a male assailant who was believed to be still in the area. They said that the assailant was believed to be the man they had been looking for in connection with several previous killings, and they showed the photographs of Charles Ma once more. There was the usual warning about not approaching him and calling the police immediately, and the number of the Cambridge Station was given in the report. They did not say whether the stabbings had been fatal.

The thing that Jerry hoped would trap Charles and allow him to be picked out from the large number of other Chinese travellers, was indeed, the telephone.

Jerry checked the Shanghai flights. Assuming the flight was to be direct, there were three likely flights, and of those, the most likely was the Virgin Atlantic flight at 10:28 pm.

That was how Charles came to receive a telephone call from the boss at about 9:00 on the Monday evening, just as he was about to tuck into his beef burger.

The scrambler made the voice sound a little strange, but the message was clear enough.

"Charles Ma, you are under arrest on suspicion of the murders of Angela Huddlestone, Nigel Crofton-Jones, Flora MacGregor, and Hamish MacGregor, the attempted murder of Sergeant Jenny Patel, and the attempted murder, on two occasions, of Rowan Pike. You do not have to say anything, but it may harm your defence if you do not mention when questioned something which you later rely on in court. Anything you do say may be given in evidence."

Charles looked round. Two tall men, obviously policemen, were standing just behind him. One of them was holding a phone to his ear.

"And just in case you did not understand because my voice was scrambled here it is again, for the avoidance of doubt," said Detective Inspector Gregory.

Tommy grabbed one arm; Jerry grabbed the other. They forced Charles's arms behind his back, applied the handcuffs and took the handcuffed Charles Ma into custody.

****

Henry had managed to resist, for the whole of Sunday, the temptation to switch on his mobile phone. He had no idea that Rowan had finally got her memory back, at least her memory leading up to the doping with Rohypnol. He had no idea that Robert and Amanda had been arrested, and were in custody. It was lunchtime on the Monday when he finally cracked and turned on his phone again. There were about twenty missed calls from Judith, a number of missed calls from his office, and one call from the boss on the pay-as-you-go.

The police had not bothered to go trawling round the South Croydon Hotels. Henry would keep. His goose was cooked anyway. As soon as he switched on his mobile phone, they got an accurate fix, and a police car was despatched to pick him up.

The car took him to Islington Station where Jerry and Tommy were still working.

"Good afternoon, Henry," said Jerry. "Was it you that tipped us off about Charles being in Hampstead?"

Henry realised there was no point in denying it.

"Do you know where he was going?" Jerry asked.

"He told me on Saturday he was going to fly to Shanghai on Monday evening to look after some of his father's business interests there," said Henry.

"Why did you tell us where he was?" Tommy asked.

"I thought he was going to kill me," said Henry. "Did he manage to kill Rowan?"

"I am sure you will be pleased to know that he did not manage that."

"I am glad," said Henry. "I wasn't really involved in the first attempt; I came back to find them pouring the paracetamol stuff down her throat. I just wish I had never shared that study with Charles and Nigel at Brassington Hall. How long do you think I am going to get?"

"At least five years I would think," said Jerry. "It's up to the CPS but I don't think you will be charged with attempted murder, unlike the others."

"Now, if you will excuse me, I think we should offer you a cup of coffee and a comfortable cell, if we have one left. Two of your friends are already enjoying our hospitality."

Epilogue

It took quite a while for the police to unravel all the forensic evidence and create a watertight case against the participants in the attempted murder, by poisoning, of Rowan Pike. It was accepted by the CPS that Henry had not been party to the administration of Rohypnol or paracetamol and was guilty only of trying to pervert the course of justice, by not reporting what he had seen on his return to Angie's room. Fingerprint evidence from the apparatus was critical, as was the presence of paracetamol traces on the pestle and mortar, and the tubing and funnel. Charles was charged with four murders and three counts of attempted murder, both attempts on the life of Rowan Pike and the attempt on Jenny Patel. Samantha was able to identify Charles's voice as that of the person who had killed Nigel. It was a significant piece of evidence in that case. Charles's fingerprints were all over the unburnt part of the house in Edinburgh where the MacGregors had been murdered. That did for him there. He had slipped up in Angela's flat as well. He had stirred the Rohypnol into the coffee with a teaspoon while Angie was in the bath and had forgotten to wipe the handle of the spoon. It was only a partial print, but, with the other evidence, it proved to be enough to convict. The two raincoats abandoned on the Caledonian Express trains gave a DNA match to Charles.

As far as the drug dealing was concerned, each of the defendants was prepared to give evidence against all the others. The main problem was trying to find the money. It was probably going to take a long time but, in the meantime, all four defendants were found guilty of drug dealing.

Charles was given a life sentence on each of the murder charges and a ten-year sentence for the attempted murder of Rowan Pike and Sergeant Patel. The judge ordered that he should serve a minimum of thirty years in prison. The prosecution left the charge of participation in the attempted poisoning of Rowan Pike on file. He showed no remorse at any stage throughout the trial, and this was remarked on by the judge before he passed the sentence.

Amanda, as the architect of the attempt on Rowan Pike's life, was given a ten-year sentence for attempted murder. As the leader of the drug dealing gang, she was given a seven-year sentence. The judge decreed that these crimes were sufficiently serious that they should be served consecutively. Amanda remained icily detached as she was described by the judge as a devious and dangerous woman.

Robert was given a nine-year sentence for the attempted murder of Rowan Pike and a seven-year sentence for drug dealing, the sentences to run concurrently. The press had a field day with him. A former president of the union, a future prime minister who had allowed greed to destroy a potentially glittering career.

Henry received a two-year sentence for perverting the course of justice, and a five-year sentence for his part in the drug dealing. His sentences too were to run concurrently. His father resigned from the high court and took early retirement. Henry destroyed not only his own life but that of his parents too. That was one of the things he found hardest to bear.

Judith was in court when Henry was sentenced. He looked towards her as he went towards the cells. The look of utter contempt on her face would haunt him for the whole duration of his sentence. It was a reminder to him of what he had lost through a combination of weakness and greed.

As for Rowan, she sailed on sublimely through life. She added Musical Theatre to her repertoire. After Grease, where she played Sandy, she took the lead in Legally Blonde. Her sport went from strength to strength, and her academic progress followed suit. Given back her life by the skill of the medical team, she was determined to make the best of every moment she had. Each minute would be sixty seconds worth of distance run.

And Sergeant Tommy Trinder did take early retirement and open his pub in Whitstable.

Ingram Content Group UK Ltd.
Milton Keynes UK
UKHW020634050423
419681UK00009B/201